RENDEZVOUS
WITH
DEATH

HELEN VAN ROOIJEN

Other Books by this Author

Rendezvous at Lock 6

Rendezvous on the Opal Fields

ISBN: 978-0-6487261-5-9

DEDICATION

To Martin ... as always

ACKNOWLEDGMENTS

This last book of my *Rendezvous* Trilogy took longer than I had planned. As they say – we plan but life happens. Friends, Rosalea and Ian especially, and with loving family support from our sons, Alex and Matthew, got us through it. Now thankfully life has got back on track so here is *Rendezvous with Death.*

Martin has been his usual amazing support. He turns my 'suggestions' into the front and back covers – with patience and forbearance. A fab job again and he has been my foremost editor this time. Not sure how anyone can edit me – the dyslexia makes my constructions sound like me fumbling along telling the story – so I've been told, rather than a literary piece.

The story highlights Sydney and Hobart as I continue my Australian setting – this is where I'm at and I love the places and the flora and fauna. OK, especially the bird life.

Mary Gudzenovs has put my book into the format for publishing, thank you. Friends from Eyre Writers continue support – Diane, Alison, Aileen, Kathy, Mary again, and others who share our retreats. I will mention Rowie and Sandy, who were instrumental assistance in another episode of – we plan but life happens.

So, my trilogy is completed. I'll quite miss my characters but maybe they will insist again that there is more story to tell about them in the future. In the mean time I'll go ahead with the other stories that buzz about in my head.

Thank you to my readers who ask – when is the next one out? You are appreciated.

Once again, my characters and the names I give them, have no association with anyone at all with us or passed on.

Best regards

Helen van Rooijen
Port Lincoln, South Australia

Chapter 1

The small flag hung a limp rag on the black bonnet as the Embassy plated Mercedes hissed into a 'No Parking' zone outside the Sydney CBD building.

A guard riding shotgun, eased his bulk out of the front seat, and opened the rear car door for the lone passenger. For a brief instant, the flowing navy silk of a full burka outlined the slender figure of the woman as she alighted. Though covered as she was, her posture and the fractional glimpse of killer navy high heels, gave any bystander the impression that she was a young woman. She stepped onto the pavement and swept toward the building with no acknowledgement to her guard who had unobtrusively moved ahead of her to activate the automatic glass doors.

Her arrival was fluid and dramatic to anyone watching.

The guards manning the security checkpoint inside the vast marble entrance hall were watching.

That morning an electronic surveillance post had been set up for a very special occasion; the annual, invitation only, Argyle Diamond Sale. Today the exquisite gem quality diamonds from the Argyle Mine in northern Western Australia were being offered to a selection of very rich potential buyers. These invitations were sought after and buyers or their representatives came personally to Sydney for the sale. The majority were from the mega rich and powerful market economies of China, Russia, and the Middle East oil royalties. Less, these days, came from the USA and Europe.

Only one or two invitations were offered to Australian multi-billionaires and Hollywood and Bollywood notables were excluded as generally perceived as not rich enough to make the first invitation cut.

The sale was that exclusive.

The Argyle Mine produced diamonds that were split into two categories. The most commonly mined were industrial diamonds but the diamonds on sale today were of the magnificent gem quality. They ranged from the more usual 4D pure whites and the unique Argyle champagne gold colours through the pinks and reds to the very rare and exquisite deep blues. The stones were cut and polished in Perth, or alternatively in Amsterdam and Brussels, for this occasion. They were expected to realise in advance of another one to two hundred million dollars in sales today.

The burka clad woman halted before the checkpoint and placed a large navy designer hand bag onto the tray for X-ray inspection. She passed innocently through the electronic gate portals but was halted immediately afterwards.

'Excuse me, madam,' a male guard said, his tone respectful but firm, 'We're required to see your face before you can proceed further.'

The woman didn't answer. Her movement and apparent look at the officer, through the mesh that concealed her eyes, was an up and down sweep. He could feel the cold distain of it. With a shrug, he moved aside and a female guard stepped forward.

'Would you be more comfortable for me viewing you in a private room?' she asked.

'Yes,' the burka clad woman said. The short answer implied; I do not show my face to any man. The woman picked up her bag from the exit security bench and followed the guard to a small room beside the check point.

'Are you going to the Argyle Diamond sale?' the ever-chatty guard asked.

The woman made no comment and carefully undid the catch that held a mesh of material in place before her face.

Her face was Middle Eastern beautiful. Dark eyes lined in smoky black liner and long lashes curled. Her olive skin was flawless and cheekbones high and shaded with a whisper of colour. Her mouth a slash of scarlet red. Before the guard could do more than draw breath, the cloth was replaced and the woman walked to the door where she waited for the guard to open it for her.

As the woman left the security area and walked in a mysterious glide towards the bank of elevators, the female guard mouthed 'Wow!' at her colleague before returning to her surveillance position.

Chapter 2

Senior Detective Inspector Harry Shaw stood at the window of his office in the New South Wales Police headquarters. He looked out over the expanse of the Sydney CDB. Over the grey of buildings, the green of parks and the splashes of the blue-water harbour and, further away, the cobweb fling of the Bridge.

His city.

Harry's reflection in the window brought his gaze back from through the glass. He ran a reflective hand across his chin and shrugged out of his suit jacket. As he loosened his tie he slung the jacket onto the back of his char and turned back to the two men who sat waiting for his evaluation of the report that had just arrived.

'Things are quiet now, well Sydney quiet anyway,' he said a grin spread over his handsome bull dog features. 'But, Lex, this may be the breakthrough we've needed.'

Lex Osei, an ex-South African detective and black as the darkest veld night, said. 'I agree. The crime scene was under the flight path of the missing plane but I'd have thought the ferocity of the crime was right outside the usual Hood MO.' He pushed the South Australian Police file towards Harry as the latter resumed his seat across the desk.

'Well, I think you're wrong. There's evidence that the plane blew up but we've always suspected that Dieter and Sean Hood escaped, somehow.   Destroying that plane would've totally shitted Sean off. He loved planes and to have his brother destroy this one would have really...' Mark Llewellen said.

Lex turned his tall rangy body towards his friend as he interjected. 'Enough to make him kill that poor bastard in the national park?'

'Yes, in spades,' Mark rejoined. He spread his hands. 'Just imagine. You've seen your brother kill two people by tossing them out of the plane at five thousand feet. That's cold blooded murder. Then he says he's fixed explosives and pulls a gun on you and tells you to jump. You'd be scared as all hell, but you'd strap on your parachute and you'd jump alright! On landing you'd be still on one hell of an adrenalin high and pissed off. But there's someone on the ground as you land. Someone who seems concerned; maybe even wants to help you. Ready to report the aircraft accident to the police. Anything. If Dieter said - kill him. You'd do what he says.'

Harry cut in. 'I agree. Sean's always been a loose cannon, but I don't think he'd killed often before. Rough up people but his main interest was women and his planes. Dieter was the bastard who didn't get his hands dirty. Hired others to do the killing.' He held up one hand as Mark looked as though he wanted to interrupt. 'We heard on that spy tape that Dieter killed those two people, just an hour before, and maybe Sean knew he'd better do what he was told.'

Harry's hands smoothed the papers of the South Australian Police report stating they had found the body of a scientist who'd worked in the remote Lincoln National Park on Eyre Peninsula, South Australia. A first solid clue. The crime scene was one of a frenzied attack. The man's tent destroyed, his papers scattered and his computer thrown into the sea. It gave the immediate impression of a robbery and was substantiated by the jeep, his wallet and clothing missing.

'The Hood bastards have a history of bombings and an uncanny knack of walking out of the smoke into their next crime,' Lex said. He rolled his shoulders under his shirt. 'I've never met them but from the reports their presence needs to be tempered.'

'Terminated is the word I'd have used,' Harry said with a cynical laugh. He looked at the two men sitting on the other side of his desk. These detectives just might be the ones who could do it with him.

Both were senior detectives on deployment from the SAPOL force and were misfits in their own state department. Mark, for bringing a case of murder to an embarrassing conclusion by proving one of their own very senior detectives was a serial killer. Then acting very gung-ho, in the departmental opinion, he had rescued a kidnapped child and the pursued to the death a vicious criminal. To make matters more difficult Mark was now engaged to the mother of the boy he'd saved.

Lex was older, brilliant but unconventional. An urban Zulu, he'd worked with Mark on the Coober Pedy case. The hierarchy couldn't follow how that black brain worked and there was an element of racism mistrust in some officers.

Harry's assignment could change things.

That assignment, to continue the search, Australia wide if necessary, to find Dieter and Sean Hood. They were missing, presumed dead but this was not a confirmed fact and Harry had carte blanch, unprecedented in the annuals of policing in Australia, to capture these men.

Dieter Hood was that cunning and that evil.

His brother had become his apt pupil in crime.

Murder and robbery by unknown persons, no, to Harry's mind it was the work of Dieter Hood, the master mind of the duo. The man Harry had let slip through his fingers to save a woman' life. It was a mark against him, despite his seniority. He glanced at the photograph on his desk. There she was, Rhette, in her red headed glory and a smile that had hooked him for life.

The SAPOL report came close to proving that the Hood brothers were alive, and meanwhile his brief was to work with the Sydney police on any other current major crime that needed his leadership.

'Lex, keep in touch with SAPOL. If we can locate that four by four vehicle we might get DNA evidence and an idea of the direction they went. My guess's they came here to Sydney.'

'On it,' Lez said. He unrolled his lanky frame from his chair and sauntered panther silent towards the door.

'Mark,' Harry continued. 'Your job is to liaise with the drug squad and see if there's been a hint of the Hood's return. I've a suspicion that they aren't welcome and maybe there's kill contracts out on them. Get on with it. I've got enough to keep me busy and we need a breakthrough.'

Mark tucked a stray brown curl of longer than regulation hair behind an ear. 'On it,' he echoed as he left the room.

With his two colleagues gone, Harry turned back to his desk and the files waiting for his clearance. Major crime dealt with murder and drugs, big league drugs. Getting the civilian guns out of the scene after the Port Arthur massacre had left lethal weapons in the hands of the criminals, and one way to prosecute them was for just owning a gun. The run of the mill crimes were more likely knife crimes these days and with drugs taking away the crime inhibitors the blade attacks were vicious, and deadly. A person wanting drugs could kill face to face and see the victim as the knife was driven into him.

Most reports he signed off to go to the prosecutors, but on one he put a yellow postie note suggesting more detail on a point of the crime investigation that could assist police at the trial. On another he wrote – 'Could use some clarification. Don't give them any suggestion that this bastard should be tried for manslaughter instead of murder.'

Chapter 3

Four hours previously.

The man, known in a previous existence as Dieter Hood, stepped from a shower through the steam cloud that billowed as he opened the fogged glass door.

The name Hood was but one of his aliases.

Water ran in rivulets through the mat of dark hair on his chest and creased down the thickset body to pool on the tiled floor. He yanked a towel from the rack beside the shower and towelled himself down then found a minimal deodorant. No expensive toiletries this morning he wasn't in the mood, and they didn't fit his plans.

Things would change today.

They had better.

He had finally traced the last member of his family using the internet. A sister who had been separated from them when the refugee camp was liberated all those years ago. He could not believe his bitch sister was such a success in her qualifications and her employment. But there were problems in her personal life and she wanted to do a huge payout robbery. Hood came up with a scheme using as bait the exact vulnerabilities he'd previously ostracised her for. And she'd agreed. Backed into a corner she'd agreed. Even given him the power he wanted, when he'd set up her escape routes.

Her escape with her life was conditional on him achieving his own aims.

Today, after a little covert surveillance and action, he would move ahead with his plans. They didn't necessarily include her and the life style she expected in the future. His reason for the family denial of her was not forgotten or forgiven.

A harlot. A whore against her own religion.

Reason enough for his mood. His tension.

He threw the towel down on to the wet floor and walked back into the bedroom of the rented unit he shared with his brother. A ragged scar creased pale through his upper chest body hair; a scar a reminder that he'd nearly died when part of one lung was removed in the make-shift Medicines Sans Frontiers hospital in the Middle East. Yet, still in his mid-twenties, the trauma of it had turned his black hair to silver at the temples. Looking older than his peers had originally played havoc with his ego but as the years went on he made use of looking distinguished, yet having the strength and vitality of a younger man.

He pulled a white t-shirt over his head and put red jocks on then sat on the bed. As usual he extended his left leg up to stretch the quad thigh muscle and his gaze lingered on the indentation scars. Every day he had to ease that muscle. That scar caused more trouble than the missing lung although doctors had insisted that his mild heart problems were as a result of the lack of oxygen at the time of operation. He reached down and his fingers pushed at the fore and aft scars where a bullet had gone through his flesh, a twin to the one through his chest, on a specific day so many years ago.

That was a day of the many total changes in his life, like this one had to be.

Again his life depended on it.

Chapter 4

Upstairs, in a Sydney CDB building, at the diamond sale rooms the Executive to the CEO of Argyle Diamonds, Sarah Wilkes, smoothed down her impeccably cut business suit and fluffed the white hint of lace at her neckline. It never hurt to advertise that you were a professional yet still a woman. She had smiled as she had told the young and nervous girl on work experience from one of Sydney's most prestigious schools, an hour ago. She nodded her approval noticing that the girl, Marion, wore the specified business attire, though obviously, the girl's clothing was not of the same quality as her own. She was relieved that the girl, chosen by the school for the special placement, was sensible and not so pseudo sophisticated that she could be a problem.

Sarah checked her straight fall of dark hair in a small hand mirror as her Personal Assistant, Ray Duke, came to stand at her side. His swarthy good looks always made him popular at these sales and she depended on him absolutely.

'I didn't know we were having a work experience girl here today,' he said. 'Thought that arrangement was next week for the second lesser sale.'

'Marion was recommended by the boss,' Sarah said. 'He assured me she's perfect for today and has studied the correct procedures for her position.' She returned her hand mirror to her handbag and placed it next to her briefcase.

Ray smiled. 'Them's the breaks. She looks the part.' He raised a quizzical eyebrow. 'A mini you?' At Sarah's returned smile he raised a hand in farewell to go from the spacious showroom to his welcoming position beside the executive lifts.

Two suited security men were on patrol in the room and in the corridor against unlikely theft attempts from the electronically locked display cases.

Overhead were specially installed cameras as required by the Argyle management.

Marion's job was to be inconspicuous and efficient as she served coffee, tea, various imported waters, juice and champagne now set was out on a discrete table at the side of the long executive showroom. An urn burbled in a whisper of bubbles. Exquisite wafers of biscuit, cheeses, honey sweets and Turkish delight were arranged on platters to go with the beverages. Sarah had supervised the setting of crystal, silverware and delicate china cups on the damask cloth herself and it was perfect.

'Remember to pour each beverage to the centre of the glass or cup, just so. Never spill a drop on the sides and offer a linen serviette every time.' Sarah said.

'Yes, Ma'am,' Marion said. She touched the tray of delicacies. A nervous straightening of the crystal tray.

'Don't fiddle!' Sarah admonished with a smile to the nubile young woman. 'Never ever serve with your fingers, always use the tongs. And remember not to speak unless you are spoken to and lower your eyes at all times. For many of our clients it is impolite to look into their faces and eyes.'

'Yes, Ma'am.'

Sarah turned away her smile lingering on her lips.

Marion's face glowed up with the excitement of the occasion. So many service rules, so many customs she'd had to learn for today. It was an honour. She had never had an idea of working in the diamond trade until she was sent to work with Miss Wilkes.

Her eyes traced along the display of diamonds. Gems she had not been allowed to touch for the possibility of leaving fingerprints to smudge the sparkle before the sales. She watched Miss Wilkes make one final tiny adjustment to a card in a display case.

Marion was mesmerised by the diamonds and had difficulty looking away from them. Miss Wilkes had promised she could look at the gems afterwards through a jeweller's loop to see the clarity, the cut and colour of the diamonds remaining unsold. It was something to look forward to. She fluffed her hair as she had seen Miss Wilkes do; then stood clasping her hands in front of her body to both stop them shaking with nervousness and to make sure that she appeared respectful in the work experience.

The small refreshment table elegance was totally overshadowed by twin long glass display cases that commanded the centre of the room under pure white light. Sumptuous black silk was a highlighting background to the brilliance of diamonds. Each large gem was placed separately with a small white numbered card, noting the carrot weight of the stone and a US dollar price. The prices of a dozen of the exquisite blue and two outstanding purple diamonds went to seven figures. On the reverse of the card was a detailed description of the gem although most knowledgeable buyers wouldn't dream of asking to look at this information. Many could tell at a glance the gem weight and others, who couldn't, would never admit that they couldn't make the estimation.

Their trust in the reputation of Argyle diamonds was complete.

There would be world millionaire and billionaire players who bought because they could and who would often have a current extravagantly dressed lady at their side. The Middle Eastern princes would buy individual large stones for their mothers or current favourite wives and multiples of the middle range gems in different colours for others. A woman could recognise her position in the household by the diamonds she received. Occasionally a single woman would buy for herself, spending the price of her widowhood or divorce on a diamond and the young and very wealthy might look for a diamond for a fiancé at this sale.

If two buyers sought the same gem, then it was possible for a silent and frenzied auction to take place with the marked price as the starting point. Sarah as the representative of the Argyle CEO, who was safely away from the game in Perth, would conduct the sale and negotiate what was necessary. It was only she who had set out the gems that morning from her black steel ordinary looking briefcase that now was placed in her office partition in the corner of the room with the electronic banking equipment.

The scene for this famous diamond sale was set.

At the moment, the first buyers moved into the sale room the sun burst through the clouds and a blast of light coming in from the windows and outshone the overhead lights.

The diamonds blazed in glory.

Chapter 5

Dieter Hood sat in a coffee shop half a Sydney block away from the building where the Argyle Diamond sale was being held.

He'd been there just long enough to drink one coffee and, at a waitress's suggestion, he'd apparently succumbed to her offer of more coffee. Terrible coffee in his taste, burned by a too high temperature set in the machine grinder. He'd said yes to the apple Danish suggested as he waited for his overdue mythical guest, he'd explained to her, was to arrive.

Bloody woman, go away, he thought as he precisely cut the Danish in two then pushed the plate aside. He shook a newspaper, he'd taken from an adjacent table, to appear be reading to any observer watching. Held high enough to dissuade the waitress and to avoid the CCTV cameras in the street. After half an hour, he checked his watch for the time, and casually made one phone call then snapped the mobile shut, and went, apparently to anyone watching, back to his newspaper.

What was about to happen had to be successful. It had to be. He was in more danger just being in Sydney. This city could be a death trap if he were seen and recognised by the police or any of the gangs he'd made deals with previously. His life was on a cliff edge and a sheen of sweat lingered at his hairline.

Staring at the newspaper he let the images from his past seep into his mind until the black type and photographs blurred.

Officially the Middle Eastern refugee camp, where he had been interned twenty years before, hadn't existed.

He, his younger brother and sister had found themselves there after opposing forces had blown his family's hamlet away with rocket fire. His father, the senior village man, had disappeared and later his step mother found his body, beheaded in a field. She was raped and shot when she argued to have her husband buried immediately as the Muslim custom decreed. Then he and the younger village children had been swept up, imprisoned by a contingent of UN soldiers who were guarding an official observer of the vicious conflict between the opposing factional militants of the Islamic religion. A make shift camp was set up.

Barbed wires imprisoned the refugees in lines of dun coloured tents. When the supply of tents was exhausted as more and more refugees came in shanties were built of flattened petrol cans, scraps of wood and cardboard. These formed in ragged clumps around the rebel leader's shack. The soldiers thought that they commanded the camp but it was this man who ran the compound of windblown debris. The door of his hut was decorated with twin skerricks of red cloth. He smiled; the stupid soldiers ignored the signal to outsiders on the distant hills that they were not to aim their big guns at this target.

The soldiers were so ignorant.

Juvenile in their understanding of the old conflicts.

Muslim against Muslim.

Sect against sect.

The attack on the UN soldiers came from within the camp. It was led by the rebel leader and was timed to hit the soldiers when they were most vulnerable.

That time each day when the soldiers lounged about watching the youngest blond soldier chop and cut the fruit to distribute it to the refugee children. For weeks, the rebels had watched the interaction between the soldier and one particular girl. A girl with a thick white streak in her black hair above the forehead; a girl who defied the soldier and got the fruit she wanted for her younger sister and herself.

Hood didn't know the girls. They were from another village and, being girls, were below his dignity and radar.

Hood knew of the impending attack and that everything had to be the same that day. Against orders he had warned his siblings to stand well clear of the soldiers.

'Hit the ground when you hear the first shots,' he'd instructed. 'They'll aim for the bastards on guard first then the ones near the fruit table. So stay clear.'

The camp children were purely the distraction and, as collateral damage fodder, disregarded in the rebel plan to flee the camp. They'd kill many of the soldiers before they went away into the hills.

The night before the attack Hood had begged for a gun. One of the rebel's few smuggled in arms. The leader had stood up for him and he'd been given a dilapidated single shot rifle and three bullets. But the gun felt good in his hands.

In the moment before machine gun fire swept towards the soldiers, the leader yelled. A warning - a scream in praise of Allah. Some of the children dropped. They been warned but some others didn't. Many fell as they were struck by the flying barrage of bullets.

Hood leaned against the window frame of the rebel's hut. Waited a millisecond until he sighted the young soldier, the one who cut the fruit, along the barrel of his gun. He fired and saw the man drop clutching his stomach. Another swarthy rebel snatched the gun from his hands and pushed him aside, cursing that his own gun had jammed.

There was minimal return of fire from the soldiers. Those still standing dragged their wounded comrades and the children into shelter and away from the bullets.

The ambush was over in minutes and in the chaos of the aftermath, the rebel group prepared to leave the camp for the hills where other insurgents waited.

'I'm coming with you,' Hood had shouted in jubilation, his adrenalin high.

'No, you're not. You're not from our village,' the leader retaliated.

'I will, I've got the boots from my brother. I can run.'

'You're a stupid bastard. If you are captured those boots will tell the infidels that you're from the camp.' The leader turned away dismissing him. 'Get ready to leave,' he said to his men.

He persisted. 'I'll get rid of the boots...' He put his hand on the leader's arm.

The man's eyes were black and cold under a straggle of dark hair. He shook the hand away and drew his pistol and shot Hood once in the chest and once in the leg. Hood recalled the shock and pain as he fell to the dirt floor.

The thief sniggered and pulled at the boots on Hood's feet.

'Fool! Leave them. Don't you listen? Don't you think?' the rebel leader snarled. His fist smashed into the man's face. 'If you weren't my cousin I'd shoot you too...'

The thief aimed a kick at Dieter's head as he lay barely conscious.

The leader spat in Hood's direction; 'Now you stay with the children,' he said.

Boots had been a symbol of trouble ever since the brothers had got them...

Chapter 6

The Argyle Diamond sale was going very well.

The early and knowing buyers had been in already, as usual.

Sarah smiled in satisfaction. Red card markers were on seven of the most expensive diamonds and more dots decorated many lesser valued stones. Only she personally and discretely made the sale from a desk behind frosted glass in one corner of the room then unlocked the glass case to place the sold markers on the cards. The diamonds would be delivered to buyers when their bank confirmed the payments, usually within hours depending on overseas banking times. The diamonds were then packed for careful shipment. After a sale, the buyers usually took refreshments.

There was a small commotion beside one table. Sarah smiled in quiet resignation. A woman, wearing a white dress adorned with huge red poppies, raised her voice to a thin older man standing beside her. 'I thought that these diamonds would be better. They look more like my costume jewellery...' she said.

'Is there a problem?' Sarah said as she approached them.

Her voice was warm. Discrete.

'No, of course not,' the man said. He frowned slightly at the woman, and then raised his eyes to Sarah in an expression of helpless exasperation.

Sarah recognised the Eurasian business man. This would be his third engagement and he had purchased diamonds from previous sales. Each time there was a different woman on his arm. They were looking at an exquisite six carrot pear shaped stone of the best quality.

'It had better look good when we get it made into my ring,' the woman stated, her face was a hard mask to Sarah. Her expression changed, softened, as she leaned down from her towering high heels towards her fiancé. 'It will, won't it?' she said.

'Yes. It will be magnificent.' Sarah said. She smiled at the couple and the woman seemed happy now that she'd had a say.

'Can we get two smaller diamonds to go each side of this diamond? Tiny little ones?' the woman asked her fiancé. Her voice was pseudo girlish and her fingers curled into shapes to show what she sought.

The man looked uncomfortable. He was already spending more than three hundred and fifty thousand dollars for the first gem. Setting the stone into a platinum ring would cost another fifty grand. He sighed and his eyes beseeched at Sarah.

'May I make a suggestion? Sarah asked smoothly. 'The stone you have chosen is so special, so exquisite that any additional set stones could detract from it. My advice is to let it tastefully be simply displayed in your ring...'

'Yes. She's right. Darling, it will look wonderful. We'll take it to my jeweller tomorrow and get it set. Then we can announce our engagement as soon as the ring is finished,' he said.

'Next week?' she whispered into his ear.

'We'll have my jeweller make a special design for us...'

The woman seemed to give a little shiver as she placed her hand on his arm and gazed down at the diamond. Sarah turned away to leave them to view their choice together. She had seen it all before and her lips twisted in a small knowing smile.

Sarah's phone rang in the additional external small office she used exclusively. She was expecting the call from her CEO who usually rang about this time on a sale day, and discretely she cast a glance around the room before she went to answer the call. Every potential client was browsing or talking amongst themselves. As she went out from the showroom for her office she picked up her handbag and briefcase and nodded to Ray. He would replace her in the sale room. He stood, hands clasped behind his back, as Sarah beckoned to the school girl indicating that she would like a cup of coffee on her return. Marion beamed in pleasure at the request as Sarah left the room.

With a quiet laugh and a murmur Sarah spoke to her CEO in Perth. She was smiling as she left her office.

In the corridor, there was a shuffle of feet and two tiny pops.

The lift doors hissed opened.

There was a cry and the sound of running feet.

A door slammed.

Marion was preparing the delicate cup, saucer and napkin when the sale room exploded into a massive fireball. She and everyone in the room were dead before their neurons could register shock or pain to their brains as the force hit.

Dead.

Blown to oblivion.

Three minutes later a second blast rattled the frame of the whole building. It sent more shattered glass raining as daggers down onto the footpath and cars parked on the street below.

Chapter 7

Harry Shaw felt a distinct thump.

It was an internal as well as an external bump.

He had felt similar before. It happens in an experienced policeman's life.

He looked up from his computer screen to listen. Either someone had dropped something very heavy on the floor above him or there had been an accident or blast somewhere close by in the city. He stood from his chair and went back to the window, moving quickly for a man who was very tall and solidly built.

All seemed calm as usual in the huge city.

Traffic still crawled past in the clogged street below. Above the sky was clear except far away there was a procession of planes taking off and swinging out over the sea and away from Sydney Airport. Others were held in the circular holding patterns waiting to land.

A whistling kite hovered over a nearby building. It dipped a wing and shied away from something in the south. Harry unconsciously held his breath and waited; his eyes following the path of the bird.

If something big had happened in Sydney, his phone would ring or bells would start their strident alarms very soon.

Nothing yet.

He drew a breath and hoped.

Harry's phone rang just as the internal alert bells started. He grabbed his coat and headed for the conference room where the first information received and initial orders would be given. Other officers and the top brass arrived.

Something big was on.

Ten minutes later he was in a car going to the scene of what would be described, by the ever alert media, as a probable terrorist attack on an office building.

Midmorning and the sky above the city block was a blotchy grey. The sun had dimmed to a dirty red orb through the mass of billowing clouds and the stink of burning overcame the usual exhaust emissions.

Harry stepped out of the car driven by Samantha 'Sam' Morton, head of the NSW Criminal Investigation team, and parked as close as she could get to the scene of the explosion. Behind them, detectives Mark and Lex slammed the car doors. Their attention was riveted to the hellish panorama.

Smoke streamed out a line of windows on the top floor. Below the red lights of dozens of fire engines pulsed and flickered. Water spurted from thick hoses to hiss and disappear into the gaping wounds of the building. Police cars flashed blue warnings and people still fled out of the building to be directed to safety by police and ambulance officers. Behind a line of yellow tapes, they waited in disarray, clutching each other in shock.

Many used mobile phones to record the incident. The perpetual selfie.

Sirens howled as more ambulance and emergency trucks arrived, to be ushered by uniformed police into a side street. Their crews moved to treat the injured and a smattering of pedestrians who lay on the glass strewn pavement. They had been hit by the falling glass.

A blue blanket covered one body shape in the middle of the

street.

Men and women, police and army in full Kevlar strip and carrying automatic arms, patrolled the area. Serious faced, their eyes continued their search under cars parked in the street, into bins to find anything that could cause further harm. They blocked the passage of any pedestrians trying to move in the vicinity of the scene. It was a favourite terrorist trick to explode another device when or after the emergency teams arrived.

The emergency services had learned.

Bali, London and Paris had taught important lessons.

As he watched, Harry thought that if it weren't so serious the scene could look like an illustration in a horror story. A film. He estimated that a hundred fire men fought the fire from truck's extension ladders or used hoses from buildings across the street. He knew that the fire fighters would be as close to the blaze as they could get from inside the building as well. A three-pronged attack learned in light of the Twin Towers 9/11 conflagration. Police, in a helicopter, hung just outside the pall of smoke watching the roof ready to pick up survivors if they appeared and inevitably media helicopters hovered as cameramen videoed for the mid-day news. For them the timing of the event was perfect.

'They've got it contained to one area,' a police officer said as he recognised Harry and let the group though the police tapes into the street below the fire. 'It's bad. They haven't got to the seat of the fire yet - they said the bastard's much too intense.' He paused, his eyes screwed up against the smarting smoke. 'They're not expecting any survivors up there.'

'Any idea of who occupied that part of the building?'

'No Sir. Not yet. The Security Chief was injured getting people out but another security chap said that the floor was booked for the week and internal security was increased.'

'Is the security chief OK?' Sam asked. As her face registered enquiry, her thoughts raced to the prediction that the extra security meant something important was happening in that building this morning or something valuable.

'Got his arm broken against the security arch when some idiot pushed into him. Another man attempted to crash through a reinforced glass door before they could get it opened. Busted his shoulder. There's blood everywhere. Looked worse than it was and neither of them's critical. They've both been taken him to St Vincent's Hospital. Panic casualties.'

Harry shrugged in sympathy. He looked closely at the officer. 'Get your eyes washed out by the ambos,' he said before he turned back to his men. 'It's too early to be questioning anyone yet, so fan out and keep eyes open for anything unusual. You know the drill and keep out of the emergency personnel's way. No heroics either.'

'We'll set up a mobile comfort station and I'll get the uniforms to do the initial witness statements as soon as the areas contained,' Samantha said.

Chapter 8

It was another two hours before the fire was out and a further five hours, as the afternoon drew to a close, that the area was cool enough for the fire investigators to go in to declare the area safe. The building was new and the reinforced steel and concrete had held despite the intense heat. The architects and builders would be satisfied.

Harry wasn't.

Not with the waiting, anyway.

He was no good at twiddling his thumbs outside a crime scene.

'We could smell right away that bombs'd been detonated. It's definitely a crime scene.' The chief of the fire investigators stated to Harry. 'We'll get a report to you as soon as we can.'

Harry nodded his thanks. They were the best and their evidence of the bomb characteristics, its composition and manufacture and their placement of it would be vital information.

Police Forensics would go in next with Harry, who had been assigned by the Commissioner to lead the entire team. Finally, they could get in and on with their investigations. Already he had sent the squad back at headquarters to get basic information.

Who owned the building?

Who were the tenants?

Why was there additional security? Who, what and why?

To get the CCTV recordings from the streets surrounding the area and building and elevator cameras and begin to analyse them. His team was capable enough for Harry to leave them to it and go to the scene to have an initial look for himself. Ditto for the detectives with him. Very experienced eyes.

The media, their spot lights aimed from their cameras hurled loud impatient questions at them from behind police barriers as Harry went into the building with the Forensic Team. He knew he'd have to face the media at some time, but not now. It was far too soon for comment let alone conjecture. He brushed past them with a brief shake of his head. The hierarchy in the form of the Police Commissioner would be holding a Media Conference later. He would wait for Harry's first reports before six am next morning in time for the early TV newscasts and printed media. The commissioner had said that the State Premier had contacted him already wanting information.

For Harry and the Major Crime Squad it was going to be a long night.

One lift, well away from the bomb zone, had been re-opened after careful checking by the Bomb Squad, men and dogs and the advanced forensic teams.

In the still smoky area the detectives pulled protective clothing and covers over their suits and shoes before they used that elevator and walked down the long passage on the top floor.

Yellow tapes defined the crime scene. Glass crunched under their feet or had melted in slick slabs onto the tiled floors. The paper covers were quickly soaked with filthy stinking water that would penetrate into the leather of their shoes. Later they would deal with the need to replace their shoes, more costs in work compensation, but Harry wasn't thinking of that now as he let his conscious mind take in every detail.

Paper shreds were everywhere; they seemed to clog any office or business chaos scene.

Black probable clothing pieces and red bits, that they weren't going to probe into, lay where they had been blasted. Some were splattered against one wall. Already they could smell the distinctive smell of fire and the flash cooked remains of human bodies. It was a nauseating smell no fireman, detective or medical person confronted with, at any time in their career, could ever forget. Some no longer ate pork.

Amazingly, and again due to the design and solid construction of the building, the

main damage was contained to one large room and the corridor outside. The internal remnants of an elevator showed that it had been on the floor when the explosions occurred. A burned shape lay on the lift floor.

Bodies, too many bodies, lay where they had died amid the shambles of the bomb blast mainly in the large room. It was difficult to exactly say how many human shapes, large and small, there were as the bodies were clumped and the extreme heat had twisted them in the rictus of their deaths. The body numbers information would be given eventually by the forensic pathologists after the teams had photographed, videoed, measured, samples collected and until finally the bodies could be removed. That would take a day at least, possibly longer.

The detectives stopped at the door of the blast and looked into the room. They would not enter in case they disturbed evidence. Phone cameras clicked and hand held video equipment whirred.

One look to get an image.

A look to get the feeling of the scene. Harry always had a personal need, almost a vendetta, to provide the evidence to give these bodies names, to return to each their human dignity. To find their killers. It was what made him the policeman he was.

After five minutes, they nodded to the police and fire forensic teams and backed away.

'Bad as you've seen in South Africa?' Harry asked Lex as they strode back towards the operating lift.

'No. Seen worse. At a shopping centre massacre and once a whole village was raised. At least they're all dead here. No mangled screaming survivors.' Lex's shoulders hunched. 'I never imagined I'd see this sort of carnage in Sydney.'

'We're getting it these days.' Harry said remembering the Martin Place siege. He'd been away on another case at the time in South Australia when incident had happened. 'No place's safe anymore.'

Chapter 9

'You've seen the TV reports?' Harry asked Rhette Ryan, his partner, as he stretched his long body back in his chair at police headquarters. His mobile was nestled between the side of his head and his shoulder. His hands sorted papers and photographs on his desk.

'Yes,' she said. Her voice a soft whisper in his ear.

It was next morning and he'd not been home, nor slept more than odd snatches overnight. Well, his thoughts flashed; she would be his fiancée if and when he got up the courage to ask her to marry him. It was expected, but how did a simple copper ask a millionaire to marry him. His stretch ended with a yawn. 'Sorry love,' he said into his mobile. 'Only grabbing a minute to call you.'

Rhette chuckled, briefly then her question became serious. 'It's bad, isn't it?'

'Yes, it's very bad. I'm just about to go to the seven am meeting. Scripted in the commissioner for the media and now we've got to get on with it.'

'Take care,' she said. 'And I guess that you might not be home for the cottage pie I'll be making for dinner.'

'Bitch,' he said the smile and longing in his voice she knew so well. 'I'll grab a bite and a session of shut eye here sometime after I get things going. Better go, love you...'

He yawned again. His hands dropped the papers. Twenty-four hours already gone without sleep wasn't unusual but both the adrenalin and shock of this case was going to make sleep unlikely and food essential for the next twenty-four hours. He'd have to look after his men and see that they were OK.

Two minutes later he strode into the conference room with the tall black figure of Lex Osei, acting as his note taker, in tow.

The Police Commissioner, Tom Phillips, was already there and the heads of the departments followed. Tom was the only officer in uniform. Harry noticed immediately that Tom had left the head of the table to him, a sign that the Commissioner was just an observer. He nodded to Tom and indicated to Lex that he was to sit beside him. John Pappaglopagus, 'Pap', head of Forensics; William Zeigler, 'Bill' the department computer wiz was cardigan clad as usual. Murray Gallwell, Surveillance slipped into his seat and Samantha Morton, 'Sam' head of the detective squad came into the room like the others all clutching coffee or tea mugs. They nodded to Tom and Harry as they hefted their own notes and pulled the pads provided on the table towards themselves.

Maxwell Tydsdale, 'Max' of the Terrorist Squad, draped his wiry body into a chair as Joyce Hudson of Finance carefully set her computer screen of broadsheets onto the table beside him. So, what was it going to be, Harry thought, a free hand with the overtime needed or were the purse strings, as ever, tight.

Dr Peter Winston, of Pathology, eased into the last place at the table his face gaunter than usual. Harry liked this man who saw more of the terrible things that man could do to other human beings than anyone should have to witness. Peter's face creased into a gentle smile when he saw Samantha and he nodded his dark head to her with a hint of a wink. Oh, thought Harry, Peter's got a friend.

Harry touched the recorder to cover the meeting. 'Morning all to this special meeting concerning the explosion and crime perpetrated against the Argyle Diamond Mine Sale yesterday,' he said.

As return greetings murmured down the table to him he ran a hand down his jaw. It was preferred that people attending official meetings were appropriately dressed and ready. Tough, he thought. He knew that he was unshaven and rumpled, but he'd been at it all night. He almost gave an armpit a nose but stopped himself in time. He's shower and shave later in the locker room, this briefing and set up meeting was more important.

'I'm not being irreverent with the seriousness of this crime but I'm calling this investigation "Diamonds Aren't Forever" or 'DAF' on all correspondence,' he said. 'It's got to have a name and I'll get it in before the journalists do.' There was movement as every person wrote DAF on their notes, a half smile on some faces. The name of the investigation was the prerogative of the commissioner or team leader and Harry's sense of humour always elicited an interesting jargon name. The James Bond film name suited, he had thought.

'Before you start with DAF, Harry, thank you for the personal briefing earlier. I've set up some breakfast for us all. It should be here in half an hour,' Tom Phillips said.

'Thank you.' Harry looked around the room. OK, so this meeting had to be short, obviously the commissioner had to be somewhere else in half an hour. 'We've all had the first email notes and really we just need to update anything not reported and let us know what's happening with each of your teams. We'll start with you, Pap. You've teamed up with Max after talking to me. Too early days let for any results?'

'It's a huge crime scene, but generally contained.' Pap glanced towards Max. 'So far, judging only by a count of apparent burned and torn bodies, we think we have twenty plus dead in the building and one on the street. We've got the street victim away and have started removing the other remains. Our teams are working with the Fire Investigation Squad. Done it before and they're good with the explosive remains.'

Max followed, shifting his bulk in the chair as his attention went from Pap to Harry. 'An interesting point so far is that the Fire Investigation team think that the devises were mainly of the type terrorists use. The residue has also pointed to some mining explosives. We feel, given these facts, there's a connection with terrorists and those probabilities have resulted in warnings sent out nationally to other agencies. Further chemical analysis will tell us more. As you said, Harry, early days but we'll move as fast as we can.'

'We've got a massive amount of debris to collect, plot and analyse. From the surrounding buildings and from more than a 100 metres area. Outside it's mostly glass and metal from windows. Paper too, But I never know where all the paper comes from in an incident like this.' Pap said.

Harry looked to the Commissioner. Got a nod. 'Tom and I'll arrange for as many uniformed officers to do this as you need. The Coroner's want everything and you never know what else may turn up.'

'Thank goodness for GPS plotting.' Samantha spoke up. 'If this can be done ASAP then we'll get the information to shape the crime scene.' She pushed her dark hair back from her face and turned to Murray. 'What's the range of the CCTV cameras in the area?'

'Surveillance there's good although some at blast height were knocked out. Pity about that, Sam, but there should be enough to assist. Those in the explosion area are toast. Especially the CCTV in the lift is gone as are the ones closest to the blasts,' Murray said. 'I've talked already to Bill. He'll get the camera analysis done as soon as he can.'

'I'm going to use the CIA facial recognition apps we got. Perfect timing. We've been waiting for something this big.' Bill shuffled the note book. 'Sorry that didn't sound right in these circumstances, but, we'll do the usual checking on suspicious computer sites. The crackpots too.'

Harry rescued him. 'Your computer geeks always look on the bright side.' There was a slight curling of mouths as the assembled group relaxed slightly.

Harry brought them back to the horror at hand. He looked to Dr Peter Winston. 'The autopsies will take some time. With the Commissioner's approval and we've drafting interstate forensic pathologists to assist us to get them done asap.' Peter shuffled his notes and looked around the room. 'As you'd expect the early reports are that the deaths were caused by the blasts and fire. There's also one poor chap on the street who died when he was hit by falling glass. This's a terrible crime, as bad as we've seen. Senseless. So senseless. So many people...' He let the last words hang in the air.

'And so far, motiveless.' Harry glanced towards the Commissioner. 'Tom has to go to another meeting and food should arrive soon. Do we have anything that stands out as immediately significant?'

'A woman arrived at the building wearing a full burka. Got her noticed by the security detail. They thought she would go up to the diamond sale but she may not have. I checked with Pap and he said that there wasn't an obvious burka wearing person among the victims. We'll be definitely checking the CCTV regarding her.' Sam shrugged. 'It's a sad sign of the times that the burka often signifies something sinister in people's eyes, but...'

'OK then. I'm passing the call to Joyce. Please tell us that we can have the money for overtime to all departments.' Harry said.

Joyce, of Finance, spoke for the first time. 'Tom and I have had a tele-conference with the Premier this morning before this meeting. We have been given additional funds because of the complexity, magnitude and possible ramifications of this crime.' She grinned. 'Not a lot so don't go mad, but please, he asked, get this crime solved as soon as possible before the coming State election. Those were his words, so don't quote me.'

Tom and Joyce prepared to leave the room as a knock on the door announced food.

'Next meeting tomorrow morning, same time, same place unless something urgent comes up.' Harry said. 'Great,' he said as a tray of breakfast rolls was uncovered. He reached for a bacon and egg roll. 'No bloody cheese sandwiches this time; the extra money might be good after all.'

Chapter 10

Rhette Ryan had never been so happy in her life.

Sydney was now her home base even after the trauma of her sister Kate dying there. There was the horror and threat from Hood and Quinn, and then the murder of her father Doug Napier in Coober Pedy before the ordeal was finally over. The good things were her friendship with Ana Foster, soon to be Ana Llewellen as she and Mark were getting married in a month or two. With Harry coming unexpectant into her life with his love and support made her memories soften and the difficult ones bearable.

It was alright being a policeman's partner. All right the long hours he did at work; as long as she knew he was coming home to her. Home to his small rented flat where they could shut out the world. She knew his work was difficult and the phone call this morning gave her concern without worry as he was confident in his job and responsibilities.

She ruffled the top of the shepherd's pie with a fork and dobbed bits of butter randomly over the potato before she put it into the oven. Harry was a meat and three vegies man and he loved shepherd's pie. After the lamb roast they'd eaten the day before the pie was a no brainer for later in the week. She chuckled remembering his reaction to his missed dinner but the pie could easily be kept or even frozen for another day.

The day now stretched before her and she went to turn the TV on for the most recent reports of Harry's latest case. It wasn't easy as she shied away from crime news but today given the enormity of the situation she was determined to watch. Usually she turned on the ABC but as she flicked through Channel 7 she saw it was Melissa Doyle who was reporting. Her favourite reporter.

Mel, her blonde hair pulled back into a business-like tail, was talking to a young woman, Penny, who had been on the street, sheltered by the veranda of a coffee shop when the bombs exploded. The TV camera zoomed into the IPad screen as Penny's voice continued, her voice small and shy. '...I'd just had coffee with a friend. We went outside to do a selfie... And it happened. A huge boom! There was another one too I think...' The news clip of the selfie showed first the two smiling faces posing with a bike courier coming down the street towards them in the background. Suddenly the images became distorted as her hands jolted then swung dizzyingly from faces, to the bombed building, to the flashing falling glass.

Penny's voice was as shaky as the images she'd captured.

Mel had obviously seen the scenes before because at one point she suddenly put her hand over the small screen. 'We don't need to show what happened next,' she said.

'No,' Penny said. 'It was horrible. A huge sheet of glass fell on the bike rider. He was cut ... his head ... almost in half. There was blood everywhere... he died. I saw him die...' Her voice crumpled into sobs.

The TV cameraman flashed the view taken before of a bicycle lying in the street and the covered figure beside it. In the background Penny's voice continued. 'I couldn't do anything to help him... there was too much glass falling. It was horrible! Awful!'

Melissa put an arm around Penny's shoulders in condolence.

The IPad miss mash of lurching scenes rolled on showing people running away, and then it swung out into the street, back to her friend and the street behind them. In the chaos, a figure in a coffee shop moved back and away from the disaster scene. To the rear of the café. Finally, the scene settled on the burning upper floors of the building.

Mel Doyle faced the cameras again to say. 'Penny was a lucky young woman to survive this terrible event. Later we'll get a comment from the police to follow up Commissioner Tom Phillip's conference this morning and...' she looked back to where a policeman was looking at the IPad images with Penny. The pause was long enough to see him begin to note her name on a pad. 'I'm sure the investigating police will find her record most useful.'

But Rhette was no longer listening. After an initial gasp she was longer breathing.

One image had riveted Rhette to the screen.

A man was shown casually putting a newspaper down, leaving his seat and seemingly moving quickly out of range of the recording IPad.

Away into the shadows.

I'm going mad, she thought. Seeing ghosts from the past everywhere I look. It's happening again. Post traumatic images. My imagination again. I've talked about this with the doctors, with the counsellors after Dad died. Seeing a shape, a person. Here it is again; that man looks like him. Moves like him. It isn't real... Can't be real...

Rhette shaking thumb fumbled at the TV remote button. The screen image of Melissa reporting to the camera snapped off.

She pushed a hand through her red fall of wayward curls, twisting them, pulling at them; then she hugged her arms to her body. She had to move; she couldn't sit still. She paced the room again and again. Finally, as she passed a framed photo of her late father she saw her reflection in the glass and she stopped. He wouldn't want her to wallow like this. Get over it, he'd have said. Get on with your life...

It was time she followed up an idea suggested made by the counsellor.

Do something new. Paint, go to art classes. Start a garden. Study even. A course she'd thought about. Something that would take up that space in her thoughts, her brain, and purge the irrational ghosts. They'll go but it would take time and effort.

One by one Rhette discounted the suggestions as not deep enough to contain her interest and thoughts. Suddenly she remembered her past interest with ancient Egypt as she tried to shake her fears away. I'll Google for a uni study on ancient Egypt. I've always been fascinated by the archaeology in the past. Time to actually do it.

She'd tell Harry about her new plans for distance study with a university.

She'd not share with him the figment of her imagination.

Her latest image of fear. Of hate.

The man in the café.

Chapter 11

It was now almost forty-four hours since Harry and most of the police teams had remained on duty. He'd showered and changed clothing from a small wardrobe he had in his locker, and had sent Samantha Morton and the detectives, who had stayed on, home at the change of shift at six am the second morning.

'I'll go if you do Harry,' Sam had said as she took her handbag from the lower drawer of her desk. 'We've covered everything we've got already and you look like shit. Smell a bit too...' The banter between them was comfortable even though they'd been in contest for the Chief Detective's job six months before. Harry'd won but they settled in well together, with Samantha as his deputy. Especially as Harry might be off on his special assignment if it eventuated. The job would be hers while he was away; it would test her team management skills.

Harry retorted. 'Yes, but I can shower and be OK, your hair is about to fall down and it will take you ages to get it right again.' A slow smile and a raised eyebrow went with the comment. Somehow Sam's hair was always immaculate, long brown hair shaped into soft becoming styles.

'Well OK I'll go, but I say that thank goodness for Rhette, at least you get your hair cut on a regular basis these days,' she said a grin on her face as she automatically pulled a strand of dark hair back behind her right ear.

'I promise. I'll just stay just long enough to brief the afternoon shift after I do a call around to all the teams, and Yes, I'll leave Lex here to assist you when you get back, he's had a few hours off.'

As Sam left his office, Harry swung back on his chair. Rested his eyes for the moment, stretched the kinks out of his neck.

We've got the best team, he thought.

Sam's so left brained. She gets the investigation lined up, a point by point re the formation of evidence. From that she'll draw inferences that the rest of us could miss.

Lex; him and his solitaire. He's way over into the right brain. When he gives his left brain a problem and leaves the right brain free to wander, he often comes up with insightful results. The weary smile came back on Harry's face at Lex's computer card playing methods. He could see him now. His long frame hunched over a computer screen, black head intent, black eyes glazed and the solitaire cards flip-flipping across the playing field. Instinctively Lex makes insightful jumps in cases way before we've thought of them.

Me and Mark, Harry thought, we seem to be an even left and right, and thankfully able to understand and act on what the others had thrown up as conjecture. The men had worked well as a team in the Hood case that he led to South Australia and he had asked for them in to the final wrap up of it.

Harry's head drooped onto his supporting hands in front of his screen as tiredness demanded he sleep.

Detective Ann Maxwell-Stuart coughed discretely at the open door. He jerked awake then sat back into his chair. His hands ran down his face as though they could brush the fatigue away.

'Caught me napping,' he said. He grinned a half smile. His hands dropped to his chest and he stretched his shoulders back, flexing his cramped muscles. Taking his time, he breathed deeply to flush some oxygen into his lungs and clear his head, then glanced directly at the young woman. His look said OK, you woke me, why?

Ann flushed. She wanted to tell him to go home and she was too recently promoted to detective sergeant in his squad to consider it. She carried a coffee mug and placed it on his desk.

'The next shifts come in early. We're all here and ready for the briefing,' she said.

'Good. Thanks Ann,' he said. He casually looked into the cup. The coffee was black as midnight and he guessed it was very sweet. Somewhere in an initial briefing to a new group of young detectives he'd once commented that black sweet tar was sometimes necessary to keep going. 'You've no need to have got this for me. Not your job. I don't expect it...'

'I know, Sir, but you looked as if you needed it.' She hovered beside his desk.

He raised a 'go on' eyebrow.

'The woman in the burka's caught my imagination. Would it be OK if I made her my main person of interest? Sam's ...' Ann paused still unable to quite adjust to the less formal name usage in Major Crime. It was a quantum professional jump on passing her examinations to this branch from the radio centre where she was previously assigned. 'She's OK'd it but...'

'Stop right there. If Sam's OK'd it then go ahead. You can possibly go where the heavy footed men can't. A good choice. And you don't need to tell me, just mark it on the board and get on with it. OK.'

'Thank you, Sir,' she said. Her step to the door was light and eager. It was good to be trusted, both in her ideas and the allowance to go ahead with the investigation.

Harry turned back to his computer. He'd manage to stop most of the 'Sirs' and he ignored it this time. It was more important that he needed to absorb as much information back as possible from the other teams for the briefing. He took an experimental sip from the cup. Cripes, he thought as the coffee strength almost burned caffeine holes down his throat. He shuddered. It was so sweet it had to give him a sugar surge.

She's got the makings of a good detective... That was condescending, he thought as he got to his feet and checked the squad room outside his door for her. She wasn't in sight. He tucked his portable computer under his arm and walked casually to the staff room. There he poured half the coffee down the sink and replaced it with boiling water from the urn and topped it up with milk.

Better he thought. Now he was ready for the meeting.

Chapter 12

Harry glanced up from his computer and looked at the faces of the afternoon shift detectives as they waited in Conference Room Number 2. It was now four o'clock at the official shift change. As he expected Lex, Mark and all the detectives were there. Harry was more than ready to go home to sleep after the briefing.

A large glass crime board was set up along one wall.

Already there were grim crime scene photos and investigation category notes on it. He noted an item with Maxwell Tydsdale's name against it.

'OK. Our only agenda item is DAF. The Argyle Mine Diamond crime. You've had time to have seen the initial reports,' he said as an acknowledgement that he was aware that they'd all come in early. 'Sam's gone home and Mark will be my liaison until I've had some kip. Other than that, the usual chain of command. Some of the early reports have come in. Well done on those.'

There was movement as the officers shuffled the reports to the top of the piles of paper in front of them. A couple shifted computer screens.

Harry continued. 'First, the human toll. We have twenty-three bodies in the morgue. One an external victim. Because the poor lad who was just doing his job on the street died, I asked them to look at him first. He was Shane Dawson, eighteen years of age, a bike courier. His wounds were from the falling glass and he was damn nearly beheaded. Instantaneous death and he wouldn't have known a thing. Sam got approval from the coroner and his body can be released today.'

Harry looked up as, Lee a young detective constable, shifted in his seat. 'We checked with his company. He was doing a regular run and was on the crime street to go his next delivery. Just collateral damage. Wrong place wrong time. Poor sod.' He said.

Harry frowned. 'It's good his family can have him back so soon, but no-one's just collateral damage, especially when there's a young life cut short. He was murdered the same as every other of the twenty-two bodies we have,' he said as the young man shifted again in embarrassment. 'I'm not pointing a finger at the way you reported and maybe it's because I'm tired but I'll never think of a murdered person like that and I'd prefer that you didn't also.'

'Sorry Sir.'

Harry nodded a half smile at the detective. 'But you did well to clear him so quickly. OK, then the other twenty-two bodies. Initial reports. There were two in the corridor. We can assume they were the security men employed for the diamond sales. Their bodies were very badly damaged from a close blast and the Peter Winston says that it was mainly a mopping up job with them. Where we can we'll use dental records for speed to confirm identities but inevitably we'll get to using DNA. Dental records are less expensive than DNA procedures, faster too. With these men bits of their uniform may also confirm their identities.'

'That'll keep Joyce happy with keeping the costs down...' came from the back of room.

Harry went on as the murmur of agreement ebbed. 'There was one body in the lift and the other nineteen dead in the sale room seem to be a range of ages and sexes. The Argyle people tell us that there would have been Sarah Wilkes, the CEO's chief executive and mining engineer, and Ray Duke, her personal assistant present. We can assume that if this is a terrorist attack that they would definitely be present.'

The young previously admonished detective spoke up. 'So, Boss, that's still a likely scenario?'

'Max and the terrorist squad have kept that it's a possible terrorist action on the table. There were some very, very rich people of many nationalities expected at the sale, especially from the Middle East. The Muslim question must arise given the levels of money and power that some of the buyers probably represented. Plus, the different Muslim factions. There've been a few groups putting hands up to claim that they've done it, not ISIS as yet, but most of them are the usual crackpots. But usual and crackpot aren't always different these days. I'm leaving that conjecture and evaluation to Max and his team. He and Bill have got the contacts and the international ear. The internet is on fire...' Harry nodded to the room. 'I'll let Mark have a few words on some of the input we've had. Give my tired vocals a breather.'

Mark pushed back his chair and stood near the crime scene board. His fingers raked his overlong crop of brown curly hair back from his face. 'I'll continue with John Pap's observations. He's plotted all the area. His initial thoughts are that the bombs, and he thinks that there may have been two, even three, in the initial blast and could have been placed right in the diamond display cases at opposing ends. That's not fact yet but its likely they were somewhere about there.' Mark put a diagram of the conference sale room up on the glass board. 'This'll be on your screens. No-one lived through those explosions. No way. Peter's pathologists got this from the patterns of injuries on all the victims. The blast, the extreme heat and shockwave, then the flying glass from the bombs hit everyone and everything. We also had witness statements that there was the sound of another explosion. Pap says that this was a smaller bomb that went off in the corridor. Maybe it was on a delayed fuse system.'

There was another bout of shuffling in the room. The pathology reports would hold things up and every detective present wanted evidence quickly. The old 24-hour potential success period was well over.

Mark continued. 'Pap said that they were expecting that maybe some of the diamonds may have survived.' He glanced about as eyebrows rose around the table. 'I know diamonds are pure carbon and they burn but Pap, and the Argyle CEO, say that diamonds need extreme heat to burn well. They would have had that from the explosions, plus oxygen in the air to burn to carbon-di-oxide, CO_2. But Pap and the Fire detectives say that the oxygen could have been burned or blasted away instantly in the explosions, so there may be the remains of diamonds still. We'll see.'

'So, is it likely that the motive for the bombings is terrorism not robbery? They'd want the diamonds intact not destroyed in a robbery.' Ann Maxwell-Smith spoke up.

'Smitty, you'll have to get your diamond some other way if that's the case. Might be your only chance,' Lee said.

"You could be right,' Ann said a flush going from her chin up her cheeks. She touched a thin gold chair around her neck. 'Maybe I've got one. Don't need another like some people.'

Harry and Mark exchanged glances. Mark, a little frustrated at the banter, but Harry was more relaxed because the squad seemed to be meshed. New detective Ann was 'Smitty' a good sign of her acceptance.

Mark went back to his place as Harry took over. 'Back to business. We're hoping to get the bodies ID'd as quickly as we can. The CCTV surveillance on the ground floor will hurry this along with photos taken as the potential diamond buyers entered the building. Most people were annoyed but are used to the added security on special occasions. The regular tenants went to their offices on lower floors. Luckily for our investigation, in the relevant area only Argyle'd booked that upper floor space. It's a pity that the camera in the lift was destroyed but CCTV in the other lifts will have captured any and all movement there. If someone went up to the top floor we hope to know. We're waiting still on all the usual office door to door reports from the uniform branch.'

Harry clicked through his computer screen.

'Melissa Doyle and the Channel Seven photographer have given us the film they took off an iPad they got shown. It'd gone up briefly on Facebook, put there by the young woman. But she took it down again at the Commissioner's personal request as the killing of the cyclist was too graphic for public viewing. Murray has that now and he's been able to increase the clarity from the original views. He's also got all the CCTV material from the area, really the whole of Sydney CBD. He'll trace vehicle movements.' Harry looked towards Ann. 'The arrival of the burka woman should be there.'

'One of the security people said that the car had an Embassy flag,' she said. 'That could be a positive.'

'Or not. One never knows with embassies,' Harry said. 'Find out what you can ASAP. It's now the usual crime and murder investigation whatever the motive. Everyone alive and dead is a person of interest. Check out Argyle Diamonds; who they are and their current financial situation. No dispersions there but insurance claims have been made before in previous cases. The loss in this case will be astronomical. I want to know more about the explosives but we'll get that from the fire investigation people. More about the security men employed and their company. Who everyone is and their associations. Fill in every gap...'

Harry reached for a glass of water. Took a sip. He nodded

again to Mark.

'I'm passing on Commissioner Tom Phillip's instructions. No talking in any way to the media, that's his duty and pitch, he's got to do the dirty work with the media. But listen and report anything, even the gossip. Everything we've got is now on your computers. Share everything new, and I'm to get all notes from everyone, please. Report everything, no matter how insignificant, how large or oddball.' Mark instructed. 'Any questions?'

There were none as the team knew their roles.

Harry stood as the team filed out, their chatter all work He clapped a hand on Lex's shoulder. 'This'll stop you playing Solitaire all day! You can help Sam line up the ducks.' The last was said quietly with a chuckle because Lex's habit of playing solitaire while he thought was well known in the squad. 'I'm going home now, so get busy.'

'Ducks?' Lex muttered. Harry must be either going bonkers or at least out of his mind with tiredness. He pulled out his mobile phone and contacted the Major Crime driver. 'The boss is coming down,' he said. 'Bit tired. Make sure he gets a lift home and doesn't drive himself, please.'

Chapter 13

So, it was done, Dieter Hood thought.

His time in the café, and the immediate moments after, had shown that the event was spectacular.

When the stupid shocked female wobbled her IPad around taking pictures, Hood had been forced to leave his seat earlier than he'd planned. The bomb blast dust had hardly subsided before the police, ambulances and the press vehicles began to arrive. Time to disappear; to slink out the back of the café and make it out of there as fast as he could. He just escaped the road blocks and sighed with relief as he closed the door to his flat.

Safe home.

He snapped on the TV. Already the channels were all over the incident.

Was it Sydney's latest terrorist attack, the first real one from ISIS? A gas explosion? Gang warfare? Speculation was rife. That bloody woman reporter had got her images on TV, dammit! Shit, he thought. Those kids and their iPads... His mind flooded with the possible repercussions from that fact of a brief moment, in the earliest reports, he could just have been seen.

Hood paced the floor. He kicked aside a boot that hindered his path. Fuck, he thought he'd have to get it out from under the dresser later. In another swipe, he kicked the other boot to join its mate. Boots!

Could he be recognised?

More than one of the drug gangs in Sydney wanted him dead, or at least sought the huge sums of money he owed. Plus interest. The bastards wanted the money and the happy interest would be him getting tickled with a baseball bat as punishment before they finished him off. A bullet in the scull, he'd had it done to non-payers, to people who had threatened his business. Before he changed his own business methods to appear clean and above board.

Over a previous decade, his reputation became that of a sound businessman. He'd hired a firm of public relations advisors and through apparent good works, donations to charities, donations to political parties and appearances at entertainment events, he became a person that the media doted upon. With a glamorous woman on his arm, himself suited expensively, he led a double life. A generous man about town, but to the police and people in the know he was a money launderer who ran an extensive drug cartel. The police watched for the merest slip up but with a battalion of lawyers to wage his wars, he stayed so called 'clean'.

This double empire had all collapsed in weeks when he was confronted by one infernal woman, the police in two states and an import export deal that crashed. His only way out was to die, and that he'd faked. It had almost worked but some elements of Sydney's criminal world would still pursue him, if he was seen.

Now he waited for contact from his own sources. He had his plan, and the necessary lever but one more person might have to be eliminated to achieve the final outcome. That person would be expendable. Many times in the past he had re-evaluated the course of his life. Had responded to his surroundings. Had routed out the expendable. Had found ways to survive and prosper.

Slumped on the bed he could just see one boot laying where he had kicked it...

Hood remembered the incident that had changed his position with the rebel group in the refugee camp. Barely out of his teens he'd fought for a place with them and his brother had almost ruined it for him. Maybe it was for the better, he'd never know. Many people died in the camp... He never knew what happened to the rebels when they fled into the hills after the ambush... Being repatriated to Australia may have been his best outcome, and the boots the best piece of luck.

Back in the camp he'd watched from a doorway as his younger brother Sean slouched his way near the fence. Small, sullen and scraggy in build, the boy didn't fit in except as a courier to take messages between the rebel leader and his men. His twelve-year-old feet were bare until that day a soldier pulled him up.

'Boy!' the soldier yelled.

One of the mangy dogs, thin flanked and pebble eyed, who ran with Sean growled, then slunk away as the soldier's huge German shepherd dog eyed them both.

His brother stopped ten metres away and turned as a young fair haired soldier beckoned to him. He took a minimal step towards the soldier he knew as the man who cut fruit for the young children each day inside the outer fence. He and his young sister went there to get their share and they'd boasted about it to the rebels. He remembered he'd been shouted at. It wasn't manly or right that they'd beg for food from the infidel soldiers. The boy stopped bragging when Hood smacked his brother with a back hander. A black eye to shut his mouth, but the boy and his younger sister continued to go to the fruit table each day.

Sean didn't bother to answer the soldier.

'Boy,' the soldier repeated. Black military boots with tied laces hung from his outstretched hand. 'I've got some boots for you. Want them? They're way too small for me and I've got new boots.'

Still he was silent. He needed boots but any minute this soldier would say please as if he was doing him a favour by accepting this gift. He was humiliated by the offer but he wanted the boots.

Sean glared at the soldier.

The young soldier shrugged and placed the boots on the ground inside the wires and walked away. Sean stayed still until the man and dog were far enough away not to hear his feet scuff the grey-brown dust of the camp as he picked up the boots, and ran.

It was one of the few times that Hood had a begrudging pride in his brother.

That night an older refugee tried to take the boots from Sean even though they were obviously too small for his big feet. The swarthy man was from a different village, an ally to the rebel commander, but Hood had backed his brother as he struggled against the dirty grasping hands. The older man pulled a knife as a threat. He was ready to cut the brothers throats if necessary then to cut the toes out of the boots to accommodate his splayed feet.

The leader stopped him with a curse.

The potential thief glared at the brothers and backed away but his eyes and stance said that he would not forget the incident. Killing someone and another body slung down a latrine was nothing, but loss of face was everything.

The boots had the odour of use. An insult. In that instant Hood made a vow that he and his brother would never again wear anything that someone else had worn before after they escaped from the camp. He smiled when he also recalled that his younger brother had waited two days before he wore the boots to show the soldier that he, and the now treasured boots, didn't matter. By that action he'd forgiven Sean for the loss of face with the soldiers and loss of favour with the rebels.

The next day Hood had taken the boots from Sean. As the

elder brother, it was right that he had the boots even if they were tight on his feet.

Boots an ongoing symbol of the changes in his life...

But maybe now it was time for a little celebration. He was optimistic. He didn't know if the plan had been a success but it had to be so that he could get away from Sydney. Perhaps he'd have a takeaway Indian dinner. Safer than going out for a meal. He went online to order the food from the best restaurant that would deliver - for a price.

He paused at the key board then booked airline seats for himself and his brother for Hobart. Sean would soon arrive back in Sydney from Adelaide. The latter had a small task to do in Coober Pedy; to retrieve things stored in a safe deposit box in the local bank. They would then have the necessary cash and conversion materials for the next stage.

Time to move and he was sick and tired of the waiting about.

The next step.

Chapter 14

Harry's sleep was disjointed, as always, in the start and middle of an investigation. He'd slept until about two am then, after he visited the bathroom, his sleep turned into a restless tossing and his feet thrashed the bed linen. Rhette had woken as the doona was pulled away when he heaved his body over to lay over onto his stomach. A shaft of moonlight pooled like milk on the end of the bed as she raised herself up onto one elbow and looked at him, concerned that his state of mind was disturbing his rest. She slipped out of bed and fumbled on the wisp of blue silk and lace that was her discarded nightdress.

Harry raised his head, partly asleep but as ever alert to her.

'Stay,' she said softly. She eased the doona off his body and began to massage his neck and shoulders. Her hands firm yet gentle, probing the muscles to ease the strain tension lumps she felt there. His breath exhaled in a groan of contentment. Slowly she worked her way past his scapulars and down his back, feeling the warmth, the smoothness of his skin and the underlying strength of him. She sculptured the vee of his shoulders down to his waist to the slope of his hard buttocks. She paused then pushed the doona lower and moved her attention down to his feet.

Her thumbs worked the curves of his ankles and then she ran fingers down the soles of his feet. His toes curled and his feet tensed. So he was ticklish there, she thought with a smile.

Something to remember for another time. Before he could protest or react more to his feet being touched she moved her hands up his legs to the strongly defined calf muscles. The backs of his knees were warm and she smoothed the tendons there that led to his thighs. The hair on his legs are as robust as the man himself, she thought, as she felt the change in skin composition.

With another smile she slowly massaged his buttocks. Firm and strong the gluteals there slightly clenched and she lightened her touch to encourage his relaxation. With long strokes, she eased the muscles from his shoulders to his knees until he seemed to be close to sleep. 'Will that help?' she whispered and leaned forward to kiss his back. Her hair fell forward against his back as though wanting to stay close and prolong the intimacy. Her body was responding to the feel of him in the semi darkness...

His man smell. His man feel.

There was a grunt from the pillow. 'Yes...but what do I do about this? He rolled onto his back and she could see what 'this' was. Rhette put her knee onto the bed and, pulling her nightdress up, she straddled him. There was a groan from both of them as his penis sank into the depths of her warm body. As they began the age-old movements and his hands reached to cup her breasts, he muttered in a gasp, 'I won't last long...Rhette I won't last...'

'Don't think...' she said and moments later his body clenched. Her shudder followed and she slumped forward to nestle onto his chest, her face into the curve of his neck. They lay that way until Rhette felt his breathing slow to a regular rhythm and his body relax before she moved off him and back to her side of the bed. Sex was the best sleep tonic of all.

He slept soundly after that until the alarm went off at five.

'Too early...' Rhette mumbled. On automatic she fumbled her feet to the floor, shivered, then started to get out of bed.

'Stay there,' he insisted. 'I'll shower and get breakfast at the office.' He found his mobile and made a call for his driver.

'Gotta pee,' she mumbled again. 'Wake me this early and I gotta pee.' She pulled her wrap around her shoulders, found her fluffy scuffs and headed for the toilet.

Harry laughed. She could always make things honest. Not an early morning person but she could light up the night. And her sleep relaxation technique beat anything he'd ever dreamed of.

'Look after yourself,' Rhette had called from the bedroom when he left the flat. As he stepped into the waiting police car he smiled as he thought of her warm womanly body and the red hair mussed on the pillow.

'G'day sir,' the driver had said. 'Headquarters?'

'Yes, please,' Harry said. He detached himself from images of Rhette, absently noticed that the police driver at the wheel looked too young to shave let alone grow a beard, then he thrust his mind to the day's DAF meetings that lay ahead. They had to start to get results from all the enquiries.

Harry Shaw clocked back onto his desk at police headquarters at six am to find that the night staff had collated what facts were available. Sam briefed him as they walked into the staff meeting.

The multiple autopsies at the morgue at St Vincent's Hospital were confirming the initial speculation that death was instantaneous to all of them; but some of the bodies had stainless steel shards in them. This pointed to one source of the blasts had come from possibly the hot water urn on the refreshment table. Other bodies had glass fragments slice through them. So, Harry thought, maybe two different sites of the explosives. Maybe they'd track more.

Sam had already ordered an investigation into where the urn had come from and who would have set it up. Good also. Who had constructed the glass display cases? When had they been installed. Were they new or simply they part of the building furniture in the conference room?

Harry added the requests that, if the display cases belonged to the corporate body of the building, where were they stored? He wanted a chain of evidence regarding the display cases, and the urn. He added that was it possible that the bomb had been placed under the food and drink table and again, where had it come from? Who had contact with it? Routine but vital investigation that could answer the over-riding question of motive. He clicked his mouse to send on his enquiries to all his detectives' computers.

The questions remained.

Was it a terrorist attack? If so by whom and why.

The Federal Police were listing all insurgents they knew were in the country but there had been no murmurs or hints that something was about to happen. This was out of the blue. Only more investigation would confirm or deny a terrorism factor. The coming elections weighed heavily and the eyes of the government were on this case. The public, who were very apprehensive about the international terror situation, were demanding answers.

Was it a robbery?

That seemed unlikely but there was minor visual evidence that some diamonds may have survived the blasts. The robbery notion had to be entertained primarily given the value and disposability of the diamonds. Argyle Diamonds' reputation was world class but people dealing with them were a different matter.

Harry needed a break-through to push the investigation further.

As he went to get himself a coffee from the squad recreation room he got it.

The first possible break-through.

Chapter 15

Lex and Ann appeared at Harry's elbow in the rec room.

They waited while he made his coffee, Ann with an excited flutter of her hands. C'mon, the hands said. Hurry up with what you're doing. They sat down at a table, Lex opened a small computer. As Ann started to talk he set it up.

'Boss, you remember that I was going to concentrate on the burka clad woman?' she said.

Harry nodded. 'And…?'

'I looked at the CCTV footage when she went into the building, all fashion,' she said.   Harry raised his eyebrows as he glanced away from the computer screen to Ann's face.

'Fashion?' he asked.

'The navy killer high heels and the matching silk burka. Plus the large leather handbag. All very expensive and all demanding to be seen. Well, I thought so looking at her image and actions. Everything she did said - look at me!' she said. Ann's voice rose at the end of the statement. Her hands danced to her words.

'And everyone did. Ordinary people who'd gone into the building on business before the blast. They remembered her and reported her at the first interviews. Especially too the security detail at the electronic gate,' Lex said. 'The woman who requested to see her face said she was a stunner. We're setting up an ID drawing with our forensic artist with her.'

'OK. So far so good,' Harry said as a go on I'm listening prompt.

He leaned back in his chair in an open posture.

'The security people expected her to go up to the diamond sale, but she didn't. The next place we sighted her was in the corridor on the floor below that of the sale.' Ann said. 'A scan from the CCTV showed she went into the toilet there, not far from the lifts. She didn't come out until after the blasts. My immediate question was why did she go all the way through security just to go up to the loo? She was there a while. And why go to that floor when there was one toilet for public use on the ground floor?'

'Here's where it gets even more interesting,' Lex interjected. He nodded to Ann, this was her investigation; her story.

'I called up the CCTV scans by the security gate on the ground floor after the blast. It was mayhem but the woman in the burka joined everyone rushing out of the building, as you would expect given the sirens were shrieking, smoke was pouring everywhere, and so on. She looked the same, a bit dishevelled as again you'd expect given what was going on and all the pushing and shoving. But I felt there was something different about her. Especially as she got outside the building and into the street. Her navy burka was there as before but I couldn't see her feet.' Ann looked towards Lex for support in her next statement. 'We noticed that her gait was slightly different.'

'I agree,' Lex said. 'There was something odd about her movements. As Ann said; her gait. Was she hurt somehow? Maybe. Did she lose her shoes in the rush to leave the building? Maybe. Was she in such shock at the bomb blast that she portrayed different characteristics from the person who'd passed through the security screen earlier? Maybe - but she looked shorter. Just the high heels gone? Was she carrying something different, heavier that she was protecting and keeping hidden? We couldn't see clearly, not even see the handbag. Where was it? Her hands were under the burka. We feel also that this was unusual.' When a person is hurry in in panic wouldn't they have their hands out?' From his sitting position Lex mimicked a person being pushed about in panic. 'For protection? For balance?'

Ann cut in. 'It struck us that possibly it wasn't the same woman. Height, build looked the same, or similar, but the changed walk?' She said.

Lex allowed a smile to grow over his black face. 'In the African bush the boys track animals and people by their footprints, by their gait. Maybe there's a bit of the tracker in me after all,' the tall urban Zulu said.

Ann looked at the blue-black face of Lex across the table not sure if he were joking as Harry huffed a laugh.

'Yes sure. Never met more of a city bloke than you, Lex,' Harry said. His eyes flickered to Ann. 'He got spooked by being out in the wide open Australian outback on our last case, but I reckon he could track someone by instinct on the internet clouds. Maybe across concrete too, but the bush... Forget it!' he said in explanation as Lex shrugged. 'OK. Back to business now.'

Ann flicked a bemused glance at Lex and continued. 'I checked back at the scans from the corridor outside that loo below the explosions. There'd been many women going in and out all day. A popular place. The burka woman left after the blasts and exactly four minutes afterwards a woman, who I hadn't recognised as going into the toilet, left and went quickly down to the lift that was still working. She made no attempt to use the lift that had been damaged. I thought first that she may have gone to her desk if she worked there to pick up something, but she didn't. She just left the floor.'

'Anything else about her?' Harry asked.

'She looked very upset as one might expect given the shock of the explosion and all,' Ann said. 'But...something in her expression wasn't quite right,' her voice trailed off.

The two detectives looked at Harry, faces lit up with expectation

'Is that it? A facial expression?' Harry said. 'Have you located that expensive handbag? Navy blue wasn't it and fashionable?'

Lex said in an aside to Ann. 'That's him. Never bloody satisfied...'

'Good observations. Now get on with it. The handbag. Who is this woman, or is it two women as I think you are supposing? Where did she go? What did she do next? Get picked up by a car? The embassy limo, heaven forbid...she's gone then if that's the case. We'll never get her back. Check with Murray in surveillance as a priority. Check the Sydney wide CCTV points. Get the geeks with their CIA facial recognition app. That'll get them happy,' Harry said.

'See Ann, I told you, he'd just want more.' Lex turned back to Harry a grin on his face. 'Getting all of that underway. We're not slouches. We're also checking the bus CCTVs – you never know she might have caught a bus.'

'Then look also at her going into another lavatory to get rid of the burka. Did she leave the bag for someone else? Was this burka just a prop, a disguise, if she or they were part of this crime? So, is it terrorism? A robbery or something we haven't thought of and was this woman part if it?' Harry mused aloud. 'Just had another thought you could follow up. Was the second person wearing the burka a woman? Could it have been a man? The burka could cover almost anyone, especially in a panic situation.'

Ann and Lex blinked at the new suggestion.

'I don't think so...' Ann ventured. 'The person walked like a woman...'

'OK, fair enough. Good work, now get on with it.'

The two detectives left the rec room talking and Harry went

back to his office. His own gait was lighter.

Yes, maybe we're getting somewhere, he thought. Something to hint at in his report to Tom at the afternoon meeting.

Chapter 16

'We've found a bullet,' Peter said as he, Harry and Lex arrived together at the door of the number two conference room for the DAF meeting at the end of the day. 'Didn't expect to find any. I've just put it into the system.' The excitement in his voice carried through the room.

'You sure?' Harry put out a hand to stop him.

'Of course, I'm sure, I'm not an idiot.' He grinned at Harry, an old friend. 'My pathologists don't make mistakes, especially with bullets. Doesn't it fit with your investigations?'

'It could…tell me more. Got a calibre yet?'

'Put me up to speak first then you'll get the whole lot.' Peter said as they went to be seated around the long table.

Harry welcomed the group leaders, and the Commissioner, as an opening to the DAF investigation day session. As Peter had requested Harry invited him to speak first with his update.

Peter Winston, whose English skin would rarely allow him to look anything but pale, sported a high red colour on his face and cheeks than usual as he looked around the room.

They could feel the rise in positive tension.

'We found a bullet,' the doctor said again in triumph. His verbal tone became quieter, more like the scientist he was.

'Where?' Harry's question was automatic.

'It was in the wall of the corridor, probably obscured by the remains of one of the security men who were blasted over it with the bang. It looks like it went through his body then into the wall. It was embedded quite deeply. One of my chaps doing the autopsy on the remains from the corridor found a hole in the sternum bone of one body. A breakthrough really that the sternum somehow remained almost intact. He got me to check and we decided that it might not have been caused by the explosion. Made us think; bullet wound?' Peter put photos of the sternum on the table and there was an excited shuffle as the detectives reached for them. 'See,' Peter said as he pointed, 'that hole is rounder than one would expect from an explosion. Still I've seen buttons bashed into bone that made a neat imprint with a bomb blast...'

Harry cut in. 'Then what...?'

'I sent a pathologist and one of the cadets back to the scene and they found a bullet obscured by all the mess. We're looking for more too.' Peter sent a look to Harry as a response to the next question he knew that he would ask. 'We don't know the calibre yet as it was mashed on impact and further damaged by the blast. But I think it was a .22. A small bullet, from maybe a small weapon.'

'How did that gun get through security?' Harry muttered. He looked up to see that Lex had made a note of this question.

Through the hubbub of voices, the Commissioner asked the obvious question. 'And now Peter, you're suggesting that there was an initial murder before the explosions? It could put a different slant on the investigation.'

'Yes, this wasn't expected. We will now look for other bullet wounds, as we are doing anyway. We do a complete and thorough autopsy...'

'I don't expect any other sort from you and your team,' the Commissioner was quick to say, 'but now what can we get from this? Are we talking terrorism or robbery or even personal vendetta?'

Quiet voices muttered around the table as comments were made.

Terrorism or robbery? Or personal?

Harry brought the meeting to order. 'We've an additional piece of evidence that also might throw another light on this case.' He told of the theory that Lex and Ann had suggested to him about from observations of the CCTV tapes of the burka clad woman. There was general comment, questions that Harry cut short. 'Although I'm pleased, and like this assumption, at this stage I'm keeping it as just that, until we get more evidence. Detective Maxwell-Smith will continue this line and I'll give her a couple of other men to assist her. Lex has other things to do and it'll all come back to me, but I'm hopeful that this will lead us somewhere.'

'What the Premier is going to want to know, with all the publicity and speculation about this case, is do you think this is terrorism or robbery? I think he'd be very pleased if I could tell him that it just a common or garden robbery, even if it is on a hideous scale...' Tom said.

'With all respects, Sir, I don't think we're at that point of the investigation yet. Bullets and the mysterious burka woman could still point to terrorism. It is probably hard for him, given the pressure of the election but until we have much more evidence I'm not willing to say which way it will go.' Harry said.

Tom Phillips gave a chuckle. 'Harry Shaw, I've never heard you being so careful and diplomatic. Surely you don't think that our premier would want to make any political mileage about this case?'

Chuckles and murmurs criss-crossed the table as the members watched Harry's discomfort as he squirmed under Tom's gaze. They knew his strong opinions of interfering politicians.

'No, Sir. That's for the record but it is too early. We can be pleased, grateful even for the additional funding for this case...but...'

'There you go again, Harry. Sure you're not a candidate for parliament?' Tom looked around the room. 'I haven't heard anything. Have any of you heard talk of this?'

Harry spluttered. 'You've got to be kidding...' as the room echoed with laughs. As it subsided he grinned then said. 'OK, back to business. Anything else?'

The murmurs around the table ceased.

'The CCTV scans from the building are proving their worth, but the cameras in the vicinity of the crime scene were all destroyed. Have the uniform guys come up with anything useful? I did get the report from their chief that not much was seen by people going in and out of the building. So far no-one has posted more useful selfies on the internet from the crime scene area but time will tell. And we have the geeks, sorry Bill, surfing away looking for anything to help this investigation,' Harry's report continued.

Bill Zeigler gave a grin. He was used to being teased but the public would never learn about being stupid and often downright self-incriminating with images on U-tube, Facebook and the like. His department was becoming an important arm of detective work. 'Sure, we'll save the porno for another day,' he said as his grin went with a sideways look at Tom Phillips. An important area of his unsavoury work was detecting areas of child pornography with interstate and overseas agencies.

Harry said. 'We should get a print photo from the security CCTV scan of the burka woman or the other woman who Lex and Ann are treating as suspicious. We'll show them around. Maybe we could get a result. A little discretion there please as I'd prefer this line of enquiry to be kept quiet for now.'

'I've got a metal detector into the crime scene and especially into the corridor. My teams are working hard but the mess from twenty-two blown apart bodies takes a while to go through. Not much time to look for slugs.' Pap said.

'Can we offer more personnel?' Harry asked.

'Maybe not for the actual searches or autopsies but additional draftspersons to do the body and parts plotting would be very good.'

Harry turned to the Commissioner. 'Is it possible that one or more police cadets who've made enquiries about working in crime scene investigation could be used as plotters? It'd give them experience too.'

Tom looked at Peter and got a nod. 'That can be arranged. I'll have a chat with the senior tutors and see if they can give us suitable candidates for the job. Good thinking...'

'So - we've got a bullet, a female mystery and many other aspects under investigation. We're now well over the first forty-eight hours when I usually really like to get a result by this time but this's a big one and looks bloody complex. Keep on with the good work. Bringing in a couple of young fresh cadets, blooding them must be useful for the future. Another DAF meeting tomorrow, unless we have more urgent things to report.' Harry looked at the tired and drawn faces around the table. 'Night all then,' he said, stifling a yawn without much luck. 'Go home. Get some rest. We all need it.'

The yawn was contagious and echoed by many detectives as they filed out of the room.

Chapter 17

Harry went home and almost nodded off over the dinner of roast beef and vegetables that Rhette had prepared for him. She had frozen the shepherd's pie for another night. It would keep and be ready for him then.

She wondered why she had spent so much time cooking the rib roast to a degree of rare to medium perfection when he was totally wrapped up in the huge investigation he was leading. The meat was browned, the garlic, herbs and salt and pepper rubbed in and by the time he came home the whole flat smelled inviting. He came through the door looking tired but he attempted to throw off his work concerns. Rhette smiled, he would probably have been content with baked beans out of a can as he was used to getting for himself when he was living alone, she thought. Still he ate the meal, drunk a glass of good red wine, and made appreciative noises about it all. That was enough.

Later, as they went to bed and he'd slept almost instantly, she wondered again how she could help this strong man who now lay spooned against her with one arm slung over her body. She snuggled into him and was content for the moment.

In the small hours of the morning her ghosts came out of the past to haunt her, especially in Sydney. She lay eyes wide then and her thoughts ran amuck as thoughts do in those still quiet times. She was very aware that the Sydney city was awake. The murmur of the city was always there. People were awake. Not just the ordinary citizens going about their legitimate night business but the underworld where evil slithered down the streets, oozed out of bars and nightclubs and walked on silent feet to linger on in the shadows of daylight.

Evil lurked like that TV moment.

She had seen it only once, before it was replaced by other footages, but she could have sworn she recognised the man image in the café. She couldn't confirm what she'd seen but she's known him more by his shape, his movements than by seeing his face.

So familiar.

Feared and so hated.

Because of him her father and sister were dead; killed by his henchman. But Hood was dead; he had to have been killed when his plane crashed out over the Southern Ocean on the fleeing flight from Coober Pedy. He was reported as dead, so he had to be dead. Her mind said it over and over as she lay beside Harry.

Hood was dead.

He was no longer a threat.

But, was he?

She was mistaken in what she had seen. She had to be wrong and she cemented her resolve not to bother Harry with her worries. He had enough of his own. She would get on with finding a study course and use that to cancel out her stresses. In the meantime, she thought through the opening movements of Tai Chi, imagined her body moving in the rhythms of the class. In bringing up the Chi she took a couple of slow even breaths concentrating on the flow of air into and out of her body, and finally slept.

Chapter 18

Harry's driver picked him up next morning at seven o'clock a little later than usual, and at his request, they drove past the smoke marked remains of the crime scene building in the CBD.

The police tapes which fluttered in the wind two days ago were down but a police presence was still evident. A smattering of the curious were there; and the press were photographing the bunches of flowers, sympathy cards and handwritten messages for the victims. Harry shook his head, he understood that people wanted to show concern, horror and empathy for others but the modern, to him, expressions were shudder worthy. A society, swathed in a shawl of needing to be seen as a part of any and all happenings. Vicariously being involved. It saddened him and he wanted to get results for the victims not just to placate the public.

Later, half an hour into the day shift Samantha Morton walked into Harry's office. Her hair was a becoming soft French twist in comparison to his already less than immaculate tufts as he'd continually run his fingers through his dark hair in frustration. And his tie was askew.

Harry looked up from his screens. 'Tell me something happy,' he said.

'Not sure if this is happy,' she said, 'but forensics have come across something that's a bit interesting.'

'I'll take interesting.'

'It appears that many of the CCTV cameras put into the crime scene were fakes. Just put there to look as though everything was being filmed. The security was terrible if this was the case, Harry. I've heard of fake cameras being done to deter crime but not in areas of high stakes like this multi-million-dollar diamond sale.'

'I think you have just changed the investigation to one of robbery, not terrorism. Sure the 9/11 bastards took months or years to prepare for the day but this diamond sale was semi-secret and only open to a few people,' Harry said. He put his fingers over his mouth, chin on hand in a reflective stance that told Sam that he was absorbing the new information. 'The time element is all wrong for terrorism. Robbery, that even takes time to set up, unless there's an inside element.'

She waited then said, 'I've thought robbery from day one. Interesting, isn't it?'

'Yes. I think the Premier will be a whole lot happier if he can tell the public that we are dealing with robbery not terrorism. It opens the investigation a whole lot wider too. What odds?' Harry suddenly threw the question at Sam. 'I say 80%...you?'

'90% robbery. I'm even surer. Even with the burka woman I've been convinced that we're after criminals not terrorists. I don't mean totally that they're out of it but this doesn't smell like an act of terrorism to me. The burka woman smells of a diversion to confuse the investigation. Maybe...'

'OK. Then let's have them work out what cameras were fakes and what could have been recorded if they hadn't been blown apart. Seems odd that the more modern pinhole spy cameras weren't in use,' Harry mused. 'Lex can get onto the questions this brings up immediately. Right up his street.'

'Nothing yet from the pathologists about the IDs of the victims?' Sam asked.

'We're waiting more information. Had many people coming

forward to claim that their family or friends were at the sale. Most are the usual crackpots but a couple may be genuine. Peter's team have taken DNA swabs and they are hopeful that they can make matches. So far there had been little from the embassies. I thought that there may be more given that a couple of embassies have high flyers who have come to Sydney for the diamond sales. Some people only fly and enter countries under the embassy flags. Makes taking the gems they buy out of Australia less amendable to taxes.'

'No sign of anyone like the burka lady from an embassy?' Sam asked. 'No diplomat's wife missing?'

'Nothing yet and I'm hoping there won't be,' Harry said. There was a shudder in his voice. 'It'd cause an international incident and bring in politicians, Foreign Affairs, Interpol and all the alphabet rest. It'll be CIA next! More media by the bucket load! We've got enough without this; and the conspiracy theorists have added speculations that are running rife in the media.'

'Not a simple case,' Sam said.

'No, not simple,' Harry echoed. 'But then again we never get the easy ones...' He looked up at her as she turned to leave the office with a grin. They both knew that the bread and butter cases were satisfying to put to bed but the more complex ones were what they excelled at.

Another hour later Samantha stood again at Harry's office door.

She paused a moment looking in at the tall dark detective, admitting she could never call him classically good looking. More like a bull dog but his features were so very attractive in their own way. If Rhette wasn't around, she thought, she might have let their working friendship develop further. She liked Rhette so that was that. Rhette. She'd asked about her name and Harry'd said that her mother loved the film "Gone with the Wind" and Rhette

Butler when she was pregnant and that was that... Her intake of amused reflective breath caused him to look away from his screens, and quickly she strode into the room and put the email copy she held down onto his desk.

'Seen this yet?' she asked. 'Just arrived from Pap.'

'Yes,' Harry said. 'I was just looking into the building specifics to see if they had put CCTV cameras into the service stairwells when it was built. Apparently they did ... '

'So why weren't they working?' Sam interjected. She wasn't surprised that Harry was so far ahead regarding this and already looking to find reasons before jumping to conclusions. She was a jumper, fact, but often the jumps were warranted. Sam suddenly realised she was leaning over Harry's desk and sat herself down beside him on an adjacent chair. He turned the computer screen so that both could then see the screen he was working on.

'That we have to find out as it could open another line of inquiry. It's very possible that persons unknown used those non-public stairs to plant the bombs, or if it were robbery to get in and then away.'

'How would they know about the cameras being off? When Argyle Diamonds booked the sale-rooms wouldn't they have been assured and confident that there was sufficient CCTV monitoring for the security of their sale. This is or must be an important factor. Do you want me to follow up, get in touch with the building owners and shake them up a little?' Sam asked.

'I rather suspect that the owners, and their insurers, are shaken up now. Could be the best time to ask. You do it.' He consulted his screen. 'I'm chasing the flight arrival time of the CEO's of Argyle's personal jet. He's due soon and will go straight to the Commissioner when he arrives. They'll want an update from me.'

'Lucky you... Anything more come through from Smitty

regarding the burka woman? I've not had a message from her yet.'

'I met her in the coffee room and she said that nothing had shown up. No embassy claims her, no hire car firm bookings, nothing. She'd even checked the CCTV re the flag on the limo and said that it was possible that the flag was tethered so it couldn't be recognised. It didn't flutter when the car moved,' Harry said.

'Tethered? The flag tied down?'

'Very hard to recognise the flag or country origin when the flag is tied. Could be very significant in ID-ing the car, the possible embassy, and the woman. Also, who was driving the car? Has the car or driver been traced? Any cars torched since the incident? Arson cases?'

'That's good work but she should have let us all know. I'll have a quiet word. She's new to the squad and has to let us know everything, the nothings too. I'll let her have another couple of hours on that burka woman enigma and then put her on chasing the car. She's spent more than enough time there and there's many more areas to cover.'

'Sounds a good plan.'

'I'll email you re the cameras when I get that information.' Sam said.

Later in the morning Samantha got an email from Harry.

'CCTV camera surveillance in service stairwells was discontinued for economic reasons. The building would have needed one more security staff to monitor them and that would mean a rent increase for the buildings tenants. A close vote decided negative on rent increase. Insurance was not happy and it could impinge on insurance payout if it is discovered that the service stairwells were used in the incident. Signs of the economic times but that's cleared up. Probable that these stairs used to prepare the crime, and escapes if any.

Who would have known about the diamond sale?

Get a detective to follow that up.'

The message ended.

Samantha Norton responded with more information for Harry.

'Have just had a call from Dr Peter Winston,' she wrote in Email.

'One female body from the crime scene appears to be younger than expected in the circumstances of the incident would suggest. Ties in with Commissioner Tom Phillips report from the parents from a Sydney top school saying their daughter Marion Delaney, aged 17, is missing. She went to do work experience at the diamond sale.

I contacted personnel of Argyle in WA. They said that it was not their policy to employ or have work experience persons at the major sale because of possible attempted robbery factors. Safety and also the confidential nature of the diamond transactions. Their staff consisted of Sarah Wilkins and Raymond Duke with two local security guards.

Who was this young female body? Is she the missing school girl?

Who allowed the work experience and for what reasons? Did Wilkins or Duke know the girl? Was it a personal favour to the school? I'll follow this up personally with Ann. Who contacted the school etc.

Peter also stated that the body in the lift was also female. Probable mid 30s. She was very unlucky to arrive when the lift doors opened the moment the first explosion occurred.

The body was at the back of the lift so she may have seen something before she died. Or perhaps she was blown there by the force of the explosion.

Comment: I'm now saying 100% robbery. You?'

Finally, Harry stuck his head around Sam's door.

'OK I'll go to 90%. Getting close to 100% because of the bullet found in the corridor. Question. Were the security guards killed before the explosions and by whom?' He said.

'At least we've still got questions to answer. But it's time the day shift ends without overtime unless it's absolutely necessary. They're knackered!' Sam suggested.

'Sure encourage some rest for all of us. I'm going home to Shepherd's pie. Mark's saying that Ana and Piet wonder who he is…they're only seeing him on Skype. He may need some time off soon to get in a quick trip to Adelaide.'

'I'll get the word out to everyone,' Sam yawned.

'OK, then add that there's the usual DAF meeting this afternoon. We'll keep it informal.'

Chapter 19

4pm DAF meeting started on time with all the department heads present.

Harry had already given the all his information gathered via Email and they had discussed these items.

Max from Surveillance said, stating the obvious, 'Most of the internal scans of the building are bloody useless. All CCTV are gone from the stairs. From the corridor and sale room where the bombs went off and the lift's camera were damaged beyond giving us nothing worth using.' His voice, usually pitched low and quiet was raised, reflecting the frustration he was experiencing with the dismal security in the building.

Harry leaned forward in his chair. 'Aren't the CCTV camera materials taped? Those in the lift and the relevant corridor?' He asked his face a question mark of incredibility.

'Not this time. The Argyle people asked that this not be done this time because of confidentiality of the buyers,' Max said. The shake of his head and closed eyes spoke volumes of his opinion of confidentiality.

'So, who ordered it?' from Harry.

'It was in the standing orders from Ms Wilkes who was running the show,' again the shake of Max's head.

'What about the second lift further down the corridor from the sale room?'

'We've checked the tapes from that and no-one went to the

top floor that day using that lift,' Max said.

'Had a thought,' Harry interrupted as he directed a question back. 'Do any of the lower floor CCTV cameras cover the entrances to the service stairs?'

'No, they don't. I thought of that too and we checked. The building surveillance is pathetic, put in by idiots. People who didn't know what they were doing and look at the bloody results.' Max paused. 'I checked the previous day, even to the week before tapes. The Argyle people'd asked that the whole floor be not viewed. Again, it's all to do with confounded confidentiality and secrecy so they could set up the diamond sale room without anyone knowing exactly what was happening and where. Except for the invitees.'

'OK, I'll check with the Argyle CEO and get his take on what was usual regarding cameras etc with a sale. So far it's sounding well planned for secrecy or if robbery then with inside connections. Robbery or terrorism? Until we get a few more answers about the victims I'm not going to rule out either. He's still pretty upset. He said he'd had a phone call from Sarah Wilkes just before the blast and she was happy with the sales. He was a very upset man. What's next?'

Max excused himself to answer a phone call from the CIA. 'I'll organise a couple of coffees on my way back,' he said.

Harry smiled as he left the room. Max had a young officer who was interested in a girl working in the coffee shop next door and he was sure that commercial percolated coffee rather than the insipid instant wouldn't be a problem. Max was so keen he was paying for them all.

Bill Zeigler said, 'The internet has been remarkably quiet in terrorism area. Not even ISIS's made a claim. Or anyone else. Seems it's off the radar and by the same criteria there's no rumours about local lads doing a robbery.'

'Any one big enough for something like this in Sydney?' Lex asked. Not being local his knowledge of the criminal scene was less that the other detectives.

'There's plenty with the scope in the gangs just no-one has shown inordinate interest in diamonds before. Drugs, money laundering and the like, sure but not diamonds so far.' Harry mused. 'It could be another method of cleaning up the profits of crime.

'I'd go so far to say that the perpetrators aren't local.' Bill hunched his shoulders in the grey cardigan he wore and peered over his half frame glasses. 'The local lads are getting clever with security but there's usually some hint that something's on the go in the internet clouds. This time nothing at all.'

'Thanks Bill.' Harry scanned the table. 'Anyone else got interesting that we haven't looked at yet or are you all still within the first days of investigations?'

Bill shuffled. 'In the interests of laying out the whole package I've used the CIA photo identification app on some of the media and other records of the immediate scene after the bombs went off.'

'And?' Harry said.

'There's a face in a café in a selfie taken by a young woman. It's very indistinct but we're working more on it. Just got a hunch that this was someone overseeing the crime.' Bill said.

'Keep at it. Anything else?' Harry asked.

'Can't be sure given that there's a question about one of the Argyle people being on Max's watch list. Low down on the list, he's not been a problem. Just Australian Muslim and a single male.'

'Now you bring a terrorist suspect back into it.' Harry's voice was incredulous.

'The FBI photo app is new, still unreliable but they've had a good look at Ray Duke.'

Harry reached for his phone. 'How long have you known about Ray Duke?' he demanded when Max Tydsdale answered.

'I'm outside your door, on my way back to see you.' There was breathlessness in Max's voice.

'Get yourself in here.' Harry said as he got to his feet and opened the door. Max put two takeaway coffees on Harry's desk. 'If the coffees an apology for me not getting this information quicker, then I accept. Where's Bill's coffee? He was the one with your news...'

'Bill's computers. He got the update directly from the CIA geeks. I had to wait for the official word.' Max said.

'You've got more I hope,' Harry said as he leaned across the desk to take the coffee. He took a swig. His lips pursed as his face said no sugar.

'Yes. A bit. Ray Duke isn't his name. His birth name was Mohammed Oman. He was a refugee who came to Australia thirty years ago from the Middle East with his family. The whole family is naturalised and the Argyle people know his history. They found a young man, educated in management, gave him the chance he deserves... They've had no problems with him at all.'

'Get a complete check on him and his family. We're back to square one if he doesn't check out,' Harry said. The Commissioner and Premier are going to be less than delighted, he thought, if the terrorism thread returns.

Chapter 20

Harry sat in Commissioner Tom Phillips' office on the top floor of the Police building, ready to give a personal report.

The chairs were deep on a carpet in a soft grey shade and his large desk, with a matching cabinet of deep red wood, shone with polish. There was none of the "I'm important" photos of the Commissioner with influential celebrities or people on the walls but a large oil painting of the Sydney city looked to be an original. Opposite was another that showed Sydney in the early days with sailing ships entering the harbour through the Heads. The two paintings looked like before and after views. A discrete family photo showed Tom's extended family, framed simply, on the desk.

The discussion was at the end of a question and answer session between Tom and Harry had regarding the DAF and other cases being handled by the Major Crime Squad.

'Overall the investigation's slow as it fits no known MO. None of the local boys seem to be involved and it looks like an outside job. We've contacted Interpol and other agencies for their views.'

Tom Phillips nodded. 'Yes. But we'll have to consider going back to normal shifts as soon as we can. In fact, give the squad leave as needed.'

Harry said. 'We're doing that already Sir. The squad's put in many additional hours since the start of the DAF bombings but now the long hard slog's starting to get answers to questions we are just beginning to ask.'

Tom checked his diary. Here it comes, the man had yet another appointment, Harry thought.

'Mark Llewellyn. 'He's getting married soon, isn't he? In Adelaide?'

Harry did a mental gulp. The Commissioner was that up to date with the squad's personal lives.

'Yes Sir. Next month.' Harry said.

'Well, he'll need a few days off to get back home. Help his fiancé with things...'

'Yes. He'd appreciate that.' Harry laughed. 'Mark will get leave. This doesn't mean the Premier's starting to worry about the extra costs in man hours that this investigation's costing?' The smile lapsed from his face. 'Now that we've not discounted terrorism as a likely scenario in the DAF bombings he hasn't got cold feet with expenditure. The election...the opposition starting to quibble...?' Harry let the statement hang.

Tom cut in before his chief investigator could sound off against politics. 'OK. Let's just say that we need to continue to treat this as any major crime and investigate it as normal. As I said before, the terrorism aspects are chilling and Max's boys will be underfoot as you can expect. So far they haven't found any connection, nothing on the wind. Nothing from the CIA, INTERPOL or the British either. They're interested as half the world is with this case.' The Commissioner leaned back in his chair. 'Keep me posted with any developments and commend your teams for the work they've done already.'

This was Harry's cue.

Meeting closed.

Outside Harry shrugged his shoulders. OK then, he thought. Everything on hold until we get this DAF concluded. I didn't expect any difference but had to ask. Keep my assignment in his agenda.

He took the stairs down to his office directly under the Commissioner's room. 'I'll get Mark to book his flight to see Ana, asap.' He said aloud.

Chapter 21

The atmosphere in the detectives' open space squad room fluctuated. They were frustrated with the dead ends they were experiencing. Most, if not all, leads were going no-where.

The burka woman.

Who was she? What had she done in the building?

Was she just there to go for a pee as one of the detectives said? Was the perceived difference in her gait significant after the bombs went off? Was it as different as they had first thought?

Her car was an embassy vehicle reported as stolen from the British compound. That was the first lead they could work on but the CCTV in the embassy grounds had been compromised and the gate lock bypassed. The British staff were conducting their own enquiries but were adamant that the Mercedes used was not of their doing.

Other investigation leads were facing dead ends and the usual criminal leaks were going nowhere.

Rhette sat at her computer.

After thinking she saw Hood on the day of the robbery on TV she wanted to clear her mind of it. She had said nothing to Harry about it.

She was looking for an off-campus university course. Study could finally give her something to do that would help her divert her fears and hopefully lay her demons at rest. If not at rest, then sidelined out of her thoughts for part of her day. Ancient Egypt had always fascinated her. Maybe there was an archaeology course somewhere that included this, something serious and worth doing. She was interested in people and usually history just told the stories of men and in these modern times was there a course that looked at the lives of women? One could only hope, she thought.

She clicked on all the state Australian museums she felt she could visit to see examples of the Egyptian female mummies, and then when looking at Hobart, Tasmania, she saw the MONA reference. She clicked on that and saw that it contained an active camera section where she could roam the exhibits and look at them in detail.

Great, there were female mummies from the Middle Kingdom, a wooden replica of a royal barge to travel on the Nile and real or imitation royal jewellery in gold and lapis. She looked at the 'live' scene from MONA – the Museum of Old and New Art. In one cross a group of infant school children played at the feet of one mummy while their teacher tried to keep their attention on what she was telling them and not on the older boy who was hiding behind the mummy case. Rhette smiled as he did a 'mummy walk.' The children laughed and the teacher smiled and tried to look cross. One very small girl from her class copied the strutting, arms out legs straight movement as the CCTV camera shifted focus.

The image, on another camera, was still in the vicinity of the Egyptian artefacts. A man stood apparently watching the teacher and children. No, he had his back to the camera and his gaze was more likely on a different exhibit. This had a large notice on it that Rhette could just make out – 'On loan from the Cairo Museum' she read. Good, a real artefact, she thought.

The man reached to touch the exhibit and a MONA attendant

stepped forward, her hand raised. Rhette could lip read the woman's words. The universal 'Don't touch please.' The man turned towards the attendant, an annoyed frown dented his forehead. The frown changed as though the man was trying to sweet talk the attendant into something. He stood close and with now a charming mile.

That face. Rhette immediately recognised that face.

Hood! Dieter Hood!

Again!

'Ahhh!' an intake of breath, of shock then denial burst from her lips. 'No!' Rhette could feel the blood drain from her face, her next breath was a gulp. Air, she needed air and it felt as if all the oxygen had been sucked out of the room around her. Sweat broke out on her face and along her hair line. She pushed her hands through her red curls as a bout of nausea threatened to make her gag. She put her hand over her mouth as she sat back to force her diaphragm to pull air into her lungs.

It was Hood.

This wasn't a figment of her imagination this time.

It was him. It was! She wasn't dreaming; she wasn't mistaken and delusional. This was the man who had nearly killed her. He had killed her father, her sister! Killed or ordered killed.

Rhette grabbed for her mobile phone and hit the speed dial for Harry's personal number.

'Go onto the MONA website,' she said without preamble. She reeled off the on-line address. 'Go to the Egyptian display. Now!'

Harry was on line and did as he was bid. 'I see children and a teacher looking at a mummy,' he said.

'Wait! The camera angle has shifted. Wait. It's got to go back to a different one. An attendant and Hood. It's Hood, he's there...' Rhette's voice trailed off. 'Please... please... I'm not going mad. He's there...'

The camera angle changed again, possibly drawn to the close discussion between the man and the attendant.

Harry peered into his screen.

'You're possibly right,' he said. 'It looks like Hood...different hair colour.'

'It is...and I saw him on the

scene of the bombed building. In that interview with Melissa Doyle. It was gone in the next news cross but he was in the café ...' Rhette realised she was babbling. Perspiration was still slicking on her top lip, her hands slippery on the mobile phone and the dread feeling was back. She was rigid in her chair.

'What?' Harry said. The incredulousness in his voice there even over the phone. 'Why didn't you say something before then?'

'I thought I was dreaming. Seeing Hood everywhere I looked. But...' Rhette's voice stumbled, 'but that time I was only going on the shape of the man and the way he moved. I was sure it was him but not sure enough to worry you with it. But Hood is in that museum right now. It is him...You want him for murder and everything else. Get him! Arrest him!'

'OK...' Harry said. There was a sharp intake of his breath, 'Betta go. Love you.'

She could hear Harry's fingers touching buttons on another phone before he dis-connected from her. To Channel 9 or to MONA? He'd get the tapes. Send a someone there...

She looked again at the MONA scene. It now showed the extensive book collection in the sale room. People browsed. Her hand was tense on the mouse. She wanted to yell at them ... there's someone very dangerous in the building.

A murderer!

Chapter 22

It was late.

A barrage of fierce change of season winds buffeted the Qantas jet as Mark returned to Adelaide on Friday night to see Ana and Piet. The winds roaring across the Adelaide plains were accompanied by a downpour of rain that tested the strength of the air-bridge to the terminal lounge. It shuddered against the frame of the plane and disembarking passengers scurried along the shaking path to the perceived safety of the terminal lounge.

Some Adelaide homecoming, Mark thought. Weatherwise anyway.

He was ready to drop; to fall into Ana's arms and melt into the perfume of her skin and hair in their wide warm bed. Bliss. Just to sleep tonight. He was too tired after the days and weeks of intensified investigation into the Sydney bombing with scant results, to do anything else. Piet would be well asleep and Ana waiting.

Tomorrow would be another day.

He slung his carry-on bag over his shoulder and stepped onto the escalator descending from the arrivals lounge to the ground floor of the terminal to where the last straggler passengers were waiting to check in tickets and baggage for the 'red eye specials' to Melbourne and Sydney. The planes to Perth would go just before the city noise curfew clamped down and would arrive in Western Australia before dawn. He didn't pity them their flight. In the other direction, he could see a large group of people who waited by the carousels to collect their luggage before they braved the outside weather to cross the paved open courtyard to find transport.

With no need to go to the carousel, Mark just wanted to clear the airport and get a taxi to Ana.

Suddenly TV lights flooded the lower escalator as a posse of reporters and photographers jumped forward to demand comments from a returning team of cricketers from England. They congregated as a rowdy mob at the base of escalator and their numbers blocked the walkway.

Shit! Mark thought. Just what I need.

People banked up behind him as he reached the mid flat break in the escalator. The procession halted. Mobile phones were aimed at the cricketers for selfies and the hubbub of noise increased. For some people, it was something to tell their families about tomorrow. A little vicarious moment.

Suddenly a man standing just below Mark threw up his arm as if to shield his eyes from the glaring lights. Nothing unusual, the lights were blinding. But then the man pulled his face into his collar and turned, pushing against Mark and the flow of people behind them, to try to return up the descending moving escalator.

Mark's immediate reaction was to check the man out. The policeman in Mark.

Questioning an unexpected action. Policing 101.

A flash of recollection passed between Mark and the man who grasped the hand rail to pull himself upwards.

Eyeball to eyeball.

There was no way he could push past Mark.

The man turned, jostled and elbowed his way through the throng and started down again. He thrust people aside left and right. Cries and shouts of annoyance and protest followed in his path.

A sleepy eyed little girl, travelling with the cricketer families, blocked his path just below where Mark stood. The man grabbed the child and physically threw her up and out of his way. She shrieked in fright as her body was jack-knifed up and over the escalator rail.

Mark lunged.

He grabbed the child's flailing leg with a handful of pyjama pants as she began the fall to the concrete floor below. The terrified child screamed louder. Mark's body was more than half over the rail, the precipice yawned wide below. He was in danger of falling as the child jerked and swung in his grip. His lower hand held the child and his upper arm grabbed for the moving escalator rail.

His fingers locked, held, and he hauled her and himself, back to safety.

He held the struggling girl to his chest, his heart pounding.

He thrust her towards a woman and she gathered the child, dark curls tousled and tears streamed down her cheeks, into her arms. Mark caught a glimpse of her shocked eyes. Grateful would come later.

Mark turned back looking for his quarry. Now having pushed past him, the man was below him, as he had made his escape from Mark and was off the descending escalator. He shoved aside the waiting reporters, TV crews and cricketers being interviewed. An indignant melee of protesting people was left in his wake.

The man ran.

'Stop!' Mark shouted. 'Stop that man!'

From his descending position and now almost at the bottom of the escalator Mark was momentarily halted by the throng of people regaining their composure. Over their heads he could see the running figure exit the doors to the outside. He followed and sped through the gap in the crowd left by the fugitive, the doors had closed and he had to wait precious seconds for the automatic doors to reopen. He raced out across the wide expanse of the forecourt. Darkness, rain and wind lashed about him. Nothing…

'Where'd the heck did you go, you bastard,' he gasped as the cold air hit him.

Mark was jerked to a halt as he was grabbed from behind.

Instinctively he blocked the hold, and swung the person attempting to detain him. No way would this man he was following get away. He stopped as he felt a second person, in uniform, fisted the material of his shirt front.

'Shit!' he groaned, his temper rising. The feds, he thought. Airport Federal Police. Bloody late when he could have used them before.

'I'm police! SAPOL!' he shouted as the smaller agent attempted to change a grip on Mark that was supposed to hold him. It didn't and Mark shook himself free.

The other airport policeman stepped back and yelled, 'Stop!' in a gasping breath. He'd managed to pull his sidearm from his belt and now he held a gun on Mark.

'Idiots! It's not me you should have nabbed but the man I was chasing,' Mark said through tight teeth. 'Now the bastard'll have got away.' Adrenalin was still raged through his body; his heart pumping.

'Identify yourself,' the smaller person demanded. She was a head shorter than Mark, and still gripped his arm with her hands. He looked down into the eyes of a fiery brunette and shook the hands away. So, the main attempted restraining officer was a female and she was fuming. The other male officer still had his gun aimed at Mark.

Mark could understand why. Airport incidents could well be terrorism.

He smiled, held his hands away from his body. 'Hold it. I'm just getting my ID badge.' He pulled his wallet free and extracted his warrant card. He held it up to them. 'I'm Senior Sergeant Mark Llewellen, South Australian Police, currently on secondment to the New South Wales Federal police. Alright?'

The gun was lowered as Mark started the move back into the terminal building out of the wind and the rain. The light was better there and the officers followed where they verified his warrant card.

'OK, Sir,' she handed the card back.

'And you are?' he said to her.

'I'm Officer Janet Betts, and this is Officer Todd James,' she said with a frown at the man, overweight and bulging out of his uniform, beside her. 'We could've stopped you, or the man you were chasing if he'd moved faster. Been more useful.' She pushed a hank of wet dark hair back under her uniform hat.

Mark suppressed a smile, and then got down to business. He had more rank than they did and he'd use that rank now. 'Well, you didn't and now he's gone. But you can be useful. I need to check what flight the man came on. Where was he from?' He stopped and recognised that he had to say the name of the criminal he'd recognised. 'He's Sean Hood, or that was one of his AKA's. I'll bet he's no longer using it but it was him.' Back from the dead, he thought.

'That's going to be difficult if you don't know his current name,' Officer James said.

Betts spoke up suddenly. 'If he didn't get his luggage when he took off we might be able to do something.'

'Damn it, you're right.' Mark said.

He looked towards the escalators where his own take-on luggage still rode the last step. In the flurry of the escape and the grabbing of the little girl he'd dropped the bag. He strode over and grabbed it, pleased that it was at least there. The small gifts for Ana and Pietie were hopefully intact.

The cricketers were gone but one male Channel Nine reporter remained with a camera man. The latter's camera was at shoulder height, obviously recording.

'Sir,' the reporter said. 'We got what you did. Saved that little girl. It was amazing...' He drew breath as Mark suspected that the next question asked would be about him.

He turned to the camera man. 'Put that away would you...did you get a shot of the man I chased?'

'Yes. Not a problem. It'll be on the news. Better stuff than the cricket mob yakking on about beating the Poms. Getting the ashes back again.'

Mark cringed. Not what he wanted. 'I need to see what you recorded. Can you show me right now?'

'Sure.'

With the rewind Mark saw that he'd been correct in his ID.

Sean Hood.

Even though Hood had shied away he was immediately recognisable. A change of hair length and even colour but the camera saw through it. Got you, he thought. Harry and I knew you were still alive. He said, 'Getting me a copy's no problem, is it? But you can't use that footage. He's a wanted criminal and I can and will have to stop you. I can get the authority as high as I need. Sorry mate.'

The reporter blustered. 'This is real news. The public has a right to know...'

'Yeah, right.' Mark handed the camera man his card. 'Get a copy to police headquarters tonight, and thanks, one day you could get a much bigger story.'

'You'll remember me when this happens. Give me an exclusive?' He pushed his own card into Mark's hands.

'Yes, that's a promise.'

Officer James came to stand beside Mark. 'The luggage carrousel from Sydney's clear but the Coober Pedy flight have one case doing the rounds. No one's claimed it.'

'Great...get that to the police headquarters too. Tonight.'

'You can't do that,' James said. 'It's not procedure...'

'Stuff your procedure. This investigation's bigger than letting that case go around and around indefinitely. Or until someone steals it. Just do it. Send it to the SAPOL Headquarters.' Mark said. As the adrenalin rush started to subside he could feel the tiredness drooping his eyes and his patience.

Mark turned with James and Betts as he headed again for the front doors. There was no hope that Sean Hood would come back for the case no matter what. It could hold DNA evidence to conclusively prove the ID. 'I'd take the suitcase myself right now and really bugger up chain of evidence, so you get it delivered as I said. OK? And get them to sign it in and to seal it − treat it as important and essential.'

Officer James decided that he had a witness in Betts that he'd been ordered by a senior officer and he'd better let it rest. In addition, Betts seemed mesmerised by this Llewellen character and he needed to take back his own seniority by the apparent importance of the task so late at night. He nodded his agreement.

Mark crossed to the Taxi stand his mobile phone in hand. The first call was to Ana as he was now very late, then to the Duty Officer at police headquarters advising him of the delivery of the suitcase. One last call, to speak to a sleepy Harry Shaw in Sydney. He'd do that after he got to Ana. He was already late and she could be concerned.

As he sat in the taxi, Mark thought, Sean Hood's alive as we guessed.

Probably Dieter Hood too. And what in the heck was the

bastard doing in Coober Pedy. Surely there was nothing there from the past that he could claim.

Chapter 23

'Sorry, Mark but I've got to get you back here with that suitcase.' Harry said his husky with excitement from Sydney.

'Shit boss, can't I just send it, priority with all the trimmings?' Mark's said. 'I only got through the door here. I'm bushed and I know Ana's got heaps she wants us to discuss and do before the wedding.'

'No way Mark, Sorry mate, but you've got to cut short your time with Ana. Pick up the case from your police headquarters and bring it here yourself. I don't want it touched or opened except here.'

There was a pause as Mark's grunt accepted Harry's order.

'I've put out a quiet "watchout" on Sean Hood. Got nothing yet as I expect he's holed up somewhere,' Mark said. 'All right, I'll book a flight, get the case and arrive in Sydney asap. You'll have to face Ana's temper when you see her next though...'

Harry laughed. He'd seen gentle Ana when her ire was up. Brave and formidable but she was a policeman's woman now and had to understand the life. Even when planning a wedding. 'I'll take my chances but you can tell her that the wedding is on, no matter what.'

'Yeah, I'll do that...see you tomorrow. I'll let you know the time etc but it won't be the early, early flight.' Mark signed off and his gaze fell on Ana who was picking up Pietie's Lego from the kitchen table. From the lounge room Mark caught her eye and shrugged. She sensed already that tonight was going to be their only time together before he had to go back to Sydney.

Mark made his phone calls and booked his flight back to Sydney with Qantas for just after midday.

Roast lamb, the way to a man's heart, served with roast vegetables, mint sauce and apricot pie to follow. Mark sat contented for the evening as Ana checked Pietie in bed and came back into the lounge to him.

Her dark hair was a cloud around her shoulders and the distinctive white comma framed her face as she sat beside him. What he wasn't expecting was the wedding folder Ana spread on her lap.

'I need decisions from you for the wedding. We can't put them off any longer,' she said.

Mark groaned. 'We've done all that. Got the date, the place and the honeymoon booked. That's it, especially the honeymoon?'

'Ah, but the details. You said I could do whatever I wanted for the wedding.' Ana looked Mark straight in the eye. 'And we're having the full works. A big white wedding, Rhette, my sister Kari and my old friend Lauren, in purple dresses. Your four groomsmen in rented suits with purple waistcoats and ties to match the girl's dresses. A reception centre with everything. Pietie as our cute page boy and ring bearer. Flowers by the bucket full, amazing food and a huge wedding cake. With you away I even got a wedding planner in on the deal. You'll love him he's such a dear...a bit expensive but...'

Visions too horrible to contemplate floated through Mark's mind. He froze looking wide eyed at Ana. 'But we didn't plan all that...' he managed. 'I thought you had it all for your first wedding?'

'I did and I want it all again,' Ana said. Her stern face dissolved into almost girlish giggles and she poked a finger into his ribs. 'Got you!' she squirmed as Mark grabbed her and the folder slid to the floor.

'There's a forfeit for scaring me like that,' Mark said and proceeded to kiss her soundly. Within seconds clothing was being abandoned as each tried to get at the other's naked flesh. The lovemaking was playful and intense, on the couch and then on the floor.

'That wasn't quite what I was expecting from our wedding plans talk…later perhaps,' Ana laughed as she lay against his chest.

His lips in her hair he retorted, 'You were nearly as ripe, as you said, that first time when we made love.'

She sat up and flushed. 'I hadn't had sex in four years when you seduced me…' she said as he grabbed for her again. 'OK it was mutual seduction. But we really do need to talk about the wedding. Are you still happy with the beach ceremony with our close family and friends, the restaurant, and all that?'

Mark stood and flopped down on the couch pulling Ana on to his lap. His fingers trailed a gentle path into the bullet scar under her right breast. A legacy of her time in a refugee camp as a child, and a ricochet in time to the police incident where they had met. 'What the purple dresses and waistcoats are gone? I think I could fancy our red headed Rhette in purple. She'd look stunning…' he teased.

Ana wound an arm about his neck. 'One more comment like that and you're dead meat,' she whispered into his ear.

'Oh! So, you're going to wear purple then…that'll be good. Ouch!' he yelped as she nipped his ear with sharp teeth.

'Well if we're not going to talk the wedding. Just leave it all to me and you'll just have to take what happens on the day and enjoy it.'

'It's the after I'm looking forward to. The rest of us, and Pietie together. How soon do we see about another one, a baby brother or sister for Pietie?' Mark said.

'You're keen for another baby soon?'

'As soon as you are ready...'

'We'll have to practice for that,' Ana laughed. 'I'm off to bed. Coming...?'

Chapter 24

Lex met Mark at the airport to get him and the suitcase back to Rustle Street headquarters for opening as quickly as possible.

'Pity about the loss of your time off,' Lex said. His black shaved head was billiard ball shiny as the sun streamed into the car.

'Time off! We had less than twenty-four hours together after I got a sighting of bloody Sean Hood and the suitcase. And it was wet and cold in Adelaide,' Mark said.

'You didn't go home for the weather.' Lex shot a grin at Mark. 'Harry's more than keen to open the suitcase. He's got all sorts of theories and he's waiting also to find the new name Hood's using? Got the passenger list but they can't confirm a name. The bugger would've changed to another alias, anyway.'

'Any advance on DAF since I've been gone?' Mark asked.

'Not enough. Mostly dead ends. Terrorism's not been ruled out and the public's jittery because the media haven't given up on the story. Tom Phillips and the Premier are trying to calm things. Robbery? That's still my guess.'

'I'm open. Like Harry, I'm sure that Dieter Hood's alive now that I've seen his brother,' Mark said.

'That's got to be one huge story. We'll need to investigate into how Dieter and Sean got away from that plane crash.' Lex pulled up at a traffic light as a huge truck's air brakes squealed in protest as it stopped very close behind their unmarked police car. Lex glanced into his mirror. The truck grill and a bull bar took up the whole view. 'Pity we're not on road patrol. Those trucks drivers always know us. Their intimidation is as bad here as in bloody South Africa,' he muttered as the vehicle behind inched forward, gunned engine held back only by the air brakes.

The lights changed and Lex crossed the intersection and sped away.

Mark leaned back, resting his head into the leather, and ignoring Lex's annoyance at the errant truck driver. 'Rhette and Ana were convinced that the Hood brothers were dead. Gone...Probably hopeful than sure...' His voice was tired. 'Those bastards gave them nightmares after that terrible time in Cooper Pedy.'

'There was always that element of doubt,' Lex agreed.

'We'd never have been still working the case, albeit from a distance, if Harry hadn't kept it open. Now we've got this suit-case and let's hope that it tells us something. I know it was Sean in Adelaide. No doubt, especially when he took off.'

' "The game's afoot," ' Lex quoted suddenly with a grin. 'And I wonder if there's links to this Sydney bombing. Harry thinks so. Rhette's adamant that she'd seen Sean Hood at the scene, and then surprisingly in Hobart.' He quickly told Mark of Rhette's claim. 'The mind boggles at what's going on.'

'Well, maybe you'll have to have a session playing Solitaire again, see what will spring into your head. OK,' Mark said. 'Anything else new with DAF?'

'The Argyle CEO is up shit creek trying to accept that it might've been a job where information leaked enough for a criminal gang to make the play. He's standing by his employees and wondering if one of them could've been blackmailed to do this. Thinks that they died for it. He's also doing a close examination of the fact that the quantity of industrial diamonds is down as well this year. Not thought of any connection. He's a worried man - likewise his board. They can't take in that it could be terrorism even given that Duke is Muslim.'

'Starting to stink like an inside job to me,' Mark said.

'Yeah. It does.'

'The burka woman question. Anything more on that? The security's a mess at the building - has that got a gang feeling? Anyone's MO?'

'Wait man and read your emails when you get a chance. Everything's there - especially the feeling that we're still just guessing. No strong leads anywhere else.' Lex drove into the underground police car park and Mark lifted the prize suitcase, now coated in plastic wrap like a silver gift, out of the boot. His own small case was dragged to the lifts by Lex.

As the lift doors opened onto the Major Crime floor loud handclapping, hoots of applause and whistles greeted Mark.

He stood dumbfounded, then light dawned and he shrugged, a slight smile on his face.

His grab and saving of the little girl at the Adelaide Airport had gone viral.

Shown on TV, Facebook. Twitter.

World-wide.

Not only the cameraman and reporter he'd spoken to had captured the rescue but the other channels pointing cameras at the cricket team had done the same. It was a better good news item than the victorious cricket team's arrival. The parents of the child, Lilly, wanted to thank him but he'd gone by the time they had realised exactly what had happened.

But no one had connected the dots regarding the man Mark was chasing that the police were aware of and his face had been obscured anyway. Instead Mark had been very visible making the rescue catch. The general public notion was that the man was annoyed at the cameras being present and just acted in a brutal angry fashion. Conspiracy theorists were alluding to other reasons.

Harry came forward and shook his hand as Mark got more embarrassed. He and Ana had not turned on the TV or looked at their computers or Facebook while he was home and he had no idea of the exposure his action had received.

'Thanks.' Mark was brief. 'You'd all have done the same,' he said and started towards Harry's office carrying the suitcase.

'You'll probably get a citation from Tom Phillips, and from SAPOL,' Harry said as he closed the door and the squad outside went back to their desks, grins firmly in place. It was not often the police got positive publicity.

'It was an instinctive action. We're trained for this sort of thing. Anyone of us would have done it,' Mark said. He flushed, shrugged and gestured towards the case.

Harry took the hint. 'OK then, well done anyway. We'll open this in the conference room. It's been set up as a forensic area. Cameras. The works. I want to be present for the examination. Just hope that there's something here we can use and we're not chasing someone's mistake and it's nothing.'

Chapter 25

Green sterile sheets covered the conference room table. A supply of tools, knives, swabs and evidence bags were ready with a supply of gloves. The plastic wrapped suitcase lay in the centre of it all waiting to be dismantled.

John Pappaglopagus, gowned like a surgeon, came forward and shook Mark's hand before gloving up. 'Good catch of that kid,' he said, and slapped him on the back.

Mark nodded. 'Thanks…' Cripes, he thought, I hope this fussing gets forgotten quickly.

An assistant pathologist sat at a small table ready with a small computer to log everything found.

Harry motioned to a camera man to begin recording and made a brief statement to identify the suitcase, where it had been recovered from and it's important in the DAF investigation. He emphasised that the bag had been tested for bombs by the dog squad. There was a shuffle amongst the detectives. All clear. Good.

Lex came into the room. 'I've stuck your own suitcase in our office,' he said to Mark as he gloved up.

Pap gave a chuckle behind the mask he wore. 'This'll take a while. I'm doing a complete examination. Enough to stand up in any court. Hope we've got something more than a heap of dirty jocks in here.' He hefted the bag and weighed it on digital scales. 'More than twelve kilos. Hmmm…heavy.' A grin. 'Very heavy dirty jocks...'

With the camera in close attendance Pap swabbed the plastic cover before he cut it free from the very ordinary looking black suitcase. Each swab was bagged and numbered. The case was then swabbed all over and the recording of evidence continued. Swabs were passed through a drug detection unit and came back positive for cocaine.

'Not unusual these days,' Pap said his voice matter of fact.

Harry kept his impatience under control, just, and finally sat back to wait for the case to be opened.

'Like Christmas when I was a kid. Not sure if you were going to get the present you wanted or just stuff in your stocking,' Lex said in an aside to Mark.

'Good kid or bad kid,' Mark breathed back. 'Bet you got stuff.'

'Hmmm... it's locked. I'll have to try to open them with the keys I have, break the locks, or send for a locksmith.' Pap said.

'Just open the damn thing. We haven't got all day. Does it always take this long to do your examinations?' Harry said, his voice was terse and his impatience showing.

Pap stood back. 'Who's doing this Harry? You or me? Just relax if you can.' He selected a set of keys, chose one and opened the case. 'Hey presto!' he spread his hands wide, eyebrows raised. The magician.

On top of the case contents was a light sports coat. This was lifted out and put to one side after the contents of the pockets were revealed and bagged. A handkerchief, tissue quality. A button that had come with the jacket when bought and placed into a pocket. In the inside pocket was an old driver's licence in the name of Peter O'Donnell. The picture ID could have been Sean Hood as a younger man and the picture quality was poor but enough to get Harry excited. He paced back and forth as Pap drew out hairs and dust from pockets, bagging them. 'Get on with it!'

Harry mouthed to the room in general.

A few smiles greeted his show of restlessness.

The next layer contained clothing. Clean and soiled in plastic bags. 'Here's the dirty jocks I was expecting!' Pap said with another chuckle. He was enjoying the audience. He gave the bags over to his assistant as Harry was standing close enough to be a nuisance. 'A likely chance of a DNA sample here.' Harry leaned over Pap's shoulder. 'Back off a bit mate, or take off and we'll call you if we find anything,' Pap said.

Harry retreated back to a chair.

'Ah,' said Pap. 'This looks more interesting.'

Harry stood again and moved back to the table.

Pap unwrapped a bulky parcel where a couple of shirts as binding and padding. Inside were four green plastic boxes, each about the size of large lunch boxes. One box rattled as if full of stones and the two others were packed with one hundred dollar bills in Australian currency. Pap handed the money over to his assistant to count while he opened the box of stones. As Harry expected they were large opals. Under the lights the solid opals flashed green and blue and gleamed in reds.

'Quality stuff,' Pap said of the opals. He raised his eyebrows at Harry. 'You were at Coober Pedy last year. Hazard a guess at the value of these?'

'A million. Easy, especially if sold to buyers in Asia,' was the reply from Harry.

Pap's assistant said as he hefted each box, feeling the weight of the money. 'There's a couple of hundred thousand dollars in each box. Probably more - about a total of half a million I'd guess. Do you want me to count them in full or run them through the drug indicator first?'

'Drug check them then make an accurate money count. Everything's being videoed so no sticky fingers,' Pap joked as he pulled sealing tape from the last heavy box. Inside was crystal ice and packed solid. 'It looks pure and the street value of this lot will be huge.' He said as the drug indicator went off, lights flashing and the needles jumping to the highest levels – off the scale.

'Are we looking at millions here? Half a million in cash, the opals must be worth a bundle and the drugs a million on their own?' Lex said.

'It'll all be checked against current prices. I'd guess three to five million...' Harry said with satisfaction in his voice. This money would not get to the Hood brothers.

One of the detectives stuck his head around the door. 'Harry. I've done a check on Peter O'Donnell and the birth date on the licence you have. It's a forgery.'

'OK. Thanks. I expected as much. It correlates with what we have here. Illicit drugs, money and opal and the tax man wouldn't get his cut,' Harry said. He turned back to Pap. 'Now show me what else. There's got to be other things. I want papers, any bits of paper...'

'Never satisfied,' Mark nodded to Sam. She grinned back.

'This chap's interested in Tasmania. And wine.' Pap sorted through shoes and trousers in the bottom of the suitcase and pulled out a fan of glossy brochures. Tasmania. Hobart attractions and wine regions. He tossed them on the table and Harry leafed through them.

'Is this all? He can't be just planning a bloody holiday,' Harry said. 'There's got to be more...'

There was. Slipped down into a small side pocket was a little IPad. Lex immediately came forward and impatiently waited while it was scanned for drugs and catalogued. Like everything else in the suitcase, it registered cocaine and ice.

Lex picked up the IPad. 'Mine, I believe,' he said. 'I may need your help Bill, if it's password locked - but this's mine!'

Chapter 26

'Isn't it a bit premature to be bringing this question to me? You're asking for a definitive time frame while this DAF investigation has just started - to go back to your original Hood Brothers assignment? I know,' Commissioner Tom Phillips said as the Harry shuffled in his seat, 'that brought Mark and Lex to be seconded to us, but this DAF investigation is still in the initial stages and too much in the public eye to have three top Dees go off it. The Premier has shown a great interest in particular in DAF and he wouldn't be agreeable.' Left unsaid was - given the forthcoming elections.

'No Sir, but can we have an estimate to work from?' Harry said. He had presented the information they had got from the suitcase, and his summation of it.

Tom Phillips leaned back in his chair. 'Harry, I know what this case means to you. Five years isn't it since you got the man in your sights and you've tried to get sufficient evidence against him for the prosecutors. There is ample evidence now, as long as that vital voice recording from the flight can be presented in a court and that's still debatable. Regardless of that DAF has to be the main case at present.'

'I know that Sir...' Harry said. 'But I know, I felt it all along that the bastard brothers were still alive. The Hoods would surface again...'

'We've still got the question of terrorism or robbery as the motive for DAF. Heaven help us if it is terrorism. The public is still jittery since the Martin Place incident and rightly so. Every day there's more bombs going off somewhere, Paris, Belgium, the UK and the Middle East as usual.'

His face was drawn. The years had been kind to Tom Phillips, but the grey shadows lurking under his eyes showed the tension of this case. He looked a man nearing retirement as his position suggested. It had taken many years to reach his rank and this case was the most serious he'd dealt with. Too many deaths, too many bodies and the case was no accident, but terrorism or murder most foul. A case that would remain in his mind even after retirement and it must be solved.

Harry respected Tom and recognised yet again that knowing and responding to politics and politicians was a great part of his work. He shuddered. Not his cup of tea being the top cop. He didn't want to go there. 'Yes. That's true, sir,' he said.

'If this is terrorism we're going to be flooded with Max's boys, plus the CIA. I can't in any honesty give you permission to leave the DAF enquiry until a resolution is reached regarding motive. Not for two months anyway so see me again about this matter at the end of this enquiry or that time span.' Again left unsaid – the state elections would be over by then.

'Then I'm to continue with DAF for now, Sir?' Harry asked.

The answer was obvious. The question premature, he thought as he left the Commissioner's office.

Rhette spent the morning sorting her desired study course with the University.

Mentally she ticked it off on her fingers. It had to be external: check. A whole degree course: check. First, she had to be accepted. Paying for study wasn't a problem. Not with the millions in money and opal she'd inherited from Doug, her father.

Rhette pushed all those thoughts aside. Her life now was what she needed to think about.

She was surprised to find that archaeology was a less fashionable study these days, Ancient Egypt in particular. One campus offered such a study. A disappointment was that it was about the queens of the late dynasties, when Alexander the Great started the Greek Pharaohs ruling Egypt. 332 – 30 BC. This era ended with Cleopatra, the most famous of the Egyptian queens. From the description, she decided it might have a feminist approach. That was not a problem, she thought.

Think about female things. She told herself. History was regularly written by men and the women were usually portrayed as handmaidens of men in history if they got a mention. The Queens of Egypt were different, she read in the course notes. There were female pharaohs. Interesting.

It was time to leave the crime areas to Harry.

Forget her anger against, her need to punish, Dieter and Sean Hood.

She tossed her mop of red gold curls. That was impossible to forget but for now she needed a distraction.

She was accepted and she enrolled, sending her study CV and course payment via the internet. Her first study assignment would arrive in days. They provided a list of readings and she went to Amazon and most of the other e-book providers and bought most of the specified books immediately. Everything done via the internet and her Kindle flickered as the book titles arrived.

In the afternoon Rhette drove into the city to bookshops to buy anything else of a serious nature she could find on ancient Egypt as background reading.

She came home loaded with books, plus a pork fillet for dinner and some fresh asparagus, the first of the Australian season. She found a new perfume to titillate Harry's nose. Just to remind him who and what was waiting for him at home each night.

Things for the mind, body and soul, Rhette thought.

Chapter 27

A roar of a Harley Davidson outside the Sydney motel room announced the return of Sean Hood to the bosom of his filial partnership.

He was three days later than expected. It wasn't going to be much of a homecoming.

Dieter opened the door grabbed Sean by the lapels of his jacket and threw him against a wall.

'Where the fuck've you been? What the fuck happened in Adelaide?' Dieter shouted. The words were punctuated by fists pummelled into his brother's shoulder and stomach.

Sean cringed away arms grasping to protect himself. He struggled for air and his gorge rose from the blows. Bigger and stronger than Dieter he finally exerted himself and shoved his brother away. 'Fuck you,' he said. 'It's been hell...'

Obviously, Dieter had seen the incident at Adelaide airport on TV, Sean thought. That was bad enough but he knew worse was to come and he almost hadn't come back to Sydney. It could have been better to go into hiding to get away from his brother and forget their plans. That would leave him broke and at the possible mercy of the gangs. Disappearing wasn't as easy as people thought, not without money or help.

Sean had neither...

Dieter stood up from the bed where he'd stumbled and looked at the still open doorway. 'Where's the case?' He slammed the door shut. 'Where the fuck is the suitcase?' he repeated.

'It's gone. I had to leave it at the airport. How the bloody hell could I wait and get it from the carousel when that blasted copper was after me? He recognised me...I only just got away.'

'Did you do anything to get it back?'

'Shit I tried! Of course, I tried! I doubled back and waited until the bastard and two other fucking Federal coppers went back inside. Then, after a while I followed them into the terminal. I wanted to grab the suitcase if it was still there. The bloody thing was gone and it was all I could do to get away myself.'

'So, the money and the ice are gone. You did leave the opal in the bank box as a reserve?'' Dieter's quieter words rose to a yell. 'Tell me you did what as I fucking well-ordered you to? That was our backup...our only fucking backup!'

'I took the lot. Didn't think we'd ever get back to Coober Pedy...' Sean raised an arm to try to protect himself from a fist he knew would come.

'You're not expected to think! Just to do as you're bloody well told!' Dieter yelled again and moved suddenly to slap Sean across the face. The blow landed. It stung.

The younger brother grabbed at his face and then cowered away. All his life Sean had expected and accepted punishment from his brother. It was the way of his people, the family and Dieter took the older brother's rights as law. Previously he had not followed the ancient family and religious laws except when he chose to but that had changed when they found their sister again.

His sister's crime could not be tolerated.

'So - we've got nothing.' Sean ventured after Dieter had cooled down and they slumped on the cheap floral quilts of the single beds.

Sean knew that Dieter had established a safe deposit box at

Coober Pedy when they were in the town. He was wary of being caught with drugs, cash and opals and the bank box hid things he didn't want to be found with. He hadn't had time to retrieve the contents when they had been forced to flee the town the year before. He just had the few thousands he called 'travelling money' in his wallet. Sean had been forced to take off from the airport virtually from a standing start. He had taxied across the runway, with Dieter screaming at him and him trying to shut the open aircraft door. They had only just got away.

Away from Rhette Ryan and the copper who had chased him in Adelaide.

The episode still gave Sean nightmares when he thought about it.

But as usual Dieter had a backup plan.

Sean had not expected that Dieter would explode the plane over the sea. That he would force Sean to parachute out or to stay and die with his beloved plane after the bomb timers were set. Dieter had a gun and Sean knew he would use it even on him. The two passengers on board had disappeared while he flew the plane southward. Dieter had thrown them out of the plane, out over the sea. Their deaths would have been horrible. Sean remembered and shuddered ... he wanted to live and he knew his brother was a psychopath, so he had obeyed.

Dieter leaned forward and pushed his hands through his hair, his face set. He reached across the bed space and grabbed his brother's chin and snarled into his face.

'Because of your fucking blunder we've lost more than five million. Probably more if I could've got a decent street value with the drugs. Even after the shit with the bikies and the Sydney gangs I had a deal lined up. That's finished, because of you.' Face set, Dieter wrenched Sean's face sideways and stood up. His body still tense and his hands fisted.

Sean knew that Dieter would continue to blame him for everything, again the way of the family. The way of his brother. Sometimes he had a small way to reduce the tension.

'Hey,' he said as Dieter moved towards the motel mirror, 'You've dyed your hair a better colour and your moustache coming on too. Looks good,'

Dieter was vain and it often worked. Usually.

It didn't today.

'The haircut's a bastard. I should've killed the bastard that cut it,' he said. The scowl stayed put. He kicked out at his dirty clothes on the floor at the end of the bed. 'Get this packed up and get ready to move. I've been here too long. Someone might have seen me or you after arriving on the fucking bike. Couldn't you have got here without the noise. Been dropped off a few blocks away. Now the bloody bikie gangs will know where we are. Someone'll shit on us and the word'll get out. Won't you ever use that brain that's between your ears or is it just the one in your bloody pants that rules?'

Sean said nothing. The bikie had been a woman and they had spent one night fucking their brains out in a motel room on the road east from Adelaide. It was the least he could do in payment for the ride. He changed the subject. 'What about...?' he started to ask.

Dieter cut in. 'The bitch'll find us. She's got the next address in Tasmania. She'd better get there, and soon! She'd better follow my instructions better than you did or she'll get what's coming to her.'

Chapter 28

The Commissioner Tom Phillips looked around the room at the assembled officers. Most sat, even slumped, in their chairs and many looked at the table rather than looking at him. This investigation had slowed to almost a standstill and failure was not a pretty sight.

'Are you telling me,' he aimed the question to Harry, 'that you've come to a virtual dead end with DAF?'

'No Sir. It's not the end of the case but we're struggling to get further with it than having just strong suspicions.'

'Lay it out Harry. What have you got?' Tom said.

'We know now that DAF was a robbery, although there is still a question because of the woman in the burka. It was probably a disguise but ... there's still a hint from that because of terrorism given world events.'

'And the hint leads where?'

'Nowhere, Sir. There's been no gang claiming they did it. No rumour on the streets. There's no recognisable MO. A new group...' Harry said. His eyes were dry, sunken, and dark rimmed as though someone had tricked him with soot covered binoculars from the days of that sort of practical joke. Harry looked his forty years of age, and then some. 'We go with robbery one hundred percent now especially after Pap made his first discovery. More have followed.'

Tom looked towards his head of forensics. 'Pap, I got your

email but tell us what exactly you mean by manufactured diamonds. Not from Argyle Diamonds? What got you suspicious?'

'I was taken by the fact that there were remnants of diamonds after the blast and fire, Sir. Diamonds are pure carbon and they burn. That's what I understood. They do burn but they can only ignite at a very high heat and they need oxygen. Lots of oxygen. Not much of that was left after the initial blast wave and fire.' Pap looked up and suddenly stopped talking. His teeth worried his bottom lip. 'I didn't mean to give you all a lecture,' he said.

The Commissioner frowned. 'That's what we want, go on...' he said.

'OK. I was a bit surprised when we found remnants at the crime scene. By my calculations they shouldn't have been there. All of them should have been burned. But some had been exploded out of the glass cabinets by the bomb and somehow been protected from the fire.' He looked around the room, his face hesitant and almost seeking support with his next words. 'I mean we didn't do much with them at the beginning as we were more concerned with the victims.'

'And then, as I would expect, your focus shifted. Fair enough,' Tom Phillips let him off the hook. He wasn't looking for a scapegoat. This was not the Commissioner's style at all. He needed answers.

'Yes, Sir. Anyway, after we found the bits of diamonds I sent specimens off to the Sydney Mineralogy experts for comment. They did their tests, looked at them under their big scopes. I got an immediate response. Who was I kidding? Was this some sort of interdepartmental joke?' There was a shuffle around the table as Pap's voice conveyed his discomfort. 'These were manufactured diamonds. They put it all in official language but the Argyle diamonds presented at that sale were fakes.'

'Fakes?' Tom's left eyebrow raised as a question.

Pap continued. 'They make diamonds now, mainly for the space program and other specialist needs, because they can make pure diamonds without the flaws that are found in natural stones. They have a signature structure in the crystal to actually differentiate them from the real diamonds. Manufactured diamonds can't be recognised by form, colour or anything other than under a very high-powered microscope. The coloured diamonds presented at the sale were manufactured too. They've been making zirconia's for years for lesser jewellery but this duplication was unexpected at this time and place.'

'I'd heard of sapphires being produced but diamonds? This was new to me too. We knew then we were definitely dealing with robbery from that point alone,' Harry said. 'And it had to be an inside job for the real advertised diamonds to be replaced.'

'And Hudson Tydesley's the CEO of Argyle Diamonds?' Tom asked.

'He had to be a suspect given that the company was struggling from other losses in the industrial diamond area. He said that right from the start and this made me factor him in initially. His Board wasn't happy with things and this could be a reason he'd try something like this. But Tydesley's a money man with extensive mining experience not a mineralogist. The Argyle mineralogist involved with the sale was Sarah Wilkes. She and her personal assistant Ray Duke set up the whole diamond sale as they had in past years. They organised everything.'

'And what have you done to take this case further?' Tom said.

'Pap found Duke's remains at the scene but Wilkes' body isn't apparently there. She's missing. We've been able to find out that before Sarah Wilkes studied at university in Western Australia and then worked for Argyle Diamonds, she didn't exist. Any and all personal CVs she presented was a fake as far as her past life went,' Harry said.

'Nothing about her before then?' Tom repeated the information. His hand massaged his cheek, drew down and rested at his chin. He leaned forward, his elbow taking the weight of his head. 'Nothing?' the repeated word a question.

Samantha Morton spoke up. 'Sarah Wilkes's become my main person of interest. When the CEO Tydesley tried to contact her at the sale that morning he was upset. He was going to have to tell her that the house, she shared with a woman named Petra Joyce, had burned down overnight. There was nothing left.' Sam shuffled a raft of papers in front of her. She pushed the fire reports out to the middle of the table.

Pap said, 'Totally burned. Just ashes. I had Jack Flexner in Perth confirm it for us. It has the definite hallmarks of arson, and of fire bombing, as the fire started in more than one area. Sounds familiar with everything in this case. Bombs, fires and more questions than answers.' Pap shrugged wide shoulders in shirtsleeves. He wasn't one to stay in his jacket even with the Commissioner in attendance. He was a pathologist first but the policeman and detective in him wanted the evidence he put up to be useful. He turned his attention back to Sam as she continued.

'Curiously before Sarah left for the sales she cleaned her office. She scrubbed it and took everything out. Said that she thought that there were mice there and would they find them and fumigate the office before she got back. No one thought that there were mice but they carried out her wishes. She'd been working hard on the diamond sale and deserved the care. Always a popular if reclusive person. Didn't go to many work functions and it was assumed she was a lesbian because she was always accompanied by Petra Joyce. They knew of no other relationship, except that Petra has a twin sister, Odele, address unknown. Just before the meeting I got word that Petra has also disappeared. Poof, gone. She wasn't in the remains of their house either. And she too, has no previous work or personal history on record, before she and Sarah Wilkes joined Argyle. Petra worked in electronics and kept a low profile,' Sam said.

'Interesting,' said Pap. 'We've been trying to get DNA samples of both women to compare with the bodies we have. None has been available and Sam's investigation explains that. Makes it all the more suspicious, doesn't it?'

'As far as I'm concerned, we have these two unknown women as chief suspects, no previous MOs, and nothing as indications at all of who they were, or are,' Harry said. 'We start again...' His tiredness seemed to seep out of his voice. 'Still we're getting somewhere just by this development. Bloody clever women... and they must have planned this robbery for a very long time. This was carefully constructed operation.'

'Surely Argyle would have photographs of her? Of them? Work ones, social stuff for the internal newsletters and the like,' Tom insisted as he nodded his agreement to Harry.

'We've got a couple of early photos. Nothing recent. Sarah didn't like to have her photo taken or would somehow manage to be the photographer of groups. When you get up that high in an organisation people forgive your little quirks. As I said she was popular as a person and with today's attitude to gay people they left her alone rather point her out as different. It's no longer a scandal and the company policies are open minded...' Sam said. She put the photos of Sarah on the table. 'See, it's they're not much help. A general photo. Could be anyone.'

'Have these enlarged and the computer experts do their stuff.'

'These have been enhanced...' Harry said.

'And a photo of her partner?' Tom said.

'None?' a raised eyebrow and a shrug from Samantha. None.

'We're waiting for driver's licence photos from the West.' Harry said. Should be faxed here today. This's all very recent.

'So, DAF has moved to a robbery investigation. Tell me more about the state of play within other departments.' Tom cleared the area in front of himself waiting for more papers.

Pap said. 'We've ID'd all of the other bodies and notifications have been done. Sadly, the young school girl, Marion Delaney, is one of them. In addition, we have one body we have no name for. The woman in the lift. The unlucky one, we felt, who'd just arrived or was leaving from the saleroom when the bombs went off. We may never know who she was unless someone comes forward to claim her.'

Pap suddenly said. 'I may have one way to get a DNA ID on Sarah Wilkes. Just thought of it a day or so ago. I got one of my staff to collect the contents of the waste paper bins in the toilets on that floor that was bombed. No one else other than the people at the sale would have used those loos. I'm not sure that these have been checked for DNA yet. We'd be lucky to get anything to fit but we'll try. Been a bit busy lately...'

Tom looked around the table. 'You're continuing investigation in all areas, aren't you?' he said.

Harry spoke up as there were nods from the other Department Heads. 'Yes, everything's going on. Max has one item that just may go somewhere.'

Max shuffled his papers. 'I said before that the bombs were made up with explosive usually easily got if you know the right people or are in the business. They were an unlikely mixture. Chemicals and elements, you'd find from legitimate mining, some favoured by opal miners and even the terrorists scatter bombs where nails etc make a shrapnel effect to do most damage to persons and property. Odd really and we're still endeavouring to trace all the components.'

Harry perked up. 'Maybe I'm jumping to a conclusion but you did mention opal mining.'

'Yes, we think that the detonators are very similar to those found being used on the opal fields. Easy to buy or to get still out there. The regulations are treated with a certain laxity despite the state government's attempts at tightening up things...' Max said.

'Tom, I'm going to get Mark to follow up on this tangent from this DAF investigation. Sean Hood was seen coming back from Coober Pedy last week. It may be a worthwhile check to see if he travelled there previously since he and Dieter Hood have been missing, presumed dead. He's travelled before as Peter O'Donnell, maybe he's done it again and been shopping there.'

'With so few current leads it may be a long shot. But the investigation's yours. Go ahead, go ahead all of you. So far good work.'

The commissioner picked up his papers and left the room. He didn't look a happy man. The state elections were looming and the premier wanted results in his 'War against Crime' platform. Still, the work done to narrow the probable criminals to the Argyle staff was promising. All they had to do now was find them.

Chapter 29

Sarah Wilkes almost fell into the motel room in Hobart, Tasmania, when Dieter opened the door at dawn almost ten days after the diamond bombing and robbery.

She was alone, distraught and her black jeans and a pale yellow t-shirt hung on her body as though she had recently lost weight. She pulled a large black non- descript suitcase as luggage. The multiple flight tags hung from the elastic bands at the handles like cryptic messengers.

'It's about fucking time you got here!' Dieter whispered, his menace a rumble like distant thunder. 'Sean's went fucking missing first and now you take your time to arrive.'

'Petra's missing. She hasn't turned up where we planned to meet here. She has to be dead,' Sarah howled, her face screwed up. She cried like a child.

Dieter slammed the door shut and clamped a hard hand over her mouth then swung her around and pushed her further into the room. Sarah could feel a gun pressed into her side. 'Shut up, bitch! You'll alert the neighbours and everyone else. Shut your face up and keep it shut.'

He shoved her across the room towards an armchair beside the motel fridge. Sarah flopped into it and saw that his gun had a silencer screwed onto the short barrel. He kept it levelled at her while he yanked the suitcase out of her hands and onto one of the bed single beds.

'It's all there,' Sarah hissed. 'That's all you care about.'

'That's right!' Dieter said. 'Just that. With a sister like you and now that your stupid brother has fucked up. Shit! I'm going to get out of this fucking country, back to civilization.' His eyes narrowed into a glare aimed at both of them.

'Well, here's your precious diamonds.' Her face crumpled as she pushed the suitcase towards him. 'I need Petra... I wish we'd never answered your email. We'd should've ignored you and finished this on our own. We had a plan. All we needed was money to get it going.'

'Well, you didn't have the money, did you?' her brother said. He bared his teeth at her. 'So, we're going to do it my way. My plan.'

He tried to open the suitcase. It was locked and he held out his hand. Sarah fumbled in her handbag and tossed the keys to him.

Dieter pushed the gun into a bedside drawer before he keyed the suitcase open. A small amount of clothing covered heavy plastic bags of grey industrial diamonds. Under those bags were hundreds of diamond presentation pouches packed together tightly. These were of paper and folded to contain one diamond each. He opened one pouch and looked at the large diamond that flashed under the light. 'You and your bitch did good job.'

'Yes, we did. You're not the only intelligent one in our family. I studied, got into Argyle diamonds then planned the whole job, as you call it, on my own. Planned it all these years. Petra became part of it when we...' she paused as her face crumbled again, then continued, '...all we needed was money, not you pushing in.'

Dieter threw a hand in the direction of his brother who hadn't said a word, just stared at the diamonds. 'You couldn't have done it without us. We put up the money for the fake diamonds from America, and for everything else. We did most of the set-up work.'

'Bullshit!' Sarah said. She leapt to her feet and aimed a punch at Dieter's chest. He grabbed her hand before it could contact and slapped her across the face. She backed off, her hand covering the welt on her cheek, and shouted. 'We did the dirty work. We did the bombing, the killing, and the stealing of the diamonds. It was our job but you had to muscle in.'

'And what a lovely assassin you turned out to be. A proper fucking psychotic. A real family member and remember who is in fucking charge of this family. Remember who is the disgusting pervert...' Dieter fired back.

Sean said from his position well out of the firing line. 'Without the bitch, how are we to get the next phase going?

'Petra had it all fixed,' Sarah wailed. 'I know she's dead. She has to be. So stupid to come to the saleroom as the bomb exploded. She wanted to help me...'

'Stupid, stupid fucking women. You're disgusting women.' Dieter said his eyes cold and dismissive. 'Now it's a good thing I've got an alternative plan. You'll help or you'll be as dead as her...'

'She wasn't supposed come up the saleroom... What made her come?' Sarah said. She collapsed down into the armchair again and her face crumpled into tears.

'We need money,' Sean said. He ignored Sarah as Dieter did. 'How're we going to get enough to finish this?'

'We'll have to do something.' Dieter turned his back on Sean. Jerked a thumb in his direction as he said to Sarah. 'This bastard lost our money. Every fucking cent of it. We can only use stolen credit cards for a while, then we'll have to do a robbery of some sort. Something soft.'

Chapter 30

Pietie sprinted down the South Australian beach, at Glenelg, as fast as five-year-old legs would carry him and flung himself at Mark's legs.

'Mummy's coming!' he whispered in a stage whisper that everyone standing in the casual semicircle heard clearly.

'You'd better go back to help her,' Mark said disentangling Pietie's arms with a huge smile. 'You're supposed to give the bride away...'

'How can I give her away? Anyway, she's not a bride, she's my mummy.' He said as he turned to sprint back up the beach. Sand flew away from under his bare feet. In blue shorts and shirt, he'd already taken off his shoes ready to go paddling after the ceremony. He stopped and yelled back, 'Here comes Mummy. She looks pretty!'

Ana was beautiful. A soft blue dress floated against her legs as the breeze flittered in the early evening moments before sun down.

Mark drew breath.

As Pietie gripped one hand, Ana's other hand was tucked into the elbow of his father, Jason, a retired policeman who Mark thought was on a Pacific cruise with his mother.

Ana wore blue forget-me-nots in her hair and Jason wore more as a button hole. Rhette followed in a green dress that brought out the red of her hair. Kari and Lauren stood smiling in welcome as Ana passed. As they reached the small table set up for the ceremony, his mother, Janice put a similar flower in Mark's button hole. After a quick kiss on Mark's cheek, she went to stand by her husband.

After the initial surprise of his parents being able to attend Mark only had eyes for his bride. The ceremony, with words written by bride and groom, was brief and moving to the very small group who watched the man, the woman and the small boy become a family.

The sun touched the horizon as Mark's lips touched those of his bride. 'I love you', they whispered almost in unison before they turned to the guests for congratulations.

'Best kept secret we've had in ages, surprising Mark for this day.' Jason laughed as he bent to give Ana a kiss. 'Welcome to our family.'

'You've wanted to say that ever since we met Ana,' Janice said to Jason as she hugged her daughter in law. 'All I ask of you, my dear, is that you and Mark be happy.'

Ana laid her hand on Janice's. 'Will you be grandparents for Pietie and any other babies we have? He has none and his late father and I were both orphans.'

Tears welled. 'We'd be delighted...' Janice said as Jason came to stand with her.

'Mummy! Mummy! Look dolphins! I can see dolphins!' Pietie shouted his feet in the sea. 'Come and look.'

Mark hoisted the child up onto his shoulder for a better look as the mammals swept in to roll in the waves close to the shoreline.

'A good omen,' said Rhette. She laughed, 'I've got a bit of the Scot's memory in me. Omens say things about the future...dolphins are very good things.'

Harry had been silent as Mark's best man during the

ceremony.

Now he bit his lip. The words had got to him, made him want to ask Rhette the question he knew she wanted to hear. What drummed in his head was that he couldn't match the millions of dollars her father had left her. He had nothing to offer except himself, and a forty-two-year-old police veteran.

She should have someone younger and richer. Someone who didn't remind her of what she had lost. Her sister, her father. Her past.

Harry stood beside Rhette, his eyes looking inward, and said nothing.

Chapter 31

Harry and Rhette returned to Sydney the morning after the wedding on the early plane.

Both were quiet.

The celebrations that lasted until late in the restaurant the previous night and then, at Jason's instance they went on to a jazz piano bar he remembered. Mark's parents lived in Melbourne and they would leave on their European cruise the following weekend. Until then they would stay in Ana and Mark's flat babysitting Pietie while the newly married couple went on a honeymoon for a week.

After that it was back to work for Mark until the DAF investigation was completed. Ana was learning that a policeman's life, when he had rank and, being the specialist he was, the job took him away for weeks at a time. It didn't matter, she had Pietie to care for and over all she was happy. Happier than she had ever been in her life.

Lex met Harry as soon as the lift stopped at their floor.

'I've managed to decipher what was on Sean Hood's IPad. OK, Bill Zeigler got it past the security for me but I was interested in the contents more than he was. I spent some time with him learning a bit more about getting through security systems on iPads. Thought I knew enough until Bill showed me …'

'Lex, for Christ's sake get on with it!' Harry said. 'What was there?'

The men arrived in Harry's office and Harry plonked himself on the edge of his desk. Lex sat in the visitor chair trying to appear calm and contained. His dark eyes shone out of his black billiard bald face.

'OK. I digressed. They've nothing to do with DAF that I can find. We could get him on underage sex charges. His taste in very young women porn verges on paedophilia if that was the only, or a quick, reason to get a warrant to arrest Sean.' No, he shrugged as Harry frowned. 'Anyway, after than getting through reams of pornography and detailed notes about the man's female fucks, it's all about Tasmania. He was researching Tasmania, MONA and also the wine industry areas. He was sending notes to Dieter and to another address. One of those anonymous ones. Routed all over the world and almost impossible to trace. I've got Bill on to it. You don't think they've changed to become honest citizens, do you?' Lex said a grin spread across his face at his own preposterous suggestion.

'You are kidding!' Harry said. 'And what or who is MONA?'

'It's not another female for him to fuck. Could have been with his record until I looked it up. MONA. It's a Museum of Old and New Art in Hobart. I'll send all the details on to you. There's a huge amount of info on line.'

'So, Tasmania, wine and MONA museum,' I'll be darned. It has to be enough to go to Tasmania and finding them if we get a break in DAF?' Harry sighed. 'Is there anything new on DAF since I've been to Mark and Ana's wedding. It was a good show and it's a pity that we had to leave you here in Sydney. Missed out on seeing Grace and the kids too. Sorry about that but you were needed here.'

'We're at the six week point in this investigation and its nada. Everything's slowed. The main areas have dried up, except for

Sarah Wilkes. Maybe the unidentified body in the lift might be the equally mysterious Petra Davidson. The dead security men check out. Argyle Diamonds check out. Petra worked in electronics and also supply. She may've had contacts we haven't been able to trace as yet. Working on it. The Argyle Diamonds Board is going ape about it all and so they should be. Until we find the perpetrators their previous good reputation has soured and their shares are going down and down.' Lex drew breath.

'I saw on the news that the stock market has put a hold on their shares.' Harry commented.

'As a last resort in the Perth area I contacted Jack Flexner, in pathology, he'll go through everything again. Through the burned house which is still cordoned off as a police crime scene; through Sarah's office looking for a hair, skin, fingernail clippings, anything that may give us their DNA. We can only hope.' Lex leaned an elbow on the arm of the chair and scratched behind his ear with long black fingers.

Harry sat now onto his own chair and clicked on his computer. After the opening page of the police logo the general crime information pages came up. He grunted. The police were having to contain radicals who wanted to upset political rallies on all sides of the election. Thank goodness, he thought, the bloody thing would be over soon. No matter which way the election went the police would go on. He didn't mind if the current party got back in, at least he knew what they thought of the police. A new police minister usually meant changes, most often financial changes.

Over the weekend there'd been a couple of senseless 'one punch' murders by drunken louts at Kings Cross and one at Jervis Bay. A more serious murder of a woman was still under investigation as were an assortment of robberies. The DAF investigation got a mention almost at the end of the daily bulletin.

Lex unwound his long thin frame from the visitor's chair. 'We having a DAF meeting at the end of this shift?' he asked.

'Yeah, I think so. Just you and Sam unless anyone else in the squad wants to be here. I'd welcome any ideas...'Harry said. 'We need a breakthrough. In the meantime, you can give me a break down on anything else that's happening. I've enough reports to finish going through otherwise.'

That breakthrough would come at the end the next shift.

It would confound them all.

Chapter 32

The huge Salamanca Markets are held every Saturday in Hobart come rain or shine.

People, families, and tourists thronged the four lanes of craft and food stalls, including centre ones that are back to back, that stretched down the long street leading to the dock complex of wharves and high-rise apartments. One tower had been constructed from an old round grain silo and their occupants paid an exorbitant price for the views overlooking the famous Yacht Club and the Constitution Dock. There they could witness the culmination of the Blue water classic boats that left Sydney Harbour on Boxing Day each year to race to Hobart.

A line of exclusive galleries and shops were permanent beside the open Salamanca road and park that came alive for the market. Today a magnificent cruise ship was docked for the day and most of the passengers were among the crowds at the market.

From Tasmania's magnificent wood many stalls displayed clocks, picture frames and smaller touristy items, bread boards, salt and pepper grinders made of Huon pine, maple, and sassafras timbers. Woollen clothing joined other clothing stalls, cheeses, jars of golden honey gleamed, everything handmade or grown. Chocolates, fudge and leather handbags, toys and food stalls the array seemed endless and the quality of merchandise magnificent. A couple of pubs sold beer and the myriad of stalls beckoned shoppers to wander; to catch a bite to eat, buy coffee and flowers. To try Tasmania's famous scallop pies. A spur of vegetable produce stalls threaded out below the Parliament House golden sandstone buildings and between the parks where a statue of Captain Cook's ship invited children to play in the water swirls. Seagulls squawked, scattering sparrows and poked their heads into potato chips debris or squabbled over hot chip bits thrown by children.

There was always something happening in the spaces where the now closed streets crossed, and the people that gathered were almost as colourful as the stalls and entertainment.

Musicians played, buskers sang or entertained blowing balloons into shapes for children.

Dressed in a long silver gown, with her face and body painted as a beautiful green alien, a woman stood as a living statue on a small dais. She used just her enticing eyes to inveigle donations into her collection pot. A crowd around her watched as she slowly moved to beckon to a middle-aged man to kiss her extended ring encrusted hand. When he complied, there was a cheer and he placed a twenty dollar note into her pot. When he finally moved on, urged by his wife and grandchildren. The statue's eyes and smile followed him.

When the morning sun changed to afternoon drizzle the crowds thinned a little.

A shadowy thief went from stall to stall down the centre aisle, ducked under canvases and picked up the unwary money bags and tins. A clever thief who bypassed the wood and large item stalls where purchases were usually paid on credit cards for the food stalls where everything was with cash transactions.

Sean arrived back at the motel in a state of heightened adrenalin. He hadn't practiced his thieving arts in years and was quite pleased with himself. He tossed the backpack he'd bought, and filled by theft, onto the bed.

A hard eyed Dieter counted the money and sneered. 'There's only a couple of thousand here. You have to get millions more to make up the money you lost from Coober Pedy.'

Sean shot back. 'What have you done? I hit that post office yesterday. Yeah, through the back door and got the cash takings from the day before they could get it to the bank. That was eleven thou. Enough for a few days. What the shit've you done to get money?'

'I don't have to. I didn't lose the fucking money. You did and you take the risks now.' Dieter said. He bundled the notes and dollar coins into his briefcase and left the shrapnel coins on the rumpled sheets. 'Here, here's your share,' he said. 'Share them with your sister.' He chuckled as though what he suggested was funny.

Sean didn't think it was funny and went next door, to the adjacent motel room, to be with Sarah and to escape the presence of Dieter.

Both of them were in the shits with him.

But Sean had managed to score a line of cocaine at Salamanca.

Something to look forward to when Dieter wasn't looking.

Chapter 33

In Perth, Western Australia, forensic pathologist Jack Flexner was true to his word. He found and had his samples analysed and rechecked, all before the end of shift at Sydney headquarters next day.

Some of the material he had, came from drains; the shower drains in the fire destroyed house. That property was largely compromised by fire, but he got more hairs from the personal bathroom of Sarah Wilkes at the Argyle Mine Headquarters, again from the drain under the sink. A fragment had escaped the chemicals and bleach used to eradicate the non-existent mice she had complained about in her plush office.

The two sets of DNA material matched each other perfectly.

'Hey, Harry,' he said with a wide grin on the Skype link. 'Call me a sewer rat! We worked all night on the material we found in the drains. Got some DNA that may be from your person of interest. It's female but she doesn't match anyone on our records here. It doesn't look like this person has got into trouble in the West. Pity, or I might've been able to give you a name. It would have helped your investigation?'

'I'm amazed that you found something. It'll be useful when we get closer to the woman. In the meantime please send it over asap then we can exclude that person from the victim list if she's there. It's possible that she's the unidentified Jane Doe in the lift,' Harry said disappointed to the core. He needed a name, even an

AKA. He let his head rest on a supported hand. His eyes bleak and tired.

'I've sent the details over to John Pap immediately, before I spoke to you even. He may be able to do a match. You've got more crims than we have,' Jack signed off with a chuckle. 'See you next time you're over here.'

As Harry said 'thank you' the screen went dark. It was obvious that Jack wanted to get off shift after probably a long night. Perth was three hours behind Sydney timewise, but Jack must have worked almost a twenty-four-hour shift to get these results. Dedication between the forces was to be admired.

Harry texted Pap. 'Tell me anything about the DNA profile you got from the West.'

Less than sixty seconds later Harry's phone buzzed.

'Are you sitting?' Pap said.

'Yes, I'm sitting. Sitting at attention; waiting...and waiting...'

'OK. I'm finding this very hard to believe but this female is a relative, a half-sister of...' Pap strung it out.

'Shit, Pap, say it! Half-sister to Prince Charles, the Pope, a half-sister to Mary Poppins - O lord, a half-sister to me. Didn't know I had one. One day I'll hang for you the way you string out information. Bloody justifiable homicide.' Harry said. There was both exasperation and humour in his voice.

'OK, it's not you or any other others. She's related to the Hood brothers. The DNA makes her a half-sister to Dieter and Sean Hood.' Pap said and repeated the information in emphasis. 'The Hood Brothers!' There was a 'how about that' note in his enthusiastic voice.

Harry sat back in his chair and tried to assimilate this data. On a slow deep breath, he said, 'You're sure about this? If this is as you say - it opens the case wide open enough to drive a truck through.'

'I'll need to check it again but I'm ninety-nine percent sure she's a half-sister to both of them, on her mother's side. Matriarchal DNA is more accurate than paternal DNA. That's why we were able to get a result quickly.'

Harry was silent for a moment. 'Have you checked this against the body in the lifts DNA?'

'Yes, and it's not her. I can say that the DNA sample we got is from Sarah Wilkes. She's the half-sister to the Hood brothers. This fact fits in with the DAF case, it has to. How we go ahead on it is another guess.'

'Sarah Wilkes is alive. She didn't die with the others.' Harry wanted to whoop around the room. 'She now becomes our chief person of interest. Linked with the Hood bastards. I'd never have guessed that.' He paused remembering Rhette's statement that she had though she saw Dieter Hood at the scene on TV. 'I'll take all this to Tom Phillips tomorrow and find out what his take is on this. Let's see what his recommendation will be given the fact that this bomb blast has just been the cover for a blatant robbery. And we've got a suspect and what a link.'

'And you've always reckoned that the Hood brothers are still alive...'

'Yes. I never thought they'd be stupid enough to blow themselves up in that plane, Pap. Thanks. I think this'll take some digestion... thanks to you and Jack.' Harry's mind raced ahead. DAF and the Hood brothers, who would have connected them. Dieter Hood with links to a crime this big. He had to be alive and this development had come out of left field.

'Sam,' Harry said by phone. 'You might like to hear this.' His voice was enthused for the first time in weeks.

Next Harry sent a text to the Commissioner asking for an immediate confidential meeting. Tom had gone for the day and the earliest appointment would be next morning at eight am, his secretary said.

'Book it for me, please,' Harry replied.

Tom Phillips met Harry at the door of his office and the two men shook hands. The Commissioner returned to his desk and shuffled through the file that Harry had prepared for this meeting.

'It's been seven weeks since this bombing,' Tom said, his face serious. 'It's hardly your fault and I know it's been difficult and your team have worked hard on this case, but...'

'Yes, Sir.' Harry said. 'I know we'd got theory and not enough hard facts but things may have changed. The new evidence is there...' He indicated the papers and left the Commissioner time to read in peace.

There was no doubt what this case was different. It still held the public interest and diverse theories of all persuasions were in newspapers, on TV and in all areas of the public domain. But the election had come and gone, the Premier led the government still. His election promise was they would solve this case soon - be it terrorism or robbery. A result was close. The latter was political speak and the assumption, even the lie, infuriated Harry and his team.

The Premier contacted the Police Commissioner weekly for any update. In private he was apologetic for his promise but, as he said, that was politics at election time when hounded by an Opposition. Or a persistent media. He needed the police to get an outcome and make arrests while he understood the amount of work done, as had the Leader of the Opposition. Games the political parties played across Parliament benches, and especially at Question Time.

Tom's face relaxed into almost a smile. 'It was promising when you found the car used in the robbery.'

That was something to report at the time, Harry thought, and they had hoped that it would lead somewhere in the overall investigation.

Chapter 34

Another dead end.

A Mercedes was found burned out in a scrubby ravine of tall eucalypts, outside the Sydney police area, by a Country Fire division on a training exercise. Although the people who lived near the ravine were lucky that the burning car had not started a bush fire, the police were unlucky as the car and the occupants they discovered inside were both totally burned to the extent they were. The local police had begun the investigation before drawing in the DAF team.

Harry, Sam and Pep had attended the scene. At first it looked to provide promising information and clues.

Inside the car were bodies of two men. Both men were large framed and decomposition was not a factor on their dried out remains.

One victim had been quickly identified as Bertie Bayley by dentistry records. He was a known criminal the police and his parole officer thought had retired after many years in prisons and a very few years on the outside. He had made his career stealing cars and driving for the gangs. He had some independent robbery convictions when he'd gone solo with lesser achievements. He was a good driver, had managed to keep himself fit in prison, and his last stint was typical of his lengthy crime sheet. Released in May of the previous year, he had apparently gone to England to visit his family. His criminal sheets attested that Bayley had never been accused of violence and his longer prison attendances occurred when the gangs he was driving for had committed violent acts. He got the same sentences his fellow criminals did. The conjecture was that this assignment was probably a retirement effort to get money to supplement his age pension.

Above the teeth, so carefully maintained by prison dentists, was a neat round hole in his scull made by a point two-two gun. The bullet was misshapen by the fire but the telling clue to the stolen car and dead driver was the remnant composition of the explosive and accelerant used to destroy the car and partly the bodies. The other man was not immediately ID'd, but that would come as he was probably also an also-ran small criminal associate of Bayley.

The find linked in with the DAF investigation and the only new lead was that the car had been stolen from the British Embassy in Canberra. Identifying engine numbers were shaved off and the car was given new registration plates, all to slow police investigations. The Mercedes also had the flag position on the bonnet that was useful decoy for the arrival of the burka woman at the building on the Argyle Diamond sale day.

It finally linked the woman and the robbery although everything they had after that was all theory.

Putting the pieces together Harry, Sam, Mark and Lex had decided that the probable scenario of the crime was that Sarah Wilkes had set up the robbery, had the manufactured diamonds made overseas, got the bombs from somewhere, probably procured by the Hood brothers, as the family link was now proven. Her decoy was the burka woman, possibly Petra Joyce her lover, if the relationship information from Argyle was correct. The magnitude of the bombing was enormous, perhaps to suggest terrorism but also to destroy evidence that the diamonds were fake. The victims hadn't a chance and the crime all the hallmarks of a determined and clever psychopath.

Tom Phillips looked up from the papers before him. 'This latest evidence opens the case, but where do you want to go from here? Interpol? They could be overseas already?' he said.

'I've a hunch that they're still in Australia,' Harry said. He outlined Mark seeing Sean in Adelaide Airport and the seized opal, drugs and especially the money, as important as the material on Tasmania. 'I think that now they're short of cash and they have to find a way to get the diamonds out of Australia. Argyle have told us that the amount in weight of missing industrial diamonds was almost, at least, ten to twelve kilos. They'd have to get themselves financed before they can find a way to ship that lot. The gem quality stones should be less difficult but we're watching all ports of departure very carefully.'

'It's not going to be easy, then, to get rid of that quantity of stone. That's a good point, Tom said.

'There's another sighting of Dieter Hood. Probably a legit one this time. My partner Rhette Ryan saw someone on an internet feed and alerted me. I saw it and I think she was correct. She'd know him as well as anyone.'

'OK then. Another sighting. And from that...?' Tom said.

'I think they're in Tasmania. Rhette was looking at the MONA gallery, that's in Hobart, when she saw Dieter. The last snippet I got from co-workers at Argyle was that Sarah and Petra holidayed in Tasmania last year.'

'I'm guessing that you and your team want to transfer to Hobart.'

'Yes, sir,' Harry said. 'We can do it quietly working from the Hobart police station and gather what we can as quickly as we can. There was a hint from Sean's brochures that he's interested in wineries. Different from his beverage of choice.' He raised an eyebrow and slowly shook his head. 'Then there's MONA and Dieter? That connection beats me for now but it's a start.' He changed the subject. 'Samantha's got her hands into DAF as well as everyone and can handle that and the general homicides with her team. I'd like to take Mark and Lex with me to Hobart and see what we can do to clear this matter up.'

Tom looked at his chief detective for a moment. 'All right then. But I'd like it if you refer things to me, keep me in the picture, and I can clear this with the Hobart police hierarchy. The Commissioner can brief his senior people... a thought struck me. It's looks like it's going to be a long haul. Mark's just back from his honeymoon and I guess that Ana will want to go to Hobart, and Rhette with you?'

'That would be a plan. We could rent a place, share it even, and keep out of the way of people. I checked and the Tassy police housing has been financially cut back so we wouldn't be treading on any toes by seeking police accommodation. Lex could share but he's a loner when away from Grace, so we'll see what he wants,' Harry concluded.

Now, Harry thought as he walked down the stairs to his office after Tom's agreement, it was going to be interesting to see Rhette's and Ana reaction to them moving to Tasmania until this case was concluded one way or another.

Rhette's eyes widened to a glaze.

The beginning of fear.

She pushed away from Harry's embrace. 'You're joking. Hobart! You're going to Hobart? When? And for how long?'

'As long as it takes to get the Hood brothers and their sister. You know we've narrowed it down to them, and it looks like they're in Tasmania. You provided one good piece of evidence seeing Dieter at that museum.'

145

'Well, I'm not coming with you. First you said that he was dead, then he's probably alive and in Sydney. This's a big city so I feel safe here. Now Hobart, that's a small place.' Rhette's hands shook as she brushed her hair away from her face. 'I was a help to you when I saw him, wasn't I? And that adds to your enquiries?'

'Yes, it does. That was vital. There's other hints and it all points to Hobart and Tasmania. I'll miss you terribly if you stay here...' His eyes crinkled as he smiled the invitation to come with him.

'Yes, but...' Rhette was weakening.

'Hobart isn't that small,' he added as he gathered her back into his arms. 'It's got about one hundred thousand people to hide in. Beautiful place too. Huge harbour and river, high mountains. They say it reminds people of England or Europe.'

She shook herself free. 'You're quite the tourist guide aren't you. You'll miss my cooking is my bet, and the bed...' Rhette paced the sitting room, touching things at random as her thoughts buzzed. Her teeth worried her bottom lip.

Harry caught her hands and pulled her to him. 'I'll keep you safe...' he said.

'OK, you win I'll come just to make you work reasonable hours for a change. I know you can't promise that. What next?' she said, her hands still and gripped together against his chest to stop them shaking.

'Mark's coming and probably Ana and Piet. They've got a house under construction in Adelaide and it would be a good time to just let the architect and builder get on with it. Lex'll be in Hobart too... but Grace'll probably stay in Adelaide with their four children.'

Rhette drew a deep breath. 'Alright. I'll get in touch with Ana. I think that we could find a house in Hobart for us all, even if they're still honeymooners. A bit of internet on-line house hunting for me tomorrow. How soon do we leave?'

Harry looked at her with amazement. First, she was too worried to think of going to Hobart and now all ready to make plans. What a woman, he thought. 'Go?' he said. 'As soon as we can get things sorted and passed over to Sam. We have to find and catch this gang before they can leave Australia. And we'd better be right in our premise of where they are.'

'OK. The kitchen's closed tonight. Take me out to dinner, a good bottle of wine and then bed.' Rhette said.

Her smile went straight to his core.

Chapter 35

'How about this one?' Rhette asked. 'It's got six bedrooms and it's divided almost into two, almost three, separate living areas.'

The 'For Rent' Excusive Homes section was shown up on Rhette's computer screen. Never let it be said, she thought, that she wasn't really trying to put her demons away and take on the task of the temporary move to Hobart. With luck they'd be back in Sydney with the job done, and once and for all and this time she'd demand to see the Hood bodies.

She just wanted to see the corpses and eradicate her demons.

Ana leaned across the table to look at the mansion in Bellerive. It was huge, an old colonial house with a garden of trees, flower beds and expanses of lawn. An iron lace veranda graced the long frontage of the two-story building. 'You are kidding,' she said. 'I'd cost a fortune.'

'Let's think about this. Sure - it's big but look,' Rhette flicked the screen to floor plan of the rooms. 'There's a central area, could have been a ball room in a past life and we could all gather there. There's two upstairs Sir and Madam rooms all with a modern bathroom. Downstairs there's a two-bedroom guest suite, again all mod conned, and at the other end of the house there's the servants' quarters. A big bedroom and a bunk room.'

Ana caught her enthusiasm. 'It might be possible but Harry and Mark would never go for it...'

'I'll print this out.' Rhette said. The printer whirled and spat out a colourful copy of the house plans. Rhette took a pen. 'The upstairs could be the honeymoon suite, to give some privacy to you and Mark,' she said with a sideways grin at Ana. 'And look there's the other room next door for Pietie. Perfect. We could have the guest rooms downstairs at the far end and Lex could have the run of the rooms at the other end. The long middle ballroom would be our common area.' She was busy marking off the rooms as she talked.

'Well, I'm not sure about all of your plans. Pietie would spend all the time racing up and down on the stairs, sliding down the bannisters I think they used to call it. Maybe we shouldn't plan putting us upstairs, the guest suite would be better. And...maybe it's a bit racist to put Lex in the old servant's quarters.'

Rhette came back in a flash. 'Worried about Lex? I wouldn't, he'd laugh at the racial notion and he could have Grace and the children visit in the holidays with all the rooms there. I'm sure the men would set up at least one space as a 'keep out' men's detective working room.'

Rhette flicked the screens to the view from the front of the riverside house. 'Wow,' Ana said. Bellerive was across the bay from the CBD of Hobart. With the house only one street back from the banks of the Derwent River they could see the huge lump of Mount Wellington above the city, the Tasman Bridge and the round tower of the casino.

'It's rentable by the month, and it's furnished. Do you think we dare rent this house?' Rhette asked. A mischievous smile spread across her face. 'It could be great fun... and there'll be a kindy or school nearby for Pietie. There has to be. No problem.'

'I saw the 'price on application' sign on the first screen. Have you checked it?' Ana cast a sideways look at her friend. Since the hunt for the Hood brothers had been moved to Tasmania Rhette had become a determined woman. Determined to see them caught for their crimes, paramount was for the deaths of her sister and father at their hand or by their orders. Her multi-millionaire legacy was from the opal and cash her father had left her, and spending it in that quest was OK.

'I can afford this house...and I will. Don't think about it. And don't worry about the major cleaning, we'll get someone in. I'll be studying but there'll be lots of time to do things together and explore Hobart,' Rhette said. 'It'll be fun...'

Chapter 36

'I'm bored. Get up, eat, go out and rob someone, come home and do it all again next day.' A week later Sean was trying, without success, to lighten the mood that hung around their necks like stinking buckets of week old prawns. 'I need a woman,' he turned and said with a sneer at Sarah. 'Maybe you do too?'

'You are a bastard!' Sarah threw the cup she was washing into the sink and slammed her way into her bedroom. The motel grade china survived the assault but the glass beaker it hit shattered. An empty whiskey bottle rolled to a stop at the edge of a map on the table as she'd rushed past it. Dieter glared after her. The siblings were now in another motel with two bedrooms and Dieter was more than annoyed at having to share a room with Sean.

'In the name of...' Dieter hissed. 'Shut the fuck up! It's your fault we're here and like this. You were seen by the cops and you've also been a dick head about getting more fucking money.' He pushed the bottle aside and reverted to staring at the map of Tasmania.

Sean shut up.

Dieter's hiss was worse than him shouting. Dieter hissing was dangerous; he'd learned that over the years. He slid a glance at his brother. He was un-shaven or showered, he smelled bad and had taken to slouching around the motel rooms they were in watching television all day. If he wasn't doing that he was mooning over the map looking for the mark he wanted. Today a newspaper, supplied by the motel, lay beside the map.

They'd moved from motel to motel, each sleazier that the last as the money ran low and in Dieter's paranoia that the police knew they were alive. It all reverted back to the Adelaide incident of Sean being discovered and the bloody lost suitcase. His vice like grip on the briefcase containing the gem grade Argyle diamonds, surrendered by Sarah, was total. A suggestion to fence a diamond was met with a blow, and more thunderous looks.

'Are you fucking mad?' Dieter hissed. 'They'll be looking for these as soon as they realise that the diamonds in the sale were fakes. It has to bloody eventually happen. You think of the cops as idiots. They're fucking well not!'

One action had caused concerns for Sean. In one motel room they'd occupied, Dieter had thrown the Bible into a bin and had taken a Koran, Sean didn't know he owned, from his suitcase. Dieter looked up some passages and left the book untouched after that. It was the first and only reminder of their Muslim roots that Sean had ever seen Dieter follow. He lived as an Australian, or whatever country they were in, a gentleman of means and a business leader, an entrepreneur. Sean was puzzled and wary.

The evening news came up on television and Sean sat to watch it as Dieter left the room for the bathroom. The Sydney bombing was old news and did not rate a mention on the parochial Tasmanian newscast, but they checked each evening.

The TV sports were over and the weather presenter, a woman worth looking at, was saying that tomorrow would be fine in Hobart before rain in the afternoon, when Dieter came back into the room.

'I'm going out,' he said.

He was showered and shaved, and dressed in one of his good suits. The change was total in comparison to the recent days.

'Where?' Sean managed as Dieter, patted his pocket for his

wallet and smoothed his hair in front of the mirror beside the television.

'I'm going to a wine tasting. It's time we got things moving...' he said and went out the door with the words, 'and get your bloody sister to clean this place up while I'm gone.'

Chapter 37

A sub division of the DAF investigation team would move to Tasmania.

The evidence for making the move was purely circumstantial but it was what Harry had been waiting for in his appointed task to bring the Hood brothers to trial.

With the formal blessing from Commissioner Tom Phillips, Harry would lead his team of Mark and Lex to Hobart. The camp followers, as Harry liked to call them, of Rhette, Ana and Pietie would established themselves, with little fuss, into the house that Rhette had found at Bellerive. The little fuss just meant that the men had just shrugged to the inevitable and concentrated on their part of the move.

Harry and Mark drove their own personal cars to Melbourne and boarded the Empress of Tasmania for the trip across Bass Straight to Devonport. It was a calm crossing. Rhette had been mysterious about where they would actually live in Hobart. They knew the suburb and that it was across the river from the CBD.

'Just trust me,' she said and exchanged a look with Ana.

Harry knew better than to question her as he had already been told that police accommodation was impossible and all she had told him was they would be living together. The ship docked early at the river port of Devonport and Rhette gave the men the GPS co-ordinates to follow. The convoy headed south, stopping for lunch in Launceston, before going on to the capital city of

Hobart.

Mark, used to the open plains and paddocks of regional South Australia, commented dryly that if someone could smooth the mountains and valleys from this landscape Tasmania would have an area as large as New South Wales. The others, over an afternoon tea stop of coffee and scones, had little idea of what he was talking about. 'See. Here they measure distance to travel on the roads in time, minutes and hours, instead of kilometres,' he said consulting the maps. 'If the place was flat then going from A to B would be a lot easier and quicker...'

'But not as pretty. Just look at those mountains. Some of them have a topping of snow and the trees are magnificent,' Ana insisted. She pushed back her trade mark white comma of hair against the black, and pointed out the many farm animals to Pietie.

Rhette was adamant that they just trust the GPS to get them to their destination and in the late evening they arrived in Bellerive after crossing the Tasman Bridge from the highway. She had organised a late meal waiting for them, similarly she had arranged for their beds to be made up and they all quickly settled in for the night.

Discoveries of the house and the surroundings would have to wait until next morning.

DAF enquiries, now led by Samantha Morton as team leader, would continue even though in Sydney, the case was cold, stone cold dead.

Newspapers and politicians alike had despaired of a result. Newspaper cartoonists found other topics to flaunt and haunt.

In the unofficial media, rabid conspiracy theorists suggested that Argyle Diamonds had engineered the crime and their shares dropped on the stock market in response.

There was still no confirmable whisper from the usual Sydney touts. Even investigation into old ex-crim Bertie Bayley driving the car that took the burka woman to the bombed building, led nowhere. He had evaded the CCTV cameras and his link to the crime was his own murder and the burned Mercedes. He'd been seen with a woman although there was no description other than she was a 'looker'. No-one could confirm or explain the murder's get away driver's alliance with the burka woman. So, who was she? Who was the un-identified female corpse in the lift? She was the only person with no name tag on her burned and damaged toe bones laying on the cold steel drawers in the morgue.

Questions.

Always questions needing answers.

There was the significant missing DNA among the victims.

Sarah Wilkes's body was not found, ergo was she alive? The most surprising fact was that she was the sibling of Dieter and Sean Hood. That was a shock that the DAF team were not expecting.

They had no DNA of the partner of Sarah Wilkes, Petra Joyce, and so they could not tie her in with the bombing, but the woman had disappeared from Perth. An Australia wide search was on for her, and in police parlance, they were concerned for her welfare.

So, in addition, was the victim in the lift just another unlucky person on her way to the Argyle Diamond sale? Pep and his team were convinced that she was the burka woman and they were still conducting tests to try to prove, or disprove this theory.

In Hobart, the DAF detectives would have an office supplied in the Police Headquarters in Liverpool Street, almost opposite the Royal Hobart Hospital. Another office set up, as suggested by the women, was to be in the Bellerive house.

Lex, when he joined the team in Hobart, would spend a four-day week there and three day weekends for trips back to Adelaide to see his family. The three aeroplane connections didn't seem to daunt him. He had his IPad and solitaire games to relax with and to allow his mind to wander and make connections.

That was his story anyway.

Chapter 38

Dieter Hood arrived late back to the unit in a better mood.

'I've found our mark,' he said to Sean. He loosened his tie, threw it across the table and placed a bottle of Pino Noir, a red wine resembling a cab sav, beside it. 'She fancies me but she's not my type. I think she'll go for you more. She's a divorcee and the stupid slut was willing to let this get into the conversation. As I said she's a perfect mark and she owns a winery. She gushed all over the place at the opening of her new vintage. It wasn't bad either, and she's definitely looking for a new market.'

'Is she worth a fuck?' Sean asked his usual question regarding any woman. His interest always started below his belt.

'That hardly matters. You'll do as you're told. You'll romance her, fuck her out of her head while I get on with taking over the winery for our next step. She's ripe and you'll pluck her,' Dieter said. He managed a smile at his brother. 'She's not bad looking so it won't be a chore for you, but you'll play bloody well hard to get for the first few meetings. Don't want to rush her. This's got to work.'

'And Sarah? What's her part in this?

'I hate that name...her name is Aisha. That's what she was born with. She takes on another infidel name here. She's just a woman, that's what her name says. She's a woman and we'll bloody well use her as I decide...' Dieter glared across the room at his brother.

Sean had heard the rant about Sarah's chosen name before. Ever since she'd contacted them for help with the diamond job Dieter had gone on and on about her name. 'She was a kid when she was brought to Australia and adopted out. Get over it. We changed our names... many times and we'll need to do it again... and soon. I've got all the new IDs we need,' Sean said.

'They'd better be fucking good,' Dieter's response was sharp. 'We're going to need more than one each when we leave this godforsaken place. At least multiples for you and me...' he left the words hanging. Not a positive foreboding for their sister.

Sean had a specialty, apart from petty thieving and flying an aeroplane.

There was an art, as he insisted, in getting false documents for them. He'd personally troll the old graveyards looking for a child's grave, preferably one that did not look as though it was attended by still grieving families, of about the similar birth date as either himself or Dieter. Usually Dieter. Applying for a copy of a birth certificate of the deceased child was next, then the rest was easy. When they chose to have an apparent different birth country there was an international organisation who could get what they needed. For a price. Both of them had at least three passports and driver's licence IDs they could still use. For reasons of simplicity they still called each other by the first names they had been given in Australia by adoptive parents. Learning the new identity had become a necessity and both brothers were adept at this, it was part of their life 'work.'

'So,' Sean repeated, 'what's Sarah's role in this?'

Dieter repeated the glare. 'She will be presented as my wife. I'll keep the bitch close and silent that way.'

This's going to be interesting Sean thought. 'So, when does this all start?' he said.

'Tomorrow. We'll get you introduced and you can start your

part of the deal, and she'd better fucking well go for you.'

'She will. When have I ever failed you in that way?' Sean went to bed confident that he'd get a woman to fuck and hopefully he'd contrive to move in with her as ordered. Anything to get away from under Dieter's bruising thumb.

Chapter 39

In the first weeks of their changing venues to Hobart, Rhette and Ana were busy exploring the city. A pretty city which Rhette confirmed was more like a large town in comparison with Sydney. Sure, it had all the major stores including David Jones and Myer, the Cat and Fiddle Arcade and the like, but it had the feel of a smaller town spread both sides along the Derwent River under the shadow of Mount Wellington.

To Ana it was new and comfortable after living in Adelaide and Port Lincoln in South Australia.

The house was one street back from the river but they could see the river traffic; the cargo and cruise ships and above it, the mountain now snow capped with the first autumn snows.

With little difficulty Rhette had persuaded Detective Mark Llewellyn, his new wife Ana and her son Piet to share the house with them. It was a continuation of the arrangement they had shared in Coober Pedy in the previous year. Pietie could go to kindergarten pre-school nearby too.

The house spoke of times gone by. Floors were of polished Tasmanian woods with expanses of Persian carpets, the ceilings high and many walls were panelled with Huon Pine timbers that glowed with golden age. The windows had been renovated from the small colonial size to tall ones, again in wooden frames, to let in ample light. Nooks and crannies invited gentle places to read books from the library wall, to look out and to enjoy the garden.

The house was furnished fittingly to the past times although modern conveniences had not been overlooked.

Very quickly the women got into a comfortable routine.

After the men had gone to work and while Ana went to take Piet to his pre-school, Rhette walked along the pathway by the river towards the group of shops. There was an upmarket coffee and lunch establishment that ladies who lunched frequented but after she was ignored by a waitress, probably due to the fact that her jeans and jumper may have been less than expected, she took her coffee at a little Asian shop that was less pretentious. They also made very good sushi rolls which she often bought to share with Ana for lunch.

One morning an ambulance pulled up outside the shop, against the traffic, and an attendant in uniform, ran into the shop. She thrust a note and smiling thanks to the small Oriental man behind the counter and departed at speed with an order of sushi and coffee. Rhette laughed at the event. It could only happen in a city like Hobart, never in Sydney or Melbourne.

Almost always on Rhette's agenda was the butcher shop. It smelled and looked as a butcher shop should; of the aromas of spices, hams, ropes of sausages and meat in chilled trays behind a counter. When the freezer doors opened a blast of even colder air flooded the shop. The only thing missing was sawdust on the floor, Rhette thought.

'Fillet steak for your man?' Dan asked. He was immaculate in his white shirt and navy blue and white striped apron.

Rhette remembered his name by saying, Dan-Dan the butcher man, to herself. He'd learned very quickly, as most butchers did, that she usually bought steak, lamb or pork for Harry. Expensive cuts except when she was doing his favourite, a slow cooked blade steak beef casserole. Lamb shanks were another dish he raved over. Harry appreciated the garlic and bay leaves she laced the meats with and it was a good sign that he was amenable to other cuisine. After her years in the arena of police protection, then the simple ordered life in the convent school, Rhette was more than ready to experiment with recipes. The internet provided all she could want and she found that Ana was fond of cooking interesting food too. They would cook together or take turns to cook for the household.

Harry, on the other hand, had lived a bachelor life of fast grabbed food. She could serve him anything except cheese sandwiches. 'They always give us tatty cheese sandwiches at meetings,' he whinged one morning when she was cutting sandwiches for his work lunch. Ham was presented and he was happy. A man of simple tastes, Rhette loved to tease him.

Rhette brought her remembrances back to the moment.

'Yes, but its rump tonight. Great flavour, better than fillet steak,' she commented to Dan. 'I'm going to pepper it. I've found an interesting blend of pepper corns to try for us all.' Rhette and Ana were cooking together that night, with Ana doing a desert, a lemon and coconut pudding.

Dan grinned an agreement. 'Cook it very quickly and rest it properly... and for you?' He knew she ate red meat only occasionally. 'I have some very good organic chicken...?'

'Another day... steak tonight.' Rhette laughed. 'But when you have some of the lovely Tasmanian salmon I'll buy it here; until then I'll have to get it from the Joe in the floating restaurant by the river wharf.'

'He's not supposed to sell uncooked fish,' Dan said. His eyes flicked at Rhette's trim figure, her tumble of red curly hair and wide smile. 'You've made a conquest there with Joe, no wonder he'll sell it raw. Now do you want some of my ham for Harry's lunch? I cure it myself...'

'...and it's delicious.' Rhette completed his sentence. 'Yes please.'

Dan wrapped her purchases and she slipped them into the hemp bag she carried before handing over two twenty dollar notes and receiving a few coins as change. The meat was good, the expenses matched the suburb, but Rhette was happy.

She bought vegetables and mushrooms from the green grocer and picked up a newspaper from the newsagent before she headed back to the river front to order fresh salmon for the next day's dinner. From there the path home went past the hotel. She paused to look back at the marina of yachts, the landing where the river taxis once stopped and a bustle of ducks and ducklings swam following her trying to entice some bread from her. Her eyes were drawn up to a flock of pelicans flying in a close vee formation and further across the river to where a huge cruise ship dwarfed the city's skyline from its berth at the Constitution Dock wharf.

This was the best part of the morning. By eleven she had fresh ingredients for dinner, and all she needed was for Harry to be on time after work to enjoy her cooking. The evening was theirs to talk, laugh and make love in their own area of the house. Some nights they all got together in the big sitting room to talk, share music or play cards.

For Rhette there were just the rest of the days to fill with her study, as she was busy with the pre-reading for the Egyptian course.

She walked along the walking path, the 'Charles Darwin Walk,' she noted from a sign. The river to one side and a line of amazing mansions occupied the area across the road. These were huge at least a century old and usually two storied. All houses had metres and metres of intricate white lace ironwork arching along wide verandas. The front gardens were ablaze with seasonal flowers and trees. The latter were almost all European, and with the coming of autumn the reds and yellows of deciduous leaves carpeted the lawns and paths. Late roses, uniform as standard white, red and pinks, had blooms that would soon be banished as the gardeners pruned them for winter. The smell of roses and decaying leaves wafted across the road to mingle with the scents of seaweed along the shoreline.

Rhette smiled to herself. The millions she had inherited could pay for one of these beautiful houses but she doubted that any would ever be for sale nor could she see herself living there. Unabashed she stopped often to gaze at the houses and to read the elegant signs discretely proclaiming the house names and their history. On one brass plate, she noted that this house was a registered rest home. They were looking for a temporary person to assist with lunches.

On impulse Rhette opened the gate and went up the central steps to the ornate entrance of the mansion to investigate.

Chapter 40

Lex had gone back to Adelaide from Sydney, to see his family before re-joining the team, on the morning when Harry and Mark went meet to the Hobart detectives in their headquarters. The police chief, Chad Lennox, introduced Detectives Tate Dempsey and Kira Regan who would be available to them as liaison with the Tasmanian Police Force. He put a small office and a couple of unmarked police cars at their disposal.

'I know Tom Phillips well. Anything we can do to help you with this case consider it done', he said.

It was that easy. Genuine smiles quickly overcame the possible problems with the interaction between states.

'At least you're not Victorians, but I suppose you play rugby?' Tate mumbled getting a smile from Harry and Mark.

'No. I'm a South Aussi, AFL and we're doing OK against Hawthorn, your mob, with the Crows this year,' Mark responded before Harry could say anything.

'God help me, football!' Kira said. 'And I suppose you're going to talk it all day?'

'Might make a mention now that the main games are under way. As long as the Crows are still in them...after that don't want to hear about it.'

'Hawthorn's going to do OK this year, you'll see. It won't be the end of conversation,' Tate said. He gave a short arm punch to the air, that mirrored his medium stature. He had to be the product of police gym clubs for boys that led many into the police ranks, Harry thought.

Harry sat back and stayed out of it as he could see that they would meld quite well. After a few more moments to let the banter die down he said, 'OK then. Football talk finished? Let me bring you up to speed about our being here. I guess that Inspector Lennox has briefed you somewhat?'

'Yes, Chad's given us a background, but these Hood brothers, never heard of them before now,' Tate said. He looked across to Kira, whose tall athletic frame was still almost at attention beside Harry's desk. She shrugged, me either, and moved to sit down on one of the chairs.

'The Hood brothers, Dieter and Sean, that's obviously just one of the AKAs they've used, have been in our sights for years. We know they, especially Dieter, have run heavy drugs, ordered and probably carried out murders and been in every sort of illegal deals. Despite everything they've managed to keep out of courts. Clever management and even cleverer lawyers. They went quiet and appeared as legit businessmen for a while, before they got involved with a criminal psycho in South Australia. That's when all hell broke loose and Mark got interested in them. He'd kidnapped a child...and the case went to Coober Pedy. I was chasing the brothers and Mark was trying to retrieve the boy.'

'That's when you two met up, unusual for such interstate co-operation,' Kira commented.

Harry turned to her with a grin that travelled across to Mark. 'We did alright. The psycho's dead and Mark saved the kid and married his mother last month. You'll meet Ana, Pietie, and my partner Rhette soon I'm sure. Detective Lex Osei'll be here tomorrow. Great detective, unusual methods.'

The two DAF detectives outlined the Sydney case and the reasons they believed that the culprits had moved to Tasmania, probably Hobart. They also asked if there had been any increase in petty or even serious crime as they thought that money was in short supply since Mark had captured the suitcase of money, opal and drugs at Adelaide airport.

'Nothing that we can't handle here. There's always light fingers amongst some of the black refugees we seem to have in abundance in Hobart, Tate said. 'Pickings from the market and one post office robbery we haven't pinged anyone for yet. Brazen but it didn't get them much. Could be your Hood brothers. As I said there's the usual gangs of thieves here, and we know most of their MOs, with a good sprinkling of things in the last years since...'

Kira cut him off with a frown. 'Crime's the same here as elsewhere else, the sad family murders, an occasional mugging, ditto knife fights. I think it's because we've a small population and hardly a target for most of the bigger gangs. We're just too limited in buyers for myriad of drugs in particular. I should know, I was with the Dog Squad for five years before I transferred to straight detective work.'

Harry said. 'Any specific reason you made the change from dogs to people investigations?'

'No. It was mainly because my dog was retired and was put out to pasture. He's a great family pet now. Gets an itchy nose some days,' Kira said smiling then she continued and her face became serious. 'Ice is here, of course and one day, I reckon, someone will find a way to infiltrate the legal medical opium poppy farms that are an industry here. It's very well regulated but we watch it.'

'I still say that crime has increased since...' Tate began again and Harry gave the tiniest suggestion of a wink across his new desk to Mark. He wondered what Tate's reaction to the tall black South African detective was going to be.

Chapter 41

But two days later it was Ana who, after Rhette had told her about it, began her first two- hour shift at the Rest Home to help with the lunch time meals so that staff could have their own breaks. After she had taken Pietie to school the day loomed long and too quiet. She wasn't used to doing nothing while Mark worked. Ana found that being partnered by a senior police officer, her security rating was quickly checked and approved.

Rhette had her distance university studies on 'Ancient Egyptian Queens' and Ana was getting restless. Perfect. The home was within walking distance and working there was going to be fun.

From the first shifts Ana became fascinated with one guest, Emily. She sat alone at a small dining room table set for two people, her gentle, softly lined face turned towards an empty chair and place setting opposite her.

Lyn, the senior nurse, had given her Emily as someone special to care for as part of her duties. 'It will always be the same,' Lyn said. 'Treat it all as normal...'

From the start Ana was intrigued. From that first day, she was introduced to her, Emily who immediately wanted to know all about her, and Mark. They talked for a few moments before Emily seemed to shut off and looked down at her plate. Ana took this as her signal that she should get on and attend to other guests. She kept close enough to see Emily's words and actions throughout her meal.

'Dear Edgar,' Ana heard Emily say sweetly, 'Do try this tuna salad. It's delicious today much better than yesterday's lamb stew. I found that quite unappealing.'

Emily paused as though listening. Her smile creases deepened as she whispered, 'I'll put some of your special pepper on it.' She fussed into her large old tapestry handbag and, producing an antique silver pepper shaker, she tapped a smidgin of pepper onto the plate. With a smile she concentrated on her own salad, occasionally making a comment towards the empty chair. Emily ate her peaches and icecream served as desert and lingered over her cup of tea. Catching Ana's attention Emily fingered a locket that lay nestled in the folds of her floral blouse. It contained a photograph of a man, presumably Edgar and locks of hair. 'My dear love … my lost love,' Emily sighed loud enough for Ana to hear her words.

At the completion of her meal Emily rose, and walking stick in hand, she nodded with a distant smile to the other residents and went back to her room and her afternoon TV programs.

'See?' said Lyn after she returned from her break. 'It happens every day, a daily performance.'

'Who's Edgar?' Ana asked.

'Her late husband. Been dead for years her records report. All the staff think it's all so very touching how she continues to care for him. They always set the extra place at her table and she prefers to eat alone, just with him.'

'It's certainly different.' Ana said. She looked keenly at Lyn. 'Do you see it as a strange thing that she does?' It was almost as if Lyn was keen to have someone new from the outside world to talk to about Emily. Someone outside the medical staff.

'Emily has her evening meal and breakfast served in her room. But this happens every day at lunch. I guess I'm just a bit tired but

I'm a bit over the old devoted, demented routine. It's almost childish… Like a child seeking attention.'

Ana raised her eyebrows. 'I know I shouldn't ask but has she been diagnosed with dementia?'

'So many of them get a bit odd in the end but Emily medical records doesn't have an official diagnosis of dementia. Her failing heart can cause similar symptoms, but this is like a play, a performance.' Lyn laughed softly. 'It's probably me; I've got dementia working so long with the elderly. I love them and I should be more used to their peculiarities.'

Chapter 42

'I will never play the part of your wife!' Sarah shouted. 'No fucking way!'

'You bloody will. You'll do as you're told.' Dieter shouted back as Sarah threw another cup, this time aimed at his head. Dieter's reaction was fast and he slapped the cup down. It shattered as it hit the tiled floor of the kitchenette.

'I'm not your slave. This is my gig. I did the diamond robbery. I got away with it. You just supplied the bombs. Now, because of Sean's idiocy, we're without the means to get on with your part of the deal. Getting the diamonds out of the country into markets that'll pay for them. I've had enough. I'm taking the stones and I'm going. I can find ways to sell them.' Sarah's face was flushed as she raked her hands through her dark hair.

'Oh, so you bloody can do it on your own, can you? You're not going anywhere. The diamonds stay with me, you're nothing without me now.' Dieter's shout became a hiss.

Sean, who was stretched out of a couch, watched on. This time it wasn't him in the fire zone.

'I can! All I have to do is wait for Petra. She knows I'm in Hobart. She must be sick, or something. There's no mention that the cops have got her and she did her job at the scene. Did it well too. She made my getaway work.' Sarah rubbed her eyes until they filled with tears as she slumped into a chair. She shook off Dieter's hand as he came towards her with a tissue.

Sean looked on hardly believing his eyes.

Dieter offering a tissue?

Dieter said, even gently. 'You're were lucky with that robbery. I'll admit the planning was good but it was a one off. The hard part starts now with the cops after you. They don't know about me and they'd think that Sean's near miss in Adelaide had no connection. We're in the clear and we have to keep it that way. We have to keep you safe...'

'Well, how about you treat me better and help me find Petra. She's not answering her phone... Why? Why...?'

Dieter moved behind her chair, out of her direct line of sight to avoid her eyes. 'Perhaps it's not working...'

'I'm ringing the burner phone you told us to get. That's the only one she has... her own phone got burned when we set the bombs on our house in Perth. I wish I had some way...' Sarah rambled as she tried to look over her shoulder towards Dieter. 'I need her... and I can't pretend to be your wife. It's disgusting...' She turned back to look at Sean and another tissue was put to work to mop up the tears that still seeped out of her eyes and down her cheeks.

'It'll be alright.' Dieter soothed. His voice like syrup. 'You were a marvellous actress working with Argyle when all you wanted was to destroy them and get rich. A superb actress then, now do it again when we set up the next part of the plan. You have some good clothes still and you don't scrub up too badly...' he tried for the smile although she couldn't see his face where his eyes were cold and distance.

'You're not a bad looking tart. You can do it,' Sean tried to follow his brother's lead.

Dieter remained behind her chair. His face became hard as he clenched his jaw, his lips a thin ribbon across his face. He narrowed his eyes at Sean to tell him to shut up. Both men knew that Sarah would never be reunited with Petra. With one well timed call to the burner phone, Dieter had sent Petra, the burka woman, to the lift and to her death in the explosion.

It was a fact he was not going to share with his sister.

After a day or so working at the rest home, over the staff lunch break, Ana told Emily and Edgar's story to Mark as an amusing comment on her day.

Frustratingly the detectives had discovered no trail of the Hood brothers actually arriving in Tasmania although they knew, or thought they did, that they were in Hobart. It would take time to find them, even with the local detectives helping.

Mark listened to Ana's story. 'You've got some imagination, my love and its working overtime. She's just an old crackpot. Are they all like that? A grin spread across his face as he watched his wife prepare their evening meal.

'No, not all of them. Well - Emily knows about you,' Ana told him. 'She wheedled it out of me that we're new to Hobart that you're a policeman. I didn't say any more, not how fabulous you are, in bed and out of it!' She laughed and made shushing noises, as Mark grabbed at her. Pietie was in the next room and waiting for his tea. The 'in bed' would come later.

Ana smiled. The tale would be fun to share with the others later that evening in the house when Pietie was tucked up in bed and they were relaxing. She didn't think she was betraying confidences when she didn't say names. It was an amusing alternative to the work the men were doing, and she watched as Rhette put in long hours of study. She was trying to learn the chronical of Egyptian Pharaoh dynasties and was fascinated that some of the Pharaohs were female. They could all use some diversion and relaxation.

Next day things changed at the nursing home.

Ana saw that a new gentleman resident, after inquiring gallantly if he may, asked to share the small dining table with Emily and the presence of Edgar.

Frank Higgins was a stooped ex-army major of ninety-two summers, who had once been tall before arthritis twisted his spine and the pain made his life miserable. Despite that and dosed up with medications, he still dressed with precision and elegance. He was a witty, chatty man and made Emily's eyes sparkle and her laugh tinkle. She gently chided both men to eat well, one from a full plate and the other from the ghost meal on the empty plate before the empty chair. Frank seemed charmed as she fussed at each lunch time offering napkins, salt and condiments.

Again, the staff watched and noted the small gathering and even began to wonder if there could be a little romance happening between Emily and Frank, with Edgar's blessing of course. But the next day all was not right at the cosy table. Emily appeared cross with Edgar and with a burst of angry words she turned her back on the empty chair and refused to speak to him. As any gentleman would Frank tried to calm the quarrel but Emily remained firmly turned away from Edgar. She coyly flirted with Frank and the meal was eaten with only Frank receiving her lavish attention and the gift of pepper.

'Edgar,' Emily finally scolded the empty chair as she left the dining room, 'you must not be so angry.' She paused and added, 'I will do it!'

At the rest home an apparent truce was called next day and the trio peacefully dined together until Frank was too ill to attend lunch. He became bedridden and died quietly of old age, arthritis and 'his old war stomach wounds'.

Emily was sad and dignified at the loss but after a respectful two-day period of mourning returned to dining in the communal room. She ate again with Edgar as her sole ghostly companion. She had obtained a lock of Frank's hair that she lovingly placed into her locket, but somehow the essence of Emily was gone too.

Within the week Emily's heart gave way and, with no surviving family or friends, the staff were her only mourners at her funereal. Ana and Lyn were surprised when, in a very recent codicil to Emily's will, it was stipulated that Lyn immediately receive the treasured silver pepper pot and Ana the locket. She took it home and placed it onto the mantel piece as a remembrance of an interesting lady and, next day, she went to do her lunch time work as usual.

However, Mark chuckled but was intrigued with the different shades of hair that the silver locket contained. Unknown to Ana he took the locket to work and twenty-four hours later he produced the silver locket and with it a sheet of paper. 'Interesting forensic results,' he dryly commented.

Chapter 43

Mark's voice was suddenly urgent, seriously urgent as a new thought struck him. 'You'd better get the pepper pot away from your friend Lyn. Quickly too.'

'Why?' Ana asked as she prepared to serve dinner for everyone that evening. A new recipe of lasagne with spinach and three cheeses. Her first attempt at a meatless dish for them all. Mark had come in from work, and lined up behind her for a smooch and eyed the bubbling browned cheese tray as she took it from the oven. It smelled enticing.

'Forget the why. Was Lyn at work as usual? Is she OK?' Mark asked brushing aside her question.

'Why?' Ana repeated. 'She's been a bit off and she went home early after lunch. Her shift doesn't finish until four so I stayed until all the guests were settled for the afternoon.'

'Do you know where she lives? Have you her phone number?'

'For Pete's sake tell me why, not keep asking questions. Lyn's become a friend and you're worrying me.' Ana said. She frowned at him as she stepped back to put the hot tray on the bench ready to serve after she got Pietie's hands washed. The table was set with delicate china.

Harry stopped her. He looked serious as he opened the paper again and showed her. 'There were five examples of hair in the locket. From five different people, all men. They all contained arsenic. Enough arsenic to kill.' Harry said, his voice insistent.

'Now tell me where she lives. I think we need to get to her.'

Ana's eyes widened in shock, then realisation. The pepper pot from Emily. She pushed their dinner back into the oven and snapped off the heat. 'Lyn lives in the next suburb. I've been there. Let's see that she's OK. Give Rhette and Harry a call will you. They can look after Pietie while we go. I'm sure it's OK.'

A serial killer in a gentle rest home? Ana thought as she sat next to Mark and navigated as he drove to Lyn's house. They arrived and without preamble Mark knocked hard on the front door.

Lyn's husband David had a startled expression on his face as he opened the door. Dressed in casual shorts and t-shirt h had obviously been preparing a meal. He smiled when he saw Ana. A boy about five years old peaked out at them from behind his father.

'Where's Lyn?' Mark demanded.

'She's unwell in bed. She's probably got a stomach wog.'

Mark grunted, his face serious. Still standing in the doorway he pulled his mobile from his pocket and dialled triple zero. 'Let's not risk this. Better we get the ambulance rather than us taking her to the Hobart Hospital ER. They've got what's needed now.'

Ana sped past David and went to the main bedroom. Lyn was propped up by pillows and looked pale and weak. A deep plastic dish was clasped in her hands and the stink of vomit hung thick in the room like a hovering miasma. From the room outside she could hear Mark explaining to David what he thought Lyn was suffering from.

Mark put his head around the door. At a nod from Ana he sussed that Lyn was very sick. He went back to David.

'What's going on...?'

'Sorry to just take over like this... but we think Lyn's been poisoned.'

'Poisoned?' David's voice echoed. 'How…?'

'Have you got someone, a relative or neighbour, who can look after your boy and we'll follow the ambulance to the hospital? Better that you don't drive with the worry and…' He gestured to a bottle on the dining table. 'you've had a beer too,' Mark said. His voice and demeanour were calm, friendly and David's hands relaxed fractionally from their clenched worry position. This man had things in hand.

'Yes, my sister lives across the street. She'll come over. I don't know the neighbours that well, they're new. They seem OK. A woman and her teenage son.' David's voice was still strained. He rambled as his thought took in what was happening.

'Give your sister a call.' He put a hand on the other man's shoulder as the wail of a siren became audible. 'I think it's going to be alright. I'm no doctor but she's awake and it looks like she's vomited. That can only be good.'

David used his mobile phone to all across the street and a woman arrived just as the ambulance backed up into the drive.

Ana watched the quiet efficiency of the ambulance crew as they checked their patient before they put her onto a stretcher. Mark had gone outside with the ambulance crew and he knew he would be advising them of his suspicions. They loaded her, the ambulance doors slammed and they transported Lyn and the vomit dish away.

David had changed his shorts for blue geans, his t-shirt for a skivvy, had insisted that only Lyn had used the pepper.

'I think Mark gave a sample of the pepper to the ambulance crew to be checked,' Ana said.

'Don't think I want it in the house. Too scary, the kids and all…' David said.

He thrust the pot towards Ana. She placed it into her purse. 'I'll keep it safe and Lyn can decide when she's better,' she said.

'Well, I never want to see it again.' David insisted. 'No matter what happens...' he seemed to realise what he had said and turned away.

'I agree with Mark. Lyn vomited and probably got rid of the poison. She must love pepper if she ate that big dose to make herself ill...' Ana managed a small joke to try to reduce the tension

David gave her a cursory smile and went for his car keys. 'I'll get my car out.'

'Hey, remember Mark said we'd take you to the hospital. No way should you be driving and worrying about Lyn...one problem not two,' she said.

It was a few moments later that Mark came back into the house. He had his note book out and stood writing in it.

They followed the ambulance across the Derwent River to the Royal Hobart Hospital and waited until a doctor had seen Lyn. She was immediately admitted to a room in the intensive care ward. Lyn was exhausted from the vomiting and the transfer to the hospital, the subsequent tests and lay still pale and wan in the bed. Ana and Mark waited in the reception area and David opted to stay with his wife until later when her condition improved. They offered to stay or at least to come back to take him home when he decided to do so.

'Not a bother,' David said. 'I've a brother who lives this side of the river and I'll give him a call.' He hugged Ana in gratitude and wrung Mark's hand. His eyes earnest and relieved. 'Thank you. I don't know how I can thank you,' he insisted before they left him and Lyn in the hospital and returned home.

Chapter 44

The lasagne was hot as Rhette dished it up to Ana and Mark when they got home.

She, Harry and Pietie had already eaten. Pietie was bathed and ready for bed by the time they returned to the house. Mark scoffed a huge serve with salad. 'Good!' he said as he stretched in contentment. Where's the meat wasn't an issue and Ana chuckled to herself. She'd made a huge tray of lasagne and there would be enough for another meal for herself, Mark and Piet tomorrow night.

The group sat about over coffee and talked the nursing home, arsenic, Lyn's sickness through.

Mark suggested, 'Perhaps Emily'd thought that Lyn was suspicious about her state of mind. With the death of Frank so quickly after his pepper-arsenic dosage she might have become worried. Or was it just that Emily knew that her heart was giving out and had the thought that she could do one more murder. She chose Lyn as her final psycho vengeance.'

'Then why did she give the locket with the hair to me? Ana asked.

'Ah...that was a stroke of her cunning. Would her crimes ever be found out? I think she considered that she was just too clever. She'd got away with Edgar's murder and why he was murdered is the first mystery. In the end, she may have enjoyed killing. Nursing homes must be boring places.' Mark said.

'Five lots of hair. Five probable victims.' Harry laughed. 'And we think that we are homicide detectives. This case'll either become a huge scandal with millions spent on it - bodies disinterred, more autopsies, coroners, and all the rest. It will all depend on Lyn and if she will press charges and bring the case to court.'

'The Nursing Home Board may want to hush it up,' Ana said. 'Lyn'll tell them. She's one forthright person.'

'Doesn't arsenic disappear over time?' Rhette asked. She held the antique locket admiring the delicate silver work.

'Not usually. It stays in the hair pretty well forever. They've found it old graves before now. Like the old hatters' graves. You've heard the term "mad as a hatter?" Well, that was because they'd used an arsenic compound when they made hats in the old days and the workers absorbed it over time. Poor sods. Arsenic is one of the easy poisons to test for and detect.' Harry said. 'It was just your nosey husband...' He grinned at Ana.

'It was the differences in the hair samples that caught my attention and why I asked for the forensic department to give the locket the once over. They were chuffed with what they found.' Mark paused and glanced at his wife. 'There are more questions in all this. Emily changed her will, why then? Was the fact that you, Ana, are married to me, a detective, and she could thumb her nose at everyone? Finally, did she then have the means to take bring on her own heart attack? To end it all?'

'Well, she's cremated now as she stipulated, and maybe we'll never know.' Ana said. 'And with all this I think that she was prepared enough, clever enough, that she would have had the means to commit suicide...'

'We may never know...' Mark agreed.

'By the way,' Ana said later after she'd gone into check on the sleeping Piet and they were bed. 'What were you writing in your notebook before we left Lyn's house? You seemed very interested in the neighbours…'

Mark laughed. 'I always have to do a report on any criminal action I come across. Part of the job. This'll have to be done tomorrow, and be followed up maybe by the local men. It will probably go to Commissioner Chad Lennox for decision. You make work for me, woman.' He paused and planted a kiss on her nose as she snuggled into him.

'Why'd you ask about the neighbours? You just seemed to have shifted mental gears when you looked over the fence. I thought it odd…' she said.

'You're getting to know me too well, my love. Possibly a person of interest was there. Someone who didn't come out to look at the ambulance when everyone else in the street did. A person who just looked through a window when a woman and child came out. Why? Always interesting. I noted the number plate of the two vehicles parked in the yard. One of them was a white van,' Mark said.

Chapter 45

'Keeping you up to date as promised,' Samantha Morton said per a Skype linkup with Harry from Sydney. Her face was fresh, her hair perfect in a French roll, and her smile was a cat that had eaten the cream smile.

'You got a new man?' Harry teased hopefully. ''Bout time too.'

'For goodness sake, Harry, this's an official link. Mind yourself,' she said with a smile that followed the flicker of a brief frown. 'I'm talking business.'

'OK, then. I'm listening. Is it pertaining to DAF?'

Yes. The Perth forensic boys did a DNA on a fragment they found at Sarah Wilkes' house. They've been treating Petra Joyce's disappearance as a potential crime which gave them the immediate go ahead on testing.'

'And...' Harry said in his usual jump ahead manner. 'I guess that this matched with the body in the lift at the DAF scene.'

Sam sighed. 'Yes, it did. It's a complication. So, if Petra was Sarah's partner why or how did her body end up there? I think she was the burka woman so, if that's the case, why was she expendable to the crime? It'd take timing to get her there as the bombs were set off. Plus, the Argyle people say that they understood that the couple were solid. I'm taking a stab in the dark but I'm guessing that there's an outside hand in her death. Could it be something we can use?'

'Keep that thought, Sam. It may be useful before we're done.'

'There's more,' Sam said. 'We've been able to follow up how the Mercedes got to be burned in the bush. A woman, who could answer to Sarah's description, but wearing what could've been a blonde wig, was spotted by the CCTV on the motorway following the Mercedes. Driving a hire car. The two cars turned off the main road, and away from the cameras. Later they picked her up again when she drove into a shopping mall. She stayed there a few minutes and the CCTV has her going into a post office. After that it was back to her car and on the road again to Sydney - where somehow she disappeared.'

Harry butted in. 'She seemed to know where the cameras are in Sydney. Kept away from them. Damn her... but I can't think why she'd need a book of stamps.' He nodded again to Sam to continue.

'The hire car firm's one of those little back street places attached to a dodgy workshop. They'd been paid off in cash. Shooting old Bayley was Sarah's way of payment to him and burning the merc. We've ID'd the driver now as Tony Angelo. The woman seemed to have no problems with shooting possible witnesses.'

'Interesting though, isn't it? She lived in Perth. That's a bloody long way from Sydney. Says to me that she had local help to set some of the things up. I'm thinking her brother Dieter Hood. Maybe you could check the phone towers and see if there was a call between throw away burner phones just before the bombs went off.'

'I don't quite follow that?' Sam said.

'Well, just a thought. Dieter Hood has been identified as seen in the café before the bombs exploded. The waitress wasn't sure but she thought he'd made a call on a mobile. If he did. Was it to Sarah, or was it to Petra? Or to someone else. Interesting and deadly perhaps. A way to cut back the witnesses. Or is there another reason? Hmmm…' Harry's voice trailed to a murmur. 'We can be sure he was using a disposable mobile. Any chance a tower could trace his calls?'

'It's unlikely given the amount of traffic through a tower in the CDB – but I'll try to get someone on it. Not something easy to do. You're good at giving impossible, if not nearly impossible, tasks to us mortals.'

'Aw…that's my job… and you're so good at doing them,' Harry said.

'OK. Are you suggesting questions about the division of the proceeds of this crime? Or could there be other reasons?' Sam changed topic. 'Has Lex arrived yet? I heard he was crook with the flu last week and stayed in Adelaide to get over it.'

'He flies in today. Mark's just about to go to the airport to pick him up. Cheers then, Sam, keep me informed with DAF – and new men in your life. You're far too good to be alone.' Harry clicked off the connection with a chuckle before she could respond.

Samantha sat shaking her head with amusement. Bloody good detective her boss. There was a hint of someone interesting; an emergency room doctor who had treated her father, and who kept phoning to enquire about his health. They had shared a coffee last evening.

Chapter 46

The stolen utility was T boned by a white "Exclusive Tasmanian Woollen Fashions" delivery van in the middle of Salamanca Square.

The snub-nosed van came off decidedly second best.

The driver, mobile phone in hand, was wedged into his seat by the explosion force of the air bags and the steering wheel as the front of his van was pushed inwards. His legs were crushed and mashed by the engine pushing into the cabin. Pain flooded his nerve pathways to his brain and he passed into the grey valleys of unconsciousness. The phone was flung from his hand and hit the front windscreen shattering it into opaque fragmentations.

The driver of the stolen ute took one look at the van, ignored the slumped driver, and took off running at speed.

He skirted a few people who were at the ANZ Bank ATM on a corner and ran into a mall square behind the main market area. The mall, lined with book shops, cafes, a shop specialising in scientific toys, and others with touristy items was quiet it being a work week day. The last anyone, sitting enjoying a coffee, saw of the fleeing man was he'd taken the first steep steps of the Kelly's Stairs – the historic set of stairs to the Battery Point streets above.

Lex Osei, was dropped off by Mark from the airport and was waiting in line for the Salamanca ATM as the accident unfolded. He needed some cash and his plan was to walk to the Police Headquarters to stretch his legs and to get a feel of Hobart. The five-kilometre distance would soon be covered by Lex's long legs.

Witnessing the whole incident he hit 000 on his mobile, stated who he was, and reading it from his phone, gave the GPS position. 'We need an ambulance and the police immediately,' he said.

Finishing the emergency call Lex looked about to see if anyone was attending to the van driver. No one was. While his whole detective instinct was to chase after the escaping driver of the ute, with reluctance he went to the aid of the trapped van driver. He bent to lift the man's head to clear his airway and to prevent him choking because of his slumped position face down into the airbag.

SAPOL Training and First Aid 101.

'You'll be OK', he said to the still unconscious van driver, as he reached into the vehicle window to continue to support the man's head. 'The ambulance's on its way...' Lex didn't think it necessary to add that he'd seen the injured driver he was attending using his mobile phone, illegally, at the time of the accident. The other driver was also at fault as he was speeding. Lex's days as a road cop were well over but he knew the rules.

'You! Get out of there! A loud boom of a voice shouted at Lex and a strong hand thumped down onto his shoulder. 'You, I mean you!' The hand grabbed and yanked him back away from the van.

Lex straightened his two-metre-tall figure to his full height and stared down at the scowling man who had pulled him away. 'Are you talking to me?' he said quietly. He nudged the hands away and reached back into the van to support the injured man's head again.

'Don't you listen, you black git? I said - fuck off!' The face was now red, the lips white with fury; eyes wide and staring up into Lex's face.

'I'm trying to...' Les said, his temper rising to match his assailant's but he kept his tone in check. With his free hand, he reached towards his jacket to try to get and show his SAPOL ID.

The man tensed.

A crowd was gathering. Hobart people of all description, and a murmur rose to cries. 'Leave him alone...' He's only helping...' 'Stupid bastard...' A tremor of hostility was aimed towards the bullish man.

Eyes fixed on Lex, the man shouted, 'No! You don't!' and pulled a gun from a service harness.

He fired.

The bullet took Lex in the left shoulder of the arm supporting the injured man's lolling head. As the head jerked then slumped forward again Lex swore in Afrikaans and clutched at his shattered shoulder. Blood quickly seeped out of the wound to stain his shirt. He staggered a step or two sideways, his legs buckled and his body slowly slid to the ground.

'What in the fuck did you do that for?' Lex said as his face drained to a pasty grey-black as the pain and shock set in.

The circling crowd of people backed off, silent at first, in fear. Screams and shouts started from them.

'Shit! Gawd, what have I done?' The shooter holstered his gun and with one hand partly covering his chin and lower mouth he started issuing orders to the crowd. 'Get an ambulance...now!' To one woman who seemed less traumatised than the others, he said, 'I'm a police officer. You, look after the man in the van.' He pushed her forward to where Lex had been standing. The plain clothed officer shouted to the crowd. 'This man was trying to steal from him. You could all see that, couldn't you?' His voice was a hoarse and dry; a desperate question.

'And I'm Lex Osei. Police Detective Sergeant. SAPOL,' Lex said through pain gritted teeth. His long strong legs pushed his body up to a standing position and he stood, wobbling, as he glared at the fellow police officer. 'This's the stupidest thing I've ever been involved in… ever witnessed…' His South African accent was broad and his eyes started to glaze. Another man jumped forward to catch Lex as he toppled again. He was lowered to the cobbled street and someone else put his coat over him for warmth. Lex mumbled 'Thanks…'

The Hobart police officer stood, head and arms down in the middle of the circle of people; oblivious to the noise and being ignored by the shocked crowd.

The sounds of an ambulance siren preceded the flashing of red lights with blue police lights forming a convoy of vehicles that sped, past the golden sandstone walls of Parliament House and the trees and lawns of Salamanca gardens, to the scene of the accident.

Chapter 47

'What in the hell were you thinking?' Inspector Chad Lennox could not help yelling at Tate Dempsey as the latter stood before him. 'Or were you thinking at all? I've never in my life encountered such idiocy… Such lack of discipline in a police action…' The senior officer stopped pacing around the object of his fury and slammed his office door shut. In controlled anger, he pulled down his uniform jacket, then marched to stand behind his desk.

Tate stood, his face drawn, jowls sagging. Grey with the shock at what he had done. 'Is the black cop OK? he asked. His voice was a whisper.

'That's what it's all about wasn't it? He's a black man. A big black man – that was all you could see.'

Dempsey opened his mouth as if to speak in response. Thought better of it and shut up.

Lennox cut him off. 'You're lucky, he'll live. His shoulder's a mess and he'll be a long time recovering. And the van driver, he'll be OK - no thanks to you. Lex Osei was applying first aid, not robbing him as you told the officers afterwards. The doctors've put him in an induced coma trying to get enough oxygen back into his brain for him to be more than a vegetable. If Lex Osei hadn't done what he did that driver'd be dead. That's what the doctors said. Now he's got a chance.' Chad Lennox paused to let the information sink in. He took a deep breath. 'That's just an aside.

Another complication that adds nothing to what you did is that the ute that hit the van was reported as stolen.'

Tate shrugged. Another piece of information he'd wished he'd known and acted upon at the time. Not that it would have made any difference to his actions.

'What a fucking mess you've made...and at this time when we're working between police states. Have you got anything to say at all?' The inspector glared. 'And it'd better be good.'

Tate took a deep breath. Things weren't good at home. He suspected, incorrectly, that his wife was having it off with one of the Ethiopian refugees she taught English in evening classes. A big black man. His son, Ben, was in trouble at school, being bullied or doing the bullying, it depended on who gave the reports – Ben or the school. The boy's grades were falling to a shocking low and Tate was thinking of changing schools for the eleven years old boy. He'd like to send him to a private school but the fees were too much for his salary. Only his daughter, Shelly, aged four made his life good. Her big blue eyes looked kisses at him but he feared for her future with so many things happening in Hobart and the world.

'No, Sir. I've no excuses. I think I must've had a brain snap. I was at lunch when it happened. The whole scene just looked all wrong. I was going back to the office afterwards to meet the new detective. He'd been on sick leave and was due. I get on OK with Harry and Mark. Didn't know anything about Lex Osei except his name.'

Tate didn't add that he had drunk a couple of whiskeys with his pub lunch as he had done in recent weeks. He'd been breathalysed after the shooting event and the Inspector knew that already.

'You know your career's probably over now. You should never've drawn your gun and fired under those circumstances. Never! Your training alone should've stopped that action... and the alcohol in your system goes against you and you can't blame that for your actions.'

'Yes sir, I know.'

Chad went back to his desk and sat. He signed a sheet of paper and Tate stepped forward to take it.

'You're on immediate paid leave until this comes formally to me and I can make an informed decision regarding your future with the police force... The only things in your favour now are your past fine record. Your partner Kira Regan speaks highly of you, and the fact that you eventually helped afterwards at the scene with the ambulances. Then you gave yourself up to the officers and confessed everything.' He sighed. 'Write your report and get it to me asap. Dismissed.'

Chapter 48

'Where the fuck have you been all his time?' Dieter stood in the doorway and pointedly looked his watch. Sean shoved his brother aside and limped into the flat. Dieter gave a quick glance out into the street before he slammed the door shut.

Sean's coat was torn and there was a bruise on his cheek where he'd hit the side window of the ute at the point of impact in the accident. He rubbed his chest. The action of the seat belt tightening and the airbag exploding would leave bruises there by the morning. It hurt and he screwed up his face. 'Give me a fucking minute to get my breath back.' He went to the fridge for a beer, uncapped it, and took a swallow before he threw himself into a chair.

Dieter pulled his brother's head up and saw Sean's bruises and dishevelled state. 'What in the shit have you done now?'

'I was in a bloody accident. A stupid dipstick was yacking on a phone as I was taking off with a ute I'd just pinched. He got in the way. I lost the lot. The fucking ute and the licence plates I'd swiped from a wrecker's yard. Then I had to bloody well leg it all the way back here. Now I'll have to start again. You wanted wheels...'

'Oh! For God's sake.' Dieter slapped at Sean's arm.

'What in the hell did you do that for? I'm doing my bit. At least I am...' Sean looked toward Sarah who glared back at him.

'I wanted a decent car. Not a bloody ute. We have to look

presentable for that Veronica woman. At least you've fucked your way in there.'

'At least I could do that! Cripes she's not much to look at but she's grateful...' Sean preened himself then cringed against the pain of his injuries.

Dieter turned his attention back to his sister. His reproving dirty look bored into her. 'And you...? Where are the industrial diamonds? Do I have to do everything myself? Do I?'

'I can't get the industrial diamonds from the lock up here until you get a vehicle. It's taken me and Petra a long time to get the rest of them away from Perth and the mines. To find and to hire a storage place here.' Her face fell again at her mention of her lover's name. She turned away from Dieter's scowl. 'Get a bloody car then we can get things done,' she snapped at Sean. 'You're bloody lucky that I've got cash and can finance at least this flat and some of the things we need...unlike some...' she said referring yet again to the lost suitcase and the money.

Dieter picked up threw a boot at Sean. A boot that he'd tripped over before that morning and already kicked out of his way. 'Yes, you'll have to go out and get another car; a better one this time,' he said. 'No fucking utes.'

'I'll wait until dark and I'll have another go then. After dinner when people are home and stuck in front of their tellies. I don't like doing jobs in the daylight. Always problems.' Sean picked up the thrown boot and chucked it towards its partner. He missed and at a scowl from Dieter he heaved himself out of the arm chair and picked up and tossed the offending boot into the bedroom.

Dieter scowled at the boots, still in his peripheral vision.

Boots meant trouble, always had. He was almost superstitious about boots. 'Get those fucking boots out of my way! They stink!' he shouted at Sean.

Sarah flicked on the TV. Dieter scowled across the room at her, then as a picture of MONA came on the screen, he said, 'Wait! Turn up the sound. Shut up. What's that all about?'

Sarah did as he asked. Turned it too loud, then after another glare from her brother, she lowered the sound to an acceptable level.

'… there is some discussion regarding the current exhibition on loan from the Cairo Museum being returned in the immediate future. This is due to current political unrest in that country and ISIS factions' attempts to destroy Egypt's antiquities. A spokesman from MONA stated that they would not send them back until the situation had become more stable. In other news regarding the marriage equality question, the Prime Minister said…'

'Turn it off. Shit that's just what we need. The fucking longer we wait to get rid of the industrial diamonds the more chances of problems. I don't want to but we may have to think of an alternative method of getting them away. They're the easy money grab.' Dieter stood and began to pace the small lounge room of the flat.

'Do industrial diamonds sell better than the real rocks?' Sean asked.

'Bloody ridiculous, isn't it? It'll take us longer to unload the good stuff than the industrial stones. They'll be used in industry – especially in illicit industry where guns and munitions are made. When countries and legitimate companies start buying new technology, they needing cutting - diamond material. They don't buy 'blood diamonds.'

'OK. What's blood got to do with diamonds.'

'Think about it, Sean. Diamond mines vary. African ones often have practices where miners are slaves in the modern meaning of the word. Fucking awful conditions. Terrorists use cheap blood diamonds to save money and this stands out to anti-terrorist agencies,' she said.

'So, our industrial stuff will compete with blood diamonds in the markets we're going to be using to sell them? Hardly seems worthwhile you stealing the bastards.'

'You'd think so wouldn't you, but all diamonds have a signature. Companies and people in the know will want these. Funny – they'd buy stolen authenticated diamonds rather than blood diamonds. Variations of sensibilities. Even in crooks.' She cast a sideways look at her elder brother before continuing. 'It's going to take a long time to sell the gem quality stones. It's all underground. People, especially the dictators and crime bosses want the best stuff to hide away in Swiss and private bank vaults against poorer days.' Sarah's eyes were alive as she explained to Sean. Her mining and industry knowledge to the fore. 'It's more exciting to have their women wear fabulous gems in private. Exotic. Erotic to some...'

Sean grinned. He rolled his eyes.

Dieter scowled at her. He didn't like it when she gave them the benefit of her industrial knowledge. He was the power brains and she had better not forget it.

Sarah shut up.

She turned away and shut up.

Dieter cast eyeball daggers crossed the room to his brother. 'Get the car tonight and make sure that dear Veronica knows who's the fucking boss. Get her sexually hooked and dependent on you. She has to do what she's bloody told, especially to where the wine is to be exported. Tell her you have me as a business partner and it's much better to sell her wine overseas. It's all planned and that has to work. I've other plans for the good diamonds. Got contacts. Big fucking money contacts.'

Chapter 49

'Lex, you're awake! The operation's over.' Ana clasped his free hand tightly. It wasn't her usual interaction method with Lex, but she felt herself as his wife, representative now. Grace was not able to come to Hobart before the surgical repair of his shoulder was done.

Lex's eyes fluttered open then closed again. There was a slight smile on his face. 'S'OK. Tell Grace I'm OK. Not to worry. She always worries...' he said then lapsed back into post-operative sleep.

Ana released his hand. She gestured, with a grin to Rhette, at the length of Lex's legs that were almost over the end of the bed, although he was propped up on pillows. The women shared a smile and sat back on visitor's chairs. They stayed with Lex waiting for the two detectives to come back. The men had been there previously, and talked to Lex, who was a little confused because of the pain relief he had been given. When he went to the operating theatre they left to find out exactly what had happened to him.

To be able to be at Lex's bedside Ana had asked Lyn to please have Pietie for the afternoon so she could be at the hospital. This was no problem as Lyn had completely recovered from the effects of the arsenic poisoning and was home again. Pietie and her son, James aged six, had become friends and she and Mark were pleased that there was a child he could play with in Hobart.

'He can stay overnight too, if you need. I'm sure that the boys would love a sleepover,' Lyn said.

The faces of the two little boys shone, they beamed with delight as they raced away to look at the bantam chooks. 'The eggs are so small...' Jimmy said to Pietie.

So much for worrying about me leaving, Ana thought. Her little boy was growing up. He'd gained confidence in other people his mother liked after the Cooper Pedy abduction. Marrying Mark had added a whole new and exciting aspect in their lives. Ana trusted Lyn with her son although she didn't know his history. He was just another child to her. The two women would always have a link after the Emily arsenic scare.

Ana looked up from her thoughts as Harry and Mark came into his private hospital room.

'He's woken up. But he's sleeping again...' Rhette started the report.

'No, I'm not,' Lex's quiet voice contradicted her. 'I'm here...'

The men came forward and shook hands with Lex. Mark dropped a bag of what looked suspiciously like chocolate on the bedside table.

'We've just spoken to your surgeon, the top orthopaedic man in Hobart. He says that your shoulder will be OK. Need some time and physiotherapy but it'll be as good as ever eventually. Tom Phillips sends his best and the VIP police plane will come and pick you up as soon as you can travel. How does that sound?' Harry said.

'Good,' Lex said. 'I hope you don't think I'm just wanting to leave this job to you two just to get back to Grace and the kids?'

'We did consider that. You're probably going to do better with her cooking than Ana's.' Mark edged away as his wife aimed an elbow at him.

'Please... if you don't mind. Rhette and I have a pact that you men are going to eat better than you have in all your lives. Eat healthy no matter what...' Ana said.

'I guess I'm saved from that then,' the patient said with a grin. His face became serious. 'I've been told that the van driver's serious but they're hopeful. And I remember just a bit about the accident. The driver of the ute I saw him for just a second, before he took off. Something familiar in his face. Does the area have CCTV? Might be worth a look.'

'Come on, no shop talk, you guys. It's too early,' Rhette protested.

'She may be right,' Harry said. He raised an eyebrow at Lex. 'Can it wait until you are able to write a report about the whole incident. Or we can get a police stenographer. All hell's loose. The cop who shot you was working with us and seemed OK, but you never know with some people...'

Lex took a deep breath. 'I don't know. Maybe he thought I was doing something wrong. In South Africa if a cop saw a black man leaning into a crashed car they might shoot first and ask questions afterwards. It's a thought...'

Rhette put up a hand as she looked closely at the patient. 'OK you two, I think that's enough for Lex now. He looks tired. The heavy stuff can come later if needs be.'

Lex raised his other hand. The intravenous drip lead wobbled as it flopped back onto the bed. 'Yeah, thanks. I'll just get a bit more shut eye before one of the beautiful nurses comes back. See you all later, and thanks.'

Chapter 50

Sean lay in the bed watching the woman sleeping next to him. She wasn't a beauty, never that, he thought but there was something about her that he'd not seen or felt in the women he was used to being with. Usually it was a quick leg over and he'd be off; like the chick on the motor bike. He smiled, she'd got good payment for the ride … they'd both ridden each other's butts off.

But this time it was different.

A whole new attitude…

He had never felt that a woman needed more than just his body. He had nothing to offer except sex and his looks. Dieter had paid out money to rid him of his past passionate entanglements before this. This Veronica woman wanted to know what he thought about all sorts of things. What was the last movie he'd seen? Did he read books? Had he been to a beach lately, or did he like clothing of natural fabrics? Sometimes it was silly things like whether he wanted to eat crackers in bed to feel the crumbs against his skin. It was actually fun to fossick for the sweet bits in interesting places with her. Or why shouldn't they drive down south towards Port Arthur when a night was clear and cold. Maybe they'd see the Southern Lights. An Arora that could spread a curtain across the sky as though the sky was falling in white or green waves. One night they made the trip south and exalted in the display. Dieter had been angry, next day, at the waste of petrol when he found out what they had done.

She was older than he was, and had a kid, for goodness sake. He remembered the night that the ambulance had come to the neighbour's house. Ever cautious he'd stayed indoors and just looked out the window.

Veronica slowly opened on eye. 'Why aren't you sleeping?' she said and snuggled into him. He could feel his body respond to her nakedness. Sometimes he had to concentrate to get an erection with a woman, especially when it was part of a job that Dieter had devised. No worries with this woman. Her skin was soft but not as firm as he was used to. She had belly lines where her skin had stretched when she'd carried her kid. He wanted to sink into that softness. And the softness of her breasts in his hands felt so good. She was real. No implanted breasts just softness. He laughed as he let her stroke him until she was satisfied that his erection as just right before he could roll over and enter her. There was no longer the urgency of their first lovemaking. And it was lovemaking, he felt and not just sex. It was almost that she decreed that he didn't have to try so hard, just let it happen. It did, and so far, he'd not felt that he would ever have to pretend with her...

'Um,' he said. He couldn't tell her that he was thinking of her...of how he felt. He couldn't even explain it. Was it gentle lust he was wondering as she spoke.

'Do those bruises on your chest hurt? From the accident?'

He had to tell her about being in a car accident, enough to get sympathy and to explain the bruises that adorned his chest like winter sunsets of red and purple. The area hurt still.

'Yes,' he said. 'I'll be OK.'

'Be right back,' she said and went to the bathroom for a tube of salve that would bring out the deep layers of blood to help them heal faster. She rubbed it into his chest with gentle hands and he did feel better. 'It's not just your bruises, is it? Something's on your mind. I can tell…' She snuggled back.

Business, Sean thought. Now he had to attend to Dieter's business. 'I've been thinking about your wine. It's good enough to go for better markets than just here in Australia. The Tasmanian wines are beginning to be recognised and liked overseas and it's time to go for that market. That's what my brother says. He knows; he's been in the wine business before. He's got contacts…'

'Go back to sleep now.' Veronica yawned, stretched like a warm puppy and settled back within his arms. 'Let's talk about it in the morning. Sounds interesting…'

Sean lay awake. Comforted by her sleeping form. Just not sleeping…

This woman was getting to him.

Chapter 51

'Lex! You are supposed to be resting. Not peering into that CCTV footage...' Ana's voice challenged him on her return to the hospital next day. 'I suppose they brought them in to you.' Her emphasis was on the they. 'Mark and Harry brought that in for you, didn't they?'

Lex was sitting out of bed, and indeed, was peering into a screen with the Salamanca Square CCTV footage of the man running from the accident the previous day. He shook his head. 'I asked for it... Dammit! It's no use he's keeping his head down. His face's hidden. I can't see him, let alone recognise him. For some reason, I thought I might.' He shrugged.

'You forget, you're in Hobart not Sydney or even Adelaide. How can you know the local car thieves? Mark told me the ute was stolen. It's just a random crime that you were unlucky enough to get involved in. He told me that you tried to help the van driver. Probably saved his life. Well done you...' Her voice had her usual smile in it.

Lex looked up at Ana. One of his favourite people. He sighed and pushed the screen to one side and leaned back in the chair. Another sigh escaped his lips. 'You're right. It's probably enough for one day,' he said.

Ana pounced. 'And look at you. I can't say you look pale,' she grinned. 'hardly that, but Grace would say that you're doing too much by getting back to work so soon after surgery. How am I to answer to her if you don't recover as quickly as the surgeons promised. Come on - back to bed.'

She helped Lex to his feet and even in his weary weakened state he towered over her. She chuckled as she ushered him back towards his bed. Muttered 'Sorry.' She gave a belly laugh as he flopped onto the bed. Quickly Ana pulled the sheets up.

'What's the matter with you?' It's this stupid hospital gown, isn't it? Lex asked. 'No privacy at all.'

Ana straightened her facial expression to a semi-serious one. It was all she could manage. 'I'm a married woman and I think I've seen it all. But I'll have to tell Grace that you flashed those long gorgeous black legs just for my benefit... I'll bring in your suitcase and get you some clothes, or pyjamas ... if you have them,' she said.

'Are you flirting with me, woman?' Lex said as a rejoinder.

'No. Certainly not. But that gown is really too short.' Another chuckle. 'But I've made you smile and that's always good.'

Ana went to the table and reached to close the laptop. Lex had left frozen one frame of the CCTV footage on the screen. She glanced at it and paused. 'Looks as though that man knows how to avoid the cameras. Something a bit familiar about him... from way back. When I was a child. That posture of not wanting to be seen. Of being where he shouldn't have been. Maybe...' She stopped.

It was an impression not a recognition. In a subconscious action, she tucked the natural thick white comma of her hair back behind her ear. A slight tremor shuddered through her body as a time long past registered that she chose not think about any more.

But sometimes there were reminders.

A look. A word or even the body language of a stranger.

'Hey! How's the patient today?' Rhette's voice was clear and cheerful as she came through the door into the private room. 'The doctor's we've just spoken to said you're doing fine. You could be discharged tomorrow. Then it's home and the family. We've brought in your suitcase so it's ready.'

Harry put the suitcase on the table. 'Any luck with the CCTV?' he asked as he shook hands with Lex.

'No, nothing. The crim kept his head down.'

'The bastard would...' Harry said.

Rhette said clicked the locks on the case. 'I'll unpack it for you if you like. Do you want me to find some pyjamas for you?' She looked startled when both Ana and Lex exchanged glances and laughed.

'It's OK. Private joke,' Lex said.

'You're quiet,' Rhette said as they got into the car to go across the Tasman Bridge to Bellerive and home. 'We'll be home in time to start dinner...' She started the car and pulled out of the parking spot. She glanced sideways at Ana as she stopped at the traffic lights. 'Are you OK?'

'Have you ever felt that someone walked over your grave? Someone from your distant past?' Ana said.

'Quite often,' Rhette laughed. 'Usually I've eaten something that didn't quite agree with my stomach.' She glanced towards her friend. 'But you're serious. What's up?'

'Just a feeling. Maybe it was that CCTV image of the car thief. The running man... I didn't recognise him but there was something.' Ana shook her head, 'No, I'd never make a detective. Too much imagination. But... there was something about that image...'

The lights changed to green and Rhette released the handbrake and the car moved forward. 'Thought about what we're going to make for dinner tonight? What would suit the men and Pietie. We'd better pick him up from Lyn.'

'Dinner's easy. Steak for the men, sausages for Pietie and whatever we want. We'll make it easy and do a barbeque. Then the men can cook, beer in hand, and we'll make salads.' Ana shook off her foreboding thoughts.

'Great, a good way to relax after this traumatic week.' Rhette said, 'and let's get something wickedly sweet and calorific out of the freezer for desert. It always helps my moods.'

Chapter 52

Next morning Harry received a mobile call from Lex. He switched it to speaker so that Mark could listen in.

'They've discharged me and I'm on my way to the airport. Full star treatment. They've even sent the VIP police plane from Adelaide to pick me up.' Lex's voice was quiet, almost a whisper, as though he was a little embarrassed.

'So, they should... after what you've been through,' Harry said. 'You saved that man's life and got banged up for your pains. It could even lead to another commendation like Mark's getting. Heroes. I'll be surrounded by heroes...'

'Hardly that man, I was just doing my job...' The embarrassment was back in Lex's voice.

'Well, you've got a couple of weeks off to recuperate? You'll need it just to get over the anaesthetic.'

'Crap! I'm fine. I'll take a day or so to make Grace happy, you know how these women worry and fuss, then I want to get back to my desk. I've got a hunch about the Hood brothers I have to follow up. We need to prove for sure that they're alive and we're not just chasing ghosts. We've not been able to do that yet, slippery bastards, always just ahead of us or have so much legal representation that they shut us out. We need a specific crime to be able to arrest them on sight...'

Harry interjected. 'You're supposed to be getting over a bullet, Lex, resting up not working.'

'Too right. Good on you, Lex. Get something no-one can challenge in court.' Mark interjected. He remembered well an incident where Dieter Hood had flummoxed him with clever legal representation. It still rankled.

'But you need to follow doctor's orders,' Harry insisted.

There was a deep sigh from Lex. 'I've got a busted shoulder not a busted brain. Can't just sit around while you lot have all the fun. Seriously, boss, I want to reinvestigate that incident on York Peninsula, back home when that scientist fell down the cliff in the national park. Coincidences in time and place after the Hood plane went missing...I never trust coincidences.'

'OK, but only when the doctors and Grace give you the all clear. Can you play solitaire one handed? I get the feeling you've been doing that...'

There was a rumble of a laugh from Lex, followed by coughing. 'O that hurts!' He said. 'Must remember to hold my chest when I laugh for a while. He got me in the shoulder but they patched me up into my chest. Anyway...and yes, I have been thinking and playing cards on the computer. Had another thought.'

'Watch those thoughts. Can be dangerous...' Harry voice chuckled into his ear.

'Yeah boss, true. But I know you'll have checked the stolen ute for finger prints...'

'None other than the owner, as we expected. Had to be a professional.'

'From the CCTV I thought he was bare handed. Should have been prints. Maybe the bastard was wearing latex gloves. He could have tossed them into a bin near those steps he raced up to get away,' Lex said.

The smile slowly faded from Harry's face. 'It's possible.'

'There's a new test to get prints from inside gloves. They doing it here yet? I read on the police net about a forensic scientist at

Sydney Uni experimenting. He'd got some useful ones. Not enough for courts but good enough for ID purposes. You've got a contact there, haven't you?'

'I do...and I suppose you'll have us rabbiting about in bins now?' The chuckle was back in Harry's voice. 'We don't have much uniform help. It'll be us doing it...'

'Worth it to get an ID. Especially if it's one of the Hoods. Gloves'll look a bit like used condoms. If nothing else you'll get an idea of the Hobartian sex life...' There was a restrained laugh and a careful intake of breath. 'Just to prove that one of them is alive would make our bosses happy.'

'You're right there. You getting hit was a shock and some of them think we're on a wild goose chase. Our time could be better spent in Sydney. It's always about the money. I'll follow this up. Be pretty unlikely that the bins wouldn't have been emptied but you never know.'

'Happy hunting, boss. We're arriving at the airport and I can see the SAPOL jet waiting. Maybe there'll be a nice hostie there too...

'Cheers Lex, and take it easy. Give our regards to Grace.'

Chapter 53

Dieter threw the burner phone across the room at Sarah. It clattered against the chair and fell to the floor. She pulled herself out of her low chair and picked it up with a scowl at her brother.

'Phone your blasted contact again. The release forms should be here by now. Fucking postal service. This hell hole is last on the list for mail delivery and I need to get the industrial diamonds installed now.' Dieter gave a sarcastic laugh. 'They pay the idiot CEO millions and he can't get postal packages on time...the fucker.'

'He sent the forms and they're safer through Australia Post than in the hands of private carriers. They'll be here soon. In the next twenty-four hours,' Sarah said. 'Have you got your side of the plan ready? Don't just scream at me. You haven't told me how you're going to get them to Egypt. And why Egypt?'

Sean cut in. 'We've got contacts there that Dieter trusts. Or he did before there was a shakeup in the antiquities departments. Now who knows?'

'I do, so you just shut your mouth! It's all arranged and he'll only take half...'

'What? Fifty percent!' Sarah glared across the room. 'You said that it was going only to be forty. Bastard! Or are you taking the extra ten?' She stalked towards her brother and stood nose to nose with him. He thrust a fist against her chest and pushed her away.

'Don't you question me, bitch. Just get the diamonds here in this room.'

'We've got the gem quality here ready, just waiting for Sean to do his part and steal the car. For pity's sake, I've told you the rest of the industrials diamonds've been sent from Western Australia. They're here in Hobart. I trust my contact more than I trust you.'

'Alright why did you code up the release forms? Didn't you trust us? An insurance against us?' Dieter strode back and towered over his sister. His voice again a hiss. 'Was it your bitch who sent them? That's it, isn't it?'

'None of your business.' Sarah turned away. Her face was grim. 'None of your fucking business...'

Insurance? Bloody true, she thought, her tongue clenched against the roof of her mouth. She'd tell him nothing now and the so-called release papers for the industrial diamonds was a lie. A hoax. Her insurance until she'd find out and approve the methods her brother'd devised to get the diamonds out of the country. He'd told her nothing. A 'need to know basis' he'd insisted. Rot. It was her plan, she'd done it and he was treating her like shit. All she needed was a car and an hour to herself when she could pick them up from the secure lockup. Petra had flown to Tasmania and put them there before they went to Sydney to do the robbery. Before...

She didn't trust her brother an inch, and for good reason.

Kira Regan's shoulders tensed as Harry and Mark pushed open the door to the squad room assigned to them. Tate Dempsey's desk seemed to take up more space in its empty state than when the top was cluttered with his papers. It was the first time that the team had come together again since Lex's return to South Australia.

Since the incident.

As she turned to face them Harry said, 'Nothing's your fault, detective, and I hope that we can work together as before. It'll be harder because Detective Inspector Lennox hasn't the man power to replace Dempsey. Pity...'

Unsure if the pity word covered the Dempsey incident or the lack of a replacement, Kira was surprised and relieved when first Harry then Mark offered a handshake to her. 'Yes, sir,' she said.

Kira went to the coffee machine unbidden and prepared coffee for herself and the men. It gave her time to relax and be comfortable again after her worries regarding possible attitudes in the investigation.

'OK, back to work,' Mark said, 'and as the Crows beat your mob convincingly I'm sure you can be entrusted with our next fun exercise.'

'And what would that be?' Kira said, catching the humour in his eyes.

'You and I are about to do a bin crawl...'

'You're kidding. What for?'

'We're serious. We're looking for latex gloves. They look like condoms I'm told. Hope you can tell the difference.' The humour spread to a wide grin as Harry interjected to explain the reasons.

'OK. But we'd better hope that the car thief dropped them outside a bin. Hobart's got a good rate of bin collection in the city centre,' Kira said. She huffed a sighed as she glanced out of the window and kicked off the shoes she was wearing. From a cupboard, she pulled out wellington boots then shoved her feet into them. She picked up her coat and took protective rubber gloves from a dispenser. 'I'm not doing this on my own I hope?' She looked the question at Mark. 'And I suppose we're going now?'

'Perfect timing...it's raining,' he said.

'It rains a lot in Hobart,' she crammed a matching hat to her coat and whizzed past Harry. 'Snows even on the mountain.'

Harry laughed. 'She's got you. Are there more boots in there?'

'He'll need them. Rain water pours down Kelly's Stairs. That's where the perp ran wasn't it?' Kira said.

'So Lex reported,' Harry said as Mark fossicked for boots that might fit him.

'The stairs are steep and maybe latex things might have washed down. All sort of latex things,' she said now grinning at Mark. 'We could be lucky...'

Chapter 54

With rain falling continuously from cloud that threatened to settle down to sea level, blotting out the Tasman Bridge to an arch of glimmering traffic lights spanning the Derwent River, Dieter took the MONA tourist boat to the museum. Few people huddled near the withdrawn face under the brim of a wide hat. His hunched posture and the rain dripping off his person did not invite conversation.

Inside the entrance, he merged into the crowd, imitating the people around him, giving up his coat, his backpack and his hat - revealing his hair.

Dieter had an impressive head of iron grey hair, which gave him a stylish air of elegance that he often used to his business authority and advantage. The grey added years to his apparent age making him look nearer fifty than early forties; a souvenir of the refugee camp experience. To counter this, he had a small wardrobe of hair pieces that changed his appearance and appealed to his vanity. For the visit to MONA he wore a small salt and pepper piece just long enough to cover his own hair and make the slight stubble on his face equate with an image he would offer to anyone making enquiries.

His voice was nondescript as he parroted the answers of the couple in front of him, of where he came from and how much he liked Hobart. Aware of the CCTV cameras he looked down at his program, fiddled with the ear piece of the electronic guide, and all the while kept his face turned from them.

When the group dispersed down a long corridor he casually wandered down the gangways and stairs to the Egyptian section looking for the ancient statue of a falcon that was on loan from the Cairo museum. There it was. He stood next to it appearing to study the bird and the plinth that it stood on, noting also the date and time a notice revealed it would be returned to that museum. These were the last days of MONA's special display of the Egyptian genuine Falcon exhibition. It would be ceremoniously packed and sent as originally planned with a mummy from the same period.

Dieter drew a large breath. Yes!

'Can I help you?'

He started.

The question was repeated by an auburn haired twenty-year old looking slip of a girl. He guessed she was a university student supplementing her Austudy income with hours of security duty at MONA.

'No, thank you.' He kept his voice low looking at her feet as though he was painfully shy. In that instant a feeling flooded over him that he wanted to strangle her for disturbing his thoughts. His frustrated plans. The holdups getting the releases. He wiggled his fingers then bunched his hands in his pockets to release his tension. Now wasn't the time... She came closer. His instincts doubled and he turned away.

The girl's smile faltered. 'You're sure, sir?'

Shit, Dieter thought. She will remember me.

He glanced about the display area.

There was no-one in the vicinity.

In the matrix of different exhibits there was a long glass case with the prone model of a young girl dressed in a blue ballet costume laying in it. Another featured a chair with an enamel bowl, a pointed sharp knife and two live goldfish swimming in water. For one mesmerising moment, he visualised killing the woman-child and shoving her in the glass case; replacing the model on the chair with the bowl and fish in her lap. The knife. They'd even supplied the weapon.

The short-term impulse almost overwhelmed him until his reason returned with his long-term plans and he forced himself to relax his hands in his pockets.

Still with his head down he managed a laugh. 'No, no, I was just thinking about bringing a class of students here to see MONA. There are so many amazing exhibits…' he lied.

She smiled and he thought that his response had put him in the category of people who praised the museum. Made him ordinary but enough to perhaps comment to her colleagues that as usual the public loved MONA.

'What age are your students, sir?' she said.

'They're grades five and six,' the lie again came easily.

'Then MONA is perfect for them but you may have to be a little careful about some exhibits. The exhibited line of vagina casts may offend some…' she said with a flushed giggle as she turned away to greet another group who had arrived nearby.

Dieter ground his teeth until his jaw hinges ached. It would have been exhilarating to off her. The prospect of discovery making it even more so. It was a long time since he had personally killed.

This second visit to MONA was a mistake but he was reassured that his plans had not changed due to the political threat in Egypt. He would not return until he had everything, especially the industrial diamonds ready to be hidden for transport. He had sussed out all he needed to know, especially the hidden doorway off the Egyptian chamber, and in his wanderings, he had worked out a plan.

He cursed his sister for the delay.

She was the orchestrator of some plot of her own but he had already acted and was sure he would foil her.

Sarah waited for Dieter to come back from MONA.

Against her better judgement, she cleaned and tidied the motel rooms. The brothers were pigs; definitely piggish. Newspapers, takeaway food boxes, dirty cups in the sink and Sean's boots were slung far under a bed. There was air freshener in a kitchen cupboard and she sprayed the rooms, especially the men's sleeping bedroom. Stinking men's farts, she thought.

In a wardrobe in Dieter's room she found what she was looking for, the small suitcase that had contained the gem quality diamonds. Ten million dollars' worth. She pried open the locks and found books wrapped in linen that weighed about the same as the diamonds had. She slammed the case shut...the bastards. Fucking bastards. Dieter had the diamonds with him. Didn't he trust anyone?

She worked herself up to an indignation of frustration. Who did they think they were? She had stolen the diamonds. She had taken the risks but they insisted that they only were to know of the plans to get them out of the country. And their destination. Trust their word – Trust was only a word since the robbery. She was even having thoughts that Petra had tricked her; their friendship a lie, their love an illusion. Was she connected in some way with her brothers?

At Sean's coded knock on the door she let him in and pounced. He had been out stealing car registration plates from a car dump. Naturally he got his news in first before she could start on him.

'I got three sets. Should be enough,' he said a grin of satisfaction on his face. He looked around the room. 'Maid been in to clean the place? It looks better...' he amended at her frown.

'I'm starving. Don't suppose you went out to get some food in. Even bread, anything…proper coffee?'

'Where are the diamonds? Has my bastard brother got them? Has he sold them already?' She physically forced Sean against the door of the men's bedroom. Her fingers jabbed- prod – prod- into the bruises on his chest. 'Tell me!'

Sean swept his arm against her sending her flying onto the hard settee in front of the TV. 'Leave off! That bloody hurts,' he said and rubbed the area. He sighed and sat down next to her. 'You went looking for them, didn't you?' She nodded and he continued. 'Not a good thing to do. Not with our brother. You'll pay. There'll be a comeback. Always is.'

'So where are my diamonds?' Sarah said dropping her head onto her hands. 'Where has he put them?'

'He was carrying a backpack when he went out, wasn't he? All casual slung over his shoulder. He won't let them out of his hands, not into our hands anyway.' He leaned forward and tapped her shoulder. 'I asked – is there anything to eat? I'm hungry.'

Sarah pushed away and went towards her bedroom. She turned. 'You're a spineless bastard too. Do you always just follow his orders? Do what he wants, always. Ever had an original thought of your own?'

'I've learned that isn't the best option with Dieter. He's always the boss and his word goes. Play him wrong and he'll hurt you. Hurt you bad. Even family.' There was a hesitation before Sean continued. 'Pays not to think, just do, until one day you can just get clear of him.'

'You're still with him…'

'Yes. Never had a reason not to…not a reason where I could go and still be sure to survive.' He shrugged with a rueful grimace. 'Survive and have enough for what I want. An aeroplane – that's always first. Then a pad and a procession of women to play with…'

'Not even if we joined forces together?'

Sean's mouth twitched in a fleeting smile. 'With this much at stake, the diamonds and getting away, he'll be watching. Always watching... not worth the risk.'

'Useless bastard,' she said and slammed the bedroom door behind her.

'But I'm still alive. Not sure how long you will be, little sister,' he leaned back into the couch and picked up the TV remote. 'Not sure at all.'

Chapter 55

Rhette was delighted with her studies of the women Pharaohs of Ancient Egypt. She ploughed through her books, enlisted the internet, and had sent off her first assignment to her university. She knew that MONA had an eclectic display of artefacts and, after Harry reassured her that Dieter Hood was unlikely to return there, had visited the museum twice in the past week. She had to trust and be confident, she thought.

Today she left the house in Bellerive with Harry, taking him to work, shopping for a couple of hours for treats for Piete, then driving on to MONA. She was especially interested in an unidentified mummy on show in a roomful of mummies, one listed as a probable female personage of rank, and the barge that used to ply the Nile. There were also some replica pieces of gold jewellery that had caught her eye in the gift shop. A book; 'The Queens of Egypt - from early dynastic times to the death of Cleopatra' she saw and immediately purchased.

It was a day of sharp preview of winter cold with early rain droplets still catching the sun on the rose garden as the sun came out after a downpour. It weaved diamonds on an orb spider web strung between a tree trunk and its overhanging branch. The female was the centre of a radius, her legs in pairs, waiting. Rhette, not a lover of spiders, let it be and just admired the beauty as she passed from the car park. Ahead she could see the conical designed wigwam containing intricate pattern of ropes and steel hooks hanging down from the apex, and off to the left she knew there was the huge rusty sculpture of a train, or was it a bottle on wheels or similar with a pergola...an apparition of whimsy metal near a tennis court. MONA delighted her especially after she had put aside her fears that she had seen Dieter Hood via the on-line CCTV.

Without intending she found she was looking at strangers in case he was there again.

She sped through the security area, took her electronic O recorder and went down the spiral staircase straight to the specific mummy of the era she was studying and especially to the statue of the falcon; dated approximately 1200 - 1100 years BC, on loan from the Egyptian museum. Good, she thought, a few more days to look and drink in almost mystic thoughts of the past the falcon conjured up, before it was sent back.

Could the mummy be from the court of Queen Nefertari Meritmut, wife of Ramesses 11, who she had decided to study. Most other student had chosen the more popular Queens, Cleopatra, Nefertiti or Hatshepsut, but she wanted some other royal personage. Queen Nefertari Meritmut suited perfectly; a woman who was highly educated and who could read and write hieroglyphs, a rare skill at the time. She was depicted as a Great Royal Wife, and her name meant beautiful companion and beloved of the Goddesses Mut and Hathor. She was a diplomat and Ramesses, who outlived her, made a lavishly decorated tomb for her in the Valley of the Queens. He constructed a temple for her at Abu Simbel next to his colossal monument there.

Rhette sat near the class case with a lying down model girl in it, and took out her notebook to sketch the falcon and make notes on the bird's dimensions. It was quiet until a bustling group from a cruise ship following their tour guide came through the exhibition. They were soon gone and as she was about to pack up when a young fresh-faced attendant, with red curls like her own, stopped at her side. The two women grinned in recognition of their similar hair and freckles, before the younger woman asked if she could be of assistance.

'Only if there are more exhibits of Egyptian things, especially those that may have belonged to women. Rich women, even possibly Pharaohs. I'm studying the female Pharaohs,' Rhette said in explanation. 'My subject, Queen Nefertari wasn't a Pharaohs in her own right but she ruled Egypt when her husband was off at war.'

The attendant looked around. The room was now empty except for themselves. She spoke into her communicator and smiled. 'Come, I've got an OK. There are some more in a store here ready to be displayed after the current material goes back to Egypt. You can have a quick look.'

She led the way to a small door, the catch barely visible, and they passed into a room about the size of a medium bathroom. There was one small stela that indicated that those chosen for burial alongside their Pharaohs were considered worthy of respect. Next to it, stacked against a wall was a stone relief that looked like it had been hacked off a wall. It was of the eagle God Horus, depicted with its elaborate wings spread in protection of the dead. Was the ancient falcon statue in the glass case outside, Horus?

Rhette drew breath. 'Wow!' she said. 'These are amazing. May I photograph them?' She wanted to touch them to feel their authenticity and to feel the past eons they represented and the generations of people. She knew that this was not a procedure that a student wanting to be professional would do but her fingers tingled with the urge. She turned instead to view a small bust of a woman. Her features were African and her hair worn long in a coiffure reminiscent of that of Egyptian Court ladies.

Another was of a simple mother with a child standing on her lap.

'That stone relief is genuine as all these are, but we have little description of where it was found. It's a pity that so much was moved or stolen long ago,' the attendant said as she peered through a small slit into the public rooms. 'We'd better get back, there are people coming.'

'Thank you so much for letting me see them,' Rhette said. 'They make my studies so much more vivid and compelling.'

Dieter Hood had visited MONA an hour before Rhette and, unknown to each other, they passed on the road as she drove through the suburbs to the facility.

Chapter 56

'Well, I'll be damned!' Kira whispered to herself as she bent and picked up what looked like a surgical glove from a under a pile of sodden leaves. 'Mark! Got something,' she shouted across the road where he was still kicking into autumn debris. Her tongs held the flaccid plastic.

'Not another condom, is it? He replied with assured knowledge that the condom joke had worn thin.

'No. It's not. I didn't think we'd find anything. Maybe the leaves aren't swept up... We'd better get it to the lab. We don't have to send it to Sydney our lab is experimental too. They can test it. Quicker too,' she said with just a hint of interstate competition surfacing.

'Well done you.' Kira stated at Mark's hint of condescension. There was none by the look of approval on his face. Rather one of relief as he stretched his tall frame to a full standing position. 'Two plus hours ruining shoes into this sodden stuff. Usually the uniform boys do this sort of search. I'll never...'

'Don't blame me about your shoes. I offered you a pair of wellingtons before we started this search,' Kira cut into his teasing tirade with a smile as they headed back to their car in Salamanca Square. 'We've got a few minutes for a coffee here? The Italian restaurant does good coffee.'

'Sure, and it will be your fault if I'm tempted by their cakes.'

'Not on your life. I'm not taking the blame for your

weaknesses and you're paying for both of us after that statement.' There was a flash of women's lib in her steel grey eyes, followed by a softening of tone. He was OK, this newly married man from SAPOL. 'And you get bigger bucks than I do.'

Mark laughed. 'OK. You win and you did find the glove...well a glove... could be any old latex glove.' He turned the laugh into a belly chortle as Kira made a noise not unlike a horse's snort of indignation.

'Want to bet that's the glove Lex was on about...? '

Mark was serious. 'Here's hoping we can prove to them in the higher offices that we aren't chasing ghosts. We're sure of it but they aren't.'

It was mid-afternoon when Lex phoned from Adelaide.

'You're not supposed to be working yet. I hope that this is just a report on your shoulder.' Harry said.

'Stop fussing. You and everyone else's fussing. I'm OK. Sore still, but I was impatient to go over the reports of that killing in the Innes National Park. I was lucky too when I spoke to the SAPOL office at Minlaton about it. He's had a follow up. A couple of local kids found white parachute material washed up on a beach a couple of klicks away from the murder. That find was during the school holidays and they'd made a tent and wanted to camp under it. They told a park ranger who passed on the info. The material wasn't new, been in the sea a while, so we didn't think it was a very recent.'

'Interesting...'

'He'd put in a general report but it hadn't been connected to the murder. He'd connected it but got no extra orders from Adelaide. The Park Ranger's been looking for more. No luck yet.'

'I don't suppose parachutes have serial numbers,' Harry said. He was scribbling notes onto a pad.

'They do but there weren't any on the bits they found. Was pretty big but battered by the sea and very rugged coastline.'

'Still it puts the Hood brothers at that location after they blew up their plane as far as I'm concerned. Good work.' Harry changed the subject. 'I sent Mark and Kira out looking for those gloves you thought that the car thief was wearing. They found one. Mark complained about messed up shoes but they were excited about the find. The lab here will look for prints. We could be lucky there too. Sean's dabs are on file. Not recently but he got a suspended sentence when he was eighteen for car theft. The only time we got him too. He's been the bag man, the driver and pilot for his brother all these years.'

'So, our hunch may be right. Rhette's sighting on MONA's CCTV, the suitcase that Mark got here in Adelaide and now perhaps the prints.'

'You have been busy with your solitaire cards,' Harry teased.

'Yes, I have the notion that those diamonds are still in Tasmania and I'm adding in the local wine leaflet too.'

'Not much escapes you, does it Lex? And Mark noted in another incident he was at that there was a van with a wine advert next door to it. He's going to check up on that today.' Harry added the wine questions to his notes.

'If nothing else he'll buy a couple of bottles for your dinner tonight...'

'If they've had their vintage he'll do that. Rather partial to a drop of pinot noir with a steak. Though Rhette's into fish here...'

'A good red goes with whatever you want. Don't listen to what the wine experts say every time. Catch you soon Harry.' Lex signed off.

Chapter 57

'I don't think you should be going to MONA so many times. Not after maybe seeing Dieter Hood there. It may not be safe,' Harry said. 'I know I said it was OK, but there's been more proof that the Hoods are alive.'

Rhette bristled. 'I need to go there to get information and atmosphere for my papers. There's only a few more days until they send two exhibits back to Egypt and they tie in with the time frame I'm working on.'

'What if Hood comes back? What will you do?' Harry asked his eyes piercing in his worry. 'There's too much history and he's a dangerous man.'

'I'll scream bloody murder. Scream enough to get everyone running,' Rhette said, almost in jest. She was not ready for his raking up the past killing of her sister and later her father. The hurt was too much gripping her stomach, her guts, when she thought about it. The study was supposed to help. Now it was doing the opposite.

'He could kill you before you could scream,' Harry insisted, his voice rising in emphasis. 'I'm not having my future wife exposed like this...'

'If this is your idea of a proposal I'm not sure what my answer is,' Rhette stormed back.

Suddenly the subject was out.

'Am I proposing?' Harry said, his jaw thrust out.

'Sounds like it and it's about time...' tears were nor far away and Rhette pushed her fingers into the bridge of her nose to stop them. I will not cry…I bloody won't, she thought.

Harry stopped short. 'Are you expecting me to propose? You can't want a man with my life, a simple copper, sure I'll be promoted again one day when I'm ready, but I'm off all over the place wherever the major crimes happen. No money to speak of, no house of my own. You couldn't call my flat in Sydney a house… shit I'm rambling on…' He took her face in her hands. 'You can do better…' His thumbs gentled away the hint of tears from her eyes.

Tears she wasn't going to shed.

'You really are a fool, Harry Shaw. What's money got to do with it? In your proposal, I was expecting flowers and chocolates and one day a ring, asked in a romantic setting. Then I'd do the maiden thing and all that, and say Yes with a great sigh. Now I'll have to think about it.'

'Have you thought?'

'Despite the setting; despite your overbearing way of saying it. Yes… Yes I'll marry you.' He gathered her into his arms and she giggled, quite disturbing the kiss he was aiming at her mouth. 'Is this the time I'm supposed do the heaving bosom thing and snuggle into you ready to obey your every command?' Harry's chuckle came from deep down. 'That's too pre-women's lib for me, 'she said.

'OK then. That's settled.' A smile of wonder, of joy that plunged into her like a warm arrow, washed over his face. 'I wasn't sure you'd have me,' he said. 'And you will stay away from MONA won't you. It's too dangerous.'

'No, Harry. I'm not promising anything…' she hesitated as he started to protest. 'It's a place where I can get the impetus to do my studies. If I see Dieter Hood I'll phone you, but I can't see any reason why he's interested in the place. Unless it something to do with the case you're working on.'

'A museum and the diamonds. It's possible…'

'It's a fucking good thing that you've finally got the rest of the industrial diamonds here, woman. Now I can get the first part of the disposal of them done.' Dieter Hood said. He heaved one of the four strong calico bags to feel the weight. 'Ten to twelve kilos with the others you brought, that's how much in dollars?' he quizzed Sarah.

'Their worth is about $100 per carat. Could be anywhere between forty grand and a hundred per kilo. These are good stones, some that could be used in lesser jewellery; or as bort diamonds, anywhere you need the best superior grinding tools. Mining, optics and so on,' she was ready to go on with her description until Dieter cut her short.

'Give me a bloody estimate! I don't need a lecture,' he said, a sneer tightened his jaw and his eyes.

'It depends on the market, everything depends on that. I'd say you have a good four hundred grand to one million there. It will depend on the buyer, and the estimate will be cut in half after you've paid your middle man in Egypt,' she snapped.

'You don't know much about fencing do you, stupid bitch.' Dieter's voice got quiet.

Sean Hood caught his sister's eye and he shook his head at his sister. He was feeling good as he had just snorted a small line of cocaine he'd bought on the street unknown to Dieter, in the bedroom. Don't go there he telegraphed.

'So, what's your plan now that you've got them? The Egypt connection? How will it work?' Sarah pressed on ignoring Sean's signal.

'MONA is the key with a statue they have of a falcon from the Egyptian museum. It's to go back to Cairo this week, and I asked for twelve kilos of industrials because that's the ballast in the box under the thing. I'll replace it with diamonds. Should be easy… All you two idiots have to do is make a distraction while I do the switch.'

'Distraction?' Sarah asked.

'For fucks sake do I have to think up everything? Do something that will have people running around in circles. Rape her Sean. Make her scream bloody murder. Rob her if that's too distasteful for her majesty.'

'You are a piece of work, Dieter. I don't know why I agreed to all this.'

Hood gave a laugh. 'You did it, dear sister, to escape a boring job, or was it just because you could dream up an exciting robbery such as this one? You have the bloody criminal gene in you to do something like this. Or was it just to impress your lesbian bitch?'

'I'm not the bloody life criminal like you are…' her voice rose.

'No? You've killed now to get what you want. If the bastards get you, you'll be inside forever. You popped the guards so you're a cold blooded killer bitch too. Don't you fucking go all high and mighty on me.' Dieter sauntered over to the freezer and pulled out a bottle of iced Smirnoff vodka, tossed a large measure into a glass and topped it with a minute amount of soda. He raised the glass almost in a salute to her and drained the drink in one gulp. 'You've got to learn how to live like us, live the life you want and to hell with everyone else. They're nothing and you're nothing yet. You're a novice but there's the spark of the creative in you.'

He lifted an eyebrow at Sean who refrained from comment. He knew he was safest by staying out of it.

'So … when…?' she asked.

'You two had better think up the distraction I need. About five minutes' worth. Could be on another floor, but we'll need to fix it so we all get out OK. Today or tomorrow. Then more work to do with the real sparklers.'

Chapter 58

Ana's world had settled down into her newly married love affair with Mark and looking after Pietie. Her volunteer job with the nursing home continued and her days were well filled. She felt a slight envy of Rhette's study but vowed and knew that she could do another university course when Pietie was older. Her degree in social psychology was still interesting but demanded more than she could give a profession right now.

The attitude at the nursing home was interesting. There was, to Ana's eyes, a definite denial of what had happened. The fact of a serial killer within the home patients was not one that came within their terms of reference nor their policies. Lyn was back at work and not pursuing her union's suggestion they she sue someone. Emily's family was non-existent to the extent that her funeral was prepaid and her scant belongings absorbed into the nursing home's store rooms. Life just went on there, or ceased, as it did with caring for the elderly.

After dropping Pietie off at kindergarten Ana started going to the police office to share morning snacks with Mark. There she had begun a good relationship with Kira, with friendship and trust growing between the women.

Trust was not high on the agenda of the Hood family, but something had to hold them together if they were to send the diamonds overseas, get there themselves and retrieve their booty.

Fear worked.

Next afternoon, very late as far as the employees at MONA would consider, Dieter Hood went through the reception doors dressed as an old man in a billowing overcoat. He paid his fee, demanding senior rates, and refused to give up the coat as he was requested.

'This place is too cold,' he whined. 'I need my coat and my hat.'

They let him pass through to the museum. He wandered through the rooms, taking the elevator rather than the stairs as an old man would, to arrive at the Egyptian exhibition. The attendant was a man of middle years. He stood hands tapping against each other behind his back. Tap tap tap. He moved from one foot to the other, his face slack and vacant as though he was just waiting for the end of the working day.

Sarah Wilkes arrived at MONA followed by, a few minutes later, Sean.

All was quiet with few remaining visitors.

The CCTV security guard yawned, until his attention was caught by a woman standing in the narrow corridor that held an exhibition row of plaster vaginas. Dozens made from actual women. He could read her disgust. Yes, he thought, noting her middle-aged dowdiness of a print dress, a dark cardigan and hair pulled back in an untidy bun at the nape of her neck. In his experience, a typical person who stayed to look and to be disgusted.

A man appeared behind her and the guard turned up the volume on the speaker to hear the exchange he thought might entertain him...

'Disgusting...' the woman said.

'Not to me, love,' the man said. He hitched up his jeans and flexed his shoulders in his black t-shirt. 'They look alright to me,' he repeated. 'Which one looks like yours?' The words were said with a leering smirk.

The woman's face registered shock and her frown deepened and she moved to get away from the exhibit. And the man.

He stepped towards her and pointed to one of the pieces- a tight small vagina.

'Don't you touch me,' she hissed.

'Lady, I was only asking if your pussy looked like that one.'

Her eyes widened in horror. 'Get away from me!'

The man laughed. 'Nah, I reckon it's that one. It looks well used...' he looked down her body to her groin area and his hand went to his pants.

The security guard spoke into his mike to the attendant in the next room, the Egyptian section. 'Got an incident happening near the pussies,' he said.

'I'm on it,' and he left his position to return with haste to the corridor.

It was empty.

The man and the woman were gone.

Dieter Hood slipped a burglar's key into the almost hidden lock of the small stock room next to his quarry. Once inside he used a plastic card to make the door appear locked from outside and settled down to wait. Bracing his shoulders, he lowered the pair of ten kilogram packs hidden under his coat, on straps made from torn motel towels, to the floor. Another pack strapped to his waist was added to the pile. He straightened and rubbed the small of his back. 'It's always me who has to carry the fucking weight of every fucking thing,' he muttered.

'We've got a partial print from that glove, and it could match to

Sean Hood.' Kira Regan said as she hung up an internal phone. 'They're sending the results through on e-mail.'

'Great. We've definitely proven that that Hood brothers are alive and in Hobart.' He sat back into his chair and listed. 'Dieter was seen at the bomb scene in the café and at MONA: and Sean in Adelaide and now these prints. Talk to me,' he threw a pencil across the room where Mark was tapping out a report on the results of the glove, into his computer.

As Kira smiled at the ease between these two senior detectives, Mark leaned down and scooped the pencil off the floor and threw it back in one fluid motion.

Mark got to his feet and walked to the crime scene board set up against one wall. He tapped Dieter's name. 'OK then. First Dieter and MONA. What's that all about we don't know but it's got to be something to do with the getting the diamonds out of the country. We're assuming that Dieter, Sean and probably Sarah are together. OK? I can't quite understand why they haven't just sent them out by post somewhere. Can't trust the post. That's unlikely. The postal service looks for drugs not diamonds...hmmm... or maybe they can't trust the person they're sending them to.'

Kira chipped in. 'That seems complicated but maybe they're not ready to try to get out of the country yet. We know they're here in Hobart and that's always been a mystery to me. Tasmania always puts a complicated step into crime here. Everything takes the extra day because we're an island. But now they're here we should have them trapped.'

Mark said. 'I'm still back on the exporting of these stones problem. We're dealing with kilos of industrial diamonds, if the Argyle reports tying in that robbery to Sarah and Petra Joyce are valid. Ten to twelve kilos, that's not parcel post that's shipping. Maybe someone at MONA is in, helping with the plan.'

'Would Hood be willing to share? From your reports he's usually tight. Just the two brothers and people who assist them don't always live,' Kira said.

'You've got a point. More questions than answers.' Harry clasped his hands behind his head and waited. 'I like the MONA industrial diamond connection. I'll follow that one up.'

'My meeting with Sean in Adelaide was a coincidence that still amazes me, but I'll take the occasional lucky ones. It was him and the suitcase led us here and has added the winery question with the brochures. They're short on money I'd guess given the wads of notes in the case. Dieter won't like that. I'm a bit suspicious about a neighbour of Lyn, the woman who was arsenic poisoned,' Mark confirmed to Kira. 'There was someone in her house. Maybe a kid, maybe who knows, but that neighbour has a winery. Remember the winery brochures. Might follow that up with Ana who's working with Lyn.'

'Do that... probably nothing but you're good at coincidences,' Harry said. 'No...I was going to put you on this, Mark, but the Hood bastards know you by sight. That's for you, Kira but gently – they're killers. I'd suggest that you have a word with Ana, she knows Lyn who knows her neighbour. Make it a roundabout questioning so that if possible the brothers don't see you.'

Harry straightened up and flicked the pencil at Kira. She fumbled in astonishment but caught it before it hit the floor. 'Good reflexes,' Mark said with a grin at her. 'I'll tell Ana to expect your call. OK?'

'OK.'

'There's still the problem of how the Hood family expect to leave Australia, from Tasmania. There's no international connections here. Could Sean have a plane lined up to use or steal? Possible. A boat?' Harry mused.

'Maybe they're staying. There's the medical heroin plantation outside Hobart, maybe that's their next target.'

'That's locked up tight security wise,' Kira said.

Mark gave a snort of laughter, 'Not if you're Dieter Hood,' he said. 'He gets in any where he wants to. Sean smooches and Dieter's devious. He uses everything from plain past contacts, coercion to murder and kidnapping. Robbery and arson are his stock weapons but he gets others to do the dirty work.' He nodded over to Kira. 'Sorry about all that but we've been trying to pin something on him for years. His stink turns to perfume when his lawyers come on the scene. I know, I was engaged to one of them.'

'Wow,' Kira mumbled.

'It was the surprise of my life to find she had been got at by the Hoods. And she paid with her life for it in one of the most horrifying ways we've ever come across. It's in the records. Have a look,' Mark said. He paused. 'Still we couldn't get him, either of them. That's when the bastards apparently died. Or so we thought. As I said devious, psychotic and without a qualm of feeling for anyone else. We've got to get them this time,' Mark had returned to his seat and he stared ahead unseeing into his computer screen.

The room was silent for a moment. Outside the traffic on Liverpool Street shuffled ahead with the lights, or turned into the hospital across the street. There was a flicker of a siren as an ambulance pulled out of the grounds heading for a job. A pigeon landed on the window sill in a flutter of wings. Sounds usually unheard as thoughts, conversations, the ping of phones and computer hums, usually drowned them out.

Kira's hand stilled on the notepad and her pen halted. She looked between the two men. Saw their tenseness. Their purpose underlying all the banter that was served and volleyed back like a ball in a tennis match between them. They were a doubles partnership team and the game wasn't a friendly against their quarry, she thought.

Harry rose and shuffled a drawing that the police artist had done with Mark of Sean, and an old newspaper clipping of Dieter at a charity event in the guise of a businessman, into a pile and dropped them onto Kira's desk. She'd seen them both but she spread them beside her computer and anchored them with weights.

Harry finally broke the silence. 'Knock off for the night. Can't do much more until we get a proper lead. Until we work out the MONA connection.' Ever Harry he continued, 'I wonder what our women have concocted for dinner?' A chortle. 'It'll be better than cold baked beans from a can I was used to … and Mark's still in the honeymoon stage so his desert should be excellent.' He said to Kira.

'And for someone else who's just got himself engaged look who's talking…' Mark retaliated to Kira. 'I wouldn't tease him too much. Harry's still in shock…'

Chapter 59

Dieter stood by the door, leading to the MONA Egyptian exhibition, listening. It was now just after eight thirty pm.

All had been quiet outside for an hour except for an occasional sound of a hammer blow on wood. He knew that they were making some modifications to the MONA layout on the floor above from where he waited. Added to that as far as he knew, from the noticeboard on the entrance floor, there were no planned activities such as parties, wedding celebrations, meetings, sports or similar in the grounds for that night. The music rotunda was quiet and on this cold autumn night only a skeleton staff should be in the buildings.

He hoped that the CCTV cameras would be off and unmanned.

He removed the card holding the door closed and looked out into the room beyond. It was dark with the emergency lighting casting figments of eerie shades of light and dark patterns across the mummy figures. Some painted eyes glowed as though their occupants were taking these moments in time to communicate with the replica Egyptian Royal Barge rowers to take the dead across the River Styx for burial in their tombs. They seemed to float above the floor. Dieter, who didn't have a superstitious bone in his body, except regarding boots as omens, turned his back on the mummies and softly walked towards the Egyptian hawk statue on his socked feet.

He had hoped the glass covering was merely positioned there

and not bolted down. Damn. Steel screws held it in place. He was ready for that eventuality and slipped a screw driver from his pocket. The screws came free with little effort and he placed them on the floor next to the plinth. Good, he thought. Easy. One stroke for him against the bastards. He lifted the cover away then grasped the stone black hawk on the plinth; it was heavy and he was surprised at finding it free standing. But it was the wooden plinth itself he was interested in. His contacts in Cairo had said that it contained weights of ten to twelve kilograms to steady it against movement. Hence his requirement of that amount of industrial diamonds from Sarah. His thoughts jarred at his use of her name. Dammit he was used to using it...but not for long, he thought.

The plinth lid came free in his hands and he groped into the dark hole that gaped before him. What was the nature of the ballast they had used? Was it safe to plunge his hands in and take it out? He hoped it was bricks, weights or something at least palatable. His hand touched web and he jerked back.

'Shit, the fucking bastards!' he said aloud.

He stopped. No immediate response to his voice. He had a small flashlight that he had been reluctant to use. Now he shielded the light and peered into the body of the plinth.

A large spider scuttled and he slapped at it. 'Shit,' he said again. The spider moved and this time his aim was better and it made a satisfying splotch on the side panel. Problem solved.

Inside there was more web and thankfully, bricks. Filthy dirty, and probably eons old clay bricks, but at least they would be easy to replace with the bags of diamonds. Getting his shoulder down into the hole he reached in and one by one he pulled out more than twenty small bricks. It was awkward elbow testing work and his thoughts were nasty against the world as a whole.

He placed his four heavy calico bags into the hole and finally the extra bag he had secreted around his waist. He topped the haul with four bricks to cover and conceal them. With no spider, or web left, he went back to the store room and found some plastic filler pieces that would cover everything. As time passed a threat over his head he replaced the plinth lid, the bird and then set to screw down the glass dome. He cursed as one screw cross threaded as he struggled with it, but finally, it went home. Everything looked as before.

In the store room was a small trolley, one that Dieter had counted on. He loaded the bricks up and set out for the toilets on the lower floor. One wheel squeaked and he cursed again. Lifting that wheel off the floor worked but made the trip slower. He finally pushed the trolley into the bathroom. Some of the bricks went into the men's waste bin and he put more into the women's bin next door. Another bin for recyclable refuse took the final few bricks.

Good that part was done.

Time for the next stage of his plan, he thought, as he took the small wobbly trolley back to the store room where it belonged. Not being neat, just covering his tracks to escape any suspicion that something had been happening there.

When would the workmen stop for a break?

For his next plan to work? He needed to be found.

He brushed himself down from the dirty bricks and possible remaining web debris and slipped back to the men's restroom. Once there he lay on the cold tiled floor next to the urinal, keeping out of the immediate sight line from the door, and waited. He needed to get his body temperature lowered to be convincing. It was uncomfortable, and hard; difficult to remain there without his joints and muscles actually beginning to protest and cramp.

He needed to act at being an old man.

As the time passed his discomfort became real. Damn...he thought as the cold seeped into his legs and hands. Into his back.

One last thing he needed to do to be get his plan to work, was for him to appear to not be too badly hurt, was to muss himself up. This was distasteful for the usually impeccably dressed man; the refugee camp had made him that way. He'd sworn never to wear old clothes again, never be dirty, unless there was a reason of his choosing. Tonight-was just such an occasion. He reached up and splashed his hands into the urinal, getting urine and water to mark his pants as though he had wet himself; to make a general smell and a mess to put people off handling him too much. Satisfied he began slapping his fists against the tiles, and moaning.

Help! Help! Help...!

His voice became louder and louder as he played the man who had fallen, knocked himself out briefly, was cold and in pain.

An old man unable to get to his feet on his own. Help!

It worked.

Soon his loud cries elicited response from the workmen, the security guards who, if they had been more thorough would have seen this poor man lying on the floor. With the guilt factor encouraged he was helped to his feet, sat onto a chair, blanketed, and given a cup of hot coffee. He played a man humbled and embarrassed and finally was able to convince them that, if they helped him to his car, he could drive himself home.

'We'll drive you home'

You should go to the hospital'

'We could get an ambulance.'

'No. No, you have been too kind. It was my own fault I slipped. No, the toilet floor isn't slippery, just my own stupid stumble. Fell over my own feet. My own fault. You're not to blame. I just need to go home to my own bed. My dear wife will check on me. I'm alright,' he insisted, a man flustered.

The MONA first aid man on duty checked him over and finding no injuries, except embarrassment in the old man, they let him go. They escorted him to his lonely car in the deserted visitors' carpark and he drove off.

The MONA security men laughed, remembering the wet and smelly old man's pants, and decided that the incident should not go into the report. The staff would look bad that they had missed him in the end of business day checks.

'Stupid old git…' they said and went back to their office and coffee.

In the car, Dieter Hood laughed too. He had got away with it and the diamonds were planted, ready for a trip back to the Cairo museum where his contact waited for them.

The Egyptian was a dead man if he reneged on his part of the deal.

Hood could call in contracts still worldwide. Calling in favours from syndicates of similar business men.

Chapter 60

Harry watched as Rhette twisted locks of her red hair into braids behind her left ear then ran her fingers through them to send the curls free.

She looked up and caught his gaze. 'What's up?' she straightened up from her crouched position over the table and sighed.

'Just looking at you so absorbed and concentrating. Are you enjoying your studies?' Harry said with a smile. He could sit and watch her for hours, feeling so lucky that this beautiful woman could love him.

'I am, but the Egyptian royal hierarchy is an amazingly complicated system to understand,' Rhette pushed her book towards him. 'The Pharaohs married their sisters, their cousins, or whomever just to keep the line pure. That's what they did no matter what. But, when things got into turmoil with the priests and the country was a mess, especially during the 24th and the 25th dynasties...' she tapped the page she was studying, 'Egypt was suddenly conquered by the ruler from the kingdom of Kush, lower on the Nile River. Piye, that was his name, was immediately crowned the new Pharaoh. That line of black Pharaohs and Queens of Egypt lasted for less than a hundred years until an Assyrian invasion put an end to the Nubian rule. You don't read about this in the history books I studied at school...' Rhette shrugged her shoulders, her eyes wide.

'I never knew that...' Ana said from across the room where she sat mending a tear in Pietie's school pants.

'Yes, and later, after Alexander the Great conquered Egypt, the Greeks became Pharaohs. Queen Cleopatra was Greek. She didn't have a drop of Egyptian blood in her.' Rhette continued. 'That black eagle in MONA sort of represents all this. I'm not sure why but it's so old and different from the mummies everyone connects with the Egyptian story. I'll be sad to see it leave MONA this week. I'll miss it even,' she said with a laugh.

'They're holding a small ceremony to send the items off,' Ana said.

'Can you take the time to go?' Harry asked.

'I'd like to but I have an on-line tutorial then,' Rhette said. 'I've got photos of that exhibition and I've seen the next items coming. That'll have to do me.'

Harry caught Mark's eye where he was sitting near Ana.

Hood and the closure of the exhibition could be worth a look. They would have to observe it without Hood knowing they were interested and the Hood brothers had met and knew them all, except Ana. Mark shook his head. No way was Ana going to be put in danger, again.

Harry pulled himself to his feet. 'With no-one else offering to get coffee I guess it will have to be me,' he said with a grin.

Coffee making was a good excuse and gave him time to make a couple of phone calls.

Next morning Kira pulled her hair free of her blue woollen hat and tossed it, her coat and scarf over the back of her chair. 'Brrr... It's supposed to be just autumn not winter already,' she said to the empty squad room.

Harry followed her, pushing the door open with his hip. 'Here, this'll warm you,' he said, putting a cup of coffee onto her desk.

'Stop complaining. You live here and you should be used to snow on the mountain.'

'Oh, is there snow up there already?'

'I saw it as I crossed on the bridge,' Harry said. 'Looked like snow anyway, though it's hard to tell. Sort of white and blown away. We don't get snow in Sydney, so how would I know?' he quipped.

'We've had snow on Mount Wellington one time at Christmas,' there was pride now in Kira's voice. She wrapped her hands around the cup and took a sip of the coffee. 'Hmmm. Lovely. Thanks.'

'Got a job for you,' Harry said. 'Have you been to MONA lately?'

Chapter 61

'Time to give the solitaire away for a few minutes…' Harry said. He sat back in his chair and swung his legs up onto his desk and crossed his ankles. There was an amused smile on his face as he spoke to Lex Osei in Adelaide by phone. 'Got a something you can do for me without leaving your desk and card game.'

'Sounds interesting…' Lex said and clicked off the spider screen. '… But hey, I'm still officially on post-operative sick leave.' His broad grin was eager.

'Do you want to do this job or not?'

'Of course, I do. I was getting bored anyway just doing routine work,' Lex said, as he straightened from a slumped position and pushed his empty tea mug away. He grabbed a pad and pen. 'OK shoot! What's the job? '

Harry laughed. 'Not sure shoot is the right word given…'

Lex cut in with a snort. 'OK. Wrong word…' He flexed his shoulder. There was still some pain and discomfort with movement from the bullet wound but he made sure he didn't flinch.

Harry continued. 'I've got a link approved from MONA into their little ceremony before they'll send back the two Egyptian artefacts. A mummy I suspect has been, or will be, interfered with to stow the diamonds from the Sydney robbery. I have no proof what so ever, just a hunch. The mummy's the obvious choice as the other's just a black bird. Both relics are due to leave for Cairo by air as soon as they're boxed up.'

'So, I'm to watch and see what? Surely they'll have security...'

'Yes, naturally they have but just watch for the chance of the placement of the haul in the packing. I suspect it's already in the mummy case but for the life of me I can't see where. The things sealed up tight as a fish's arse,' Harry said.

Lex laughed. 'You say tight like a fish's arse but they shit out of there. Not as sealed as you think... '

Harry became serious after a grin had fleetingly softened his ugly-handsome features. 'And you've got the FBI's face recognition system now. I'm interested in seeing who'll be there to see the goods go on their way. Any one of interest...'

'CCTV everywhere?'

'MONA has surveillance in every department during opening hours. We've been assured that they've seen nothing otherwise to make them suspicious of problems. But it's like a niggling toothache reminding me that Rhette was so sure she'd seen Dieter Hood right in position near the Egyptian exhibits. Why was he there? The bastards not interested in antiquities, nothing has ever said that - so why now? I've just got that feeling. A hunch that there's a definite reason for him being there.' Harry's voice trailed off and he sat forward in his chair. He wasn't one usually for acting on unsubstantiated notions.

'It'll be a good exercise for practice with the FBI's app. OK, when and what time, boss?' Lex said.

Harry smiled again. He liked working with the tall urban Zulu who would usually never say 'boss'. Even in jest. The man was bored out of his skull and obviously delighted to be back and given a job. 'I've set it up with MONA. Eleven Tassy time tomorrow morning. Will this fit in with your schedules?' A poke at his bored status. 'Oh, and Kira Regan will be there too. A friendly face in case you need some action. You've got her mobile number?'

'Sure have. It'll be good to talk to her. OK. So, ten thirty my time. I'll start the surveillance at nine, just in case there's anything starting early. That smart bird catches etc...' Lex said as he signed off.

Next morning in Dieter's, Sean's and Sarah's new furnished apartment, where they had moved yet again, things were as usual.

A mixture of surly temper and silence.

Dieter was dismissive of Sarah's attempt at the variety in the groceries she had bought from a large supermarket in Moonah and had put them on the table ready to pack away. He had come out of his bedroom and stalked towards her.

He waved a hand at her selection of mainly vegetables and salads with the already cooked chicken and one other packet of pre-prepared meats. 'I hate fucking chicken! Where's the steak? Decent food, not this crap you've bought,' he hissed.

Sean heard the hiss, sensed danger as always, and casually pulled a newspaper over the line of cocaine he had prepared for himself on the edge of the table. So far Dieter had not seen it. Reacting to the movement Dieter spotted the white powder and swung a fist at Sean. He ducked but the finely chopped drug flew in all directions.

'Shit!' Sean shouted. 'That was my last one!'

'You buy any more of that muck and I'll kill you,' Dieter grabbed his brother by the neck and drew him close. 'I'll kill you,' he repeated. He thrust Sean away. 'Get back to that woman and consolidate your position at the vineyard.'

Sean rubbed his neck. 'You mean fuck her stupid...It'll be a pleasure in more ways than one. Getting away from you being the first. Bastard...' he said as he moved further out of Dieter's range.

Dieter turned on Sarah. 'You! Get ready to go to MONA. You'll be my witness that the diamonds are bloody well on their way.'

Sarah looked at her half-brother. 'Why the hell me? You set them up. You check them out...'

'I'm not going back. The bastards could recognise me. You'll fucking well do as you're told, woman.' The hiss had turned to a snarl.

'No! I'm not going either...I don't know where or anything...'

Dieter leaned in close to her face. His glare seemed to soften as though he was being reasonable in his demand.

She didn't buy it.

'It's simple.' He insisted. I'll tell you what you'll do. You're going to MONA's just to check that they're going to load up the mummy and the bird on its stand. That they're sending them back to Egypt. Nothing to it... You might even get a drop of champagne as the idiots celebrate the returning of the stuff.'

Sarah flicked the powder off her blouse and went to brush her hair before she left the unit.

Chapter 62

A crowd gathered in the Egyptian room at MONA waiting for the small ceremony of thanks at the end of the current exhibition. Some people were there to actually witness the event, others were drawn to the gathering by curiosity and the laid out spread of drinks, cheese and nibbles for guests and the public alike.

It had been a significant exchange in that it was rare for a private museum gallery had been permitted to have genuine artefacts of great age from Cairo. Now it was time for their return as the political situation had become safe and quieter than a month or so ago.

It was time to send them home.

Lex, in Adelaide, cast an eye over the group via the instant transmitted CCTV cameras in MONA gallery in Hobart.

On the whole, it appeared an ordinary mix of people.

He chuckled. 'That you Kira?'

One of the little crowd was an apparently blind person in wrap around dark glasses, and a guide dog at her side. When she arrived, she had been given the courtesy of a chair at the front, near the exhibits. She lifted her head towards the CCTV camera. Nodded.

'Looking good,' Lex said into the mike that was connected to Kira's earpiece. She straightened her blue jacket and fluffed her long, and now loose, brunette hair that covered the lead. 'That your dog?'

A tiny nod of Kira's head.

'Good looking fellow,' he continued as she leant down and whispered a soft command to a huge German Shepherd dog. Its demeaner went from a patiently waiting attitude to an animal on duty. It sniffed the air and then tugged forward on the lead.

'Hold,' Kira said. The dog sat at her feet, it's eyes still intent and not straying from something in front of him

'What's he looking at?' Lex said.

Kira gave the dog another 'hold' hand signal. Behind the glasses she looked up again towards the camera.

A MONA speaker had finished his spiel on the Egyptian mummy from the early dynasty and moved towards the black eagle on its stand. Kira felt the dog tense via her lead.

Lex said. 'He's interested in the bird?'

The tiniest nod from Kira.

'Could we just let him go? Would it be a regrettable accident if he knocked the bird off the stand?' Lex instructed. 'Wait a moment. Mark's phoned and he's just pulled into the car park and I want to have a closer look at the crowd.'

Kira brought her hand up to her mouth as though stifling a cough. 'Good. I think I can see that one of the screws holding the lid on the eagle's stand has been put in crookedly. That's interesting … 'She managed to mutter into her own mike. '…and Duke's on to something! Could be drugs … or even explosives. Less likely explosives.'

'Wait… Got a possible match…' Lex said, as the computer image zeroed in on one face. The image focussed. 'Dammit. I think it's the woman, Sarah Wilkes from Sydney. I put her face, from her driver's licence, into the app as one to seek out. We know she's in Tassy. Kira make an incident! Do something that'll get people on the move. I'll have Mark to block the exit! Now!'

'Go! Search!' Kira said to Duke.

The dog lunged its massive frame at the bird on the plinth.

Kira purposely lurched then stumbled as the dog's great body pulled her forward off her chair. She found her footing, then swayed. She yelled at the animal as the leash seemed to jerk her off her feet again.

The glass lid shattered as the whole exhibit flew off under the weight of the dog and the apparently blind stumbling woman.

The stone bird bounced with a heavy thud onto the concrete floor.

Crash! The wooden plinth split as the lesser ply wood of the base came free of the nails that held it in place.

There was a shocked moment - then pandemonium broke out.

Kira, spread eagled out on the floor, moaned as thought hurt.

Duke barked in an apparent frenzy as he had been trained to do.

The assembled crowd of people backed away from the barking dog. Others shouted in shock and horror. Official gasped.

'Wilkes's gone!' Kira heard in her ear piece as she got to her feet. Next, she could hear Lex talking to Mark.

'Duke! Heel!' she commanded her dog in a quiet aside voice as she got to her feet. He returned to her side and sat, still quivering with excitement at being successful in his action. 'Good boy,' Kira petted him as his reward. She straightened and stood tall, removed her dark glasses, and eyed the split in the plinth where the large packages and the grey bricks were now visible.

There was a gasp. 'Bomb!' someone said from the now distant crowd.

'Are they bombs?'

'No!' Kira said in a loud voice. 'Wait! Every thing's alright!' Duke barked until Kira shushed him. 'Heel! – dammit!'

'Bombs!' The word repeated from the crowd.

Someone screamed.

A child cried a long, frightened shrieking wail.

There was a rush, almost a stampede, as the crowd made for the stairs and elevator.

Chapter 63

'No! Stay calm.' Kira shouted again and moved quickly, Duke at her side, to attempt to stem the rush of people. 'I'm police. Detective Kira Regan, Hobart Police. There's no bomb, but please move now to the evacuation areas. It is safe, but we'll check to make sure...'

Interesting, she thought the reaction, as she smiled to reassure and help the crowd leave the area. People are so afraid these days of terrorism. They act before they think, but maybe that's better than waiting as a target when something looks wrong.

It took only a few minutes for the area to clear before an official, who had stood flat footed as the events occurred, moved. He now rushed to her side from the podium where before he was one of the speakers about the Egyptian exhibition.

Kira flashed her police badge.

'What! What's going on?' the MONA official demanded as he stepped closer.

'I'm sorry but my dog detected drugs and rushed the exhibit. The crowd panicked when they saw this,' she pointed to the spilled plinth contents. 'They thought they were bombs. I'm pretty sure they're not but I'm pleased that they've gone just in case. The bomb squad and other detectives are on their way.'

The man looked dumbfounded at her. 'Everything was quiet until your dog...'

'He did what he's trained to do... There're drugs here right now or there's the smell of drugs here previously,' Kira said. She pulled latex gloves from her pocket and motioned the man to stand clear.

'I'm Jason Petrie. This's my area.' The tall thin man swung long arms in a 'round here' motion. 'These items were cleared by customs when they arrived months ago. How in the hell can they be contaminated by drugs now?' he said.

'Mr Petrie,' she reintroduced herself, 'Well sir, that's the question. We'll need to check what's here now.'

Kira offered her hand and they shook.

Petrie leaned closer. 'There were bricks as ballast in the plinth. I've no idea what those other packages are...' he said, his eyes wide as he stared at the broken structure. He ran a hand down a thin tangle of beard, his face distraught as he contemplated the black stone eagle laying almost underfoot. 'That item is thousands of years old. Egyptian Middle kingdom. Priceless! Just priceless.' His voice was scratchy with worry. 'Can I retrieve it please? It shouldn't be left there like that.'

'Please, wait a moment.' Kira said. She signalled 'Search!' to Duke to sniff the eagle. The dog reacted again to the smell of drugs, less so than to the packages remaining in the plinth and scattered about the floor. 'Someone has touched this piece after maybe they handled drugs, or were in the vicinity of drugs,' she said. 'But, yes. Remove the item to a safe position if this will satisfy you.'

Petrie picked up the black carved bird and wrapped protective arms about it before placing it in the centre of a nearby table. He motioned a uniformed woman to stand guard on the piece before he stared into the remains of the plinth. Turning back to Kira, he repeated. 'What are those things? Those packages? I haven't seen them before...'

'I don't think that they're dangerous but we can't be sure, sir. Let's clear the area until the rest of my team arrive. They're on their way...' Kira said and turned away to listen through her earpiece.

'She's got away! The bitch must have gone out another door. Damn!' Mark said, exasperation deadening his voice to a hoarse rasp on the police connection. 'I bloody well missed her!' He thought a moment, 'I'm not sure I'd have recognised her anyway, but that's not the point.'

Chapter 64

'Them's the breaks!' Lex told Mark via the police connection. 'We've got to get them soon. Talk about lucky. They seem to be able to vanish whenever we're near them. First Sydney, then my run in with Sean in Adelaide and now here...' he muttered.

'Has Kira had a look at the packages inside that plinth yet?' Harry broke into the conversation. 'I'm just about at MONA now.' He pulled his car into a slot reserved for the Manager's wife.

'No, not to my knowledge. Someone whispered terrorism and MONA went into close down immediately,' Mark said to Lex.

'That must have caused a stir...' Lex replied.

'Shit Yes! It was a nightmare getting everyone out from that underground multi layered building. Hole in the ground's a better word. Fabulous design for keeping precious things safe, they told me, but they'll have to look more closely on emergency procedures for the future.' Mark said. He was walking fast and had flashed his police ID as he came into the main entrance. He headed towards the elevator leading to the lower area.

'The staff were efficient in handling people. Everything's OK but it took a while to get everyone out to the evacuation points. All in all, it's been a good practice run for them and the place is empty except for us.' Kira gave a chortle. 'Duke was a help in ushering people down the ramps. He hasn't forgotten his training.'

'Good,' Harry said as he passed under the police tapes that

Kira had ordered strung by the lifts. 'Be with you soon…'

'Right boss,' Kira said.

'I'm signing off now,' Les said. 'Count me into tomorrow's update session, please Harry.'

'OK. Lex and thanks for today. Good work. You've stayed a vital part of this team even if you're in Adelaide. Seven thirty our time tomorrow then. OK?'

'Right boss,' Lex said a repeat of Kira's words. 'And Kira. Most impressive work, you and Duke.'

There was another chuckle from Kira. 'Thanks Lex. And you can sleep in – that's eight o'clock your time.'

'I'll be in pyjamas working from home. Coffee in hand. Remember - I'm still on sick leave. They say I'm a sick man…' Lex's grin belayed his words.

'Yeah, right!' Mark said as he arrived at Kira's position.

'I'm not reading those packages as bombs,' the policewoman said as she walked around the plinth. 'Duke is not responding to explosives either.' She gave a chuckle. 'I pushed him to violently rush this lot as a suspicion of drugs. Someone'd handled drugs sometime in the vicinity of the packages but I don't think they contain drugs either…'

Mark reached down to let Duke smell his hands. The dog wagged his tail. 'You've trained him well to obey your commands over his instincts. He's a search dog, primarily, isn't he?'

'Yes, but with only a few trained police dogs, he leaned to do just about everything. It was tough when I had to retire him. Too old, after a knife wound, but I'd still stake my life on him.' The huge dog slumped to the floor with a sigh and laid his head on Kira's shoe. 'He's just a lazy layabout these days. I reckon he enjoyed today though…'

'And I reckon we know what's in these packages given the Hood brothers involvement.' Mark said as he pulled a pen knife from his pocket. Kira raised a 'should you' eyebrow. 'O yes, I should and I'm right...'

A dull sparkle of industrial diamonds oozed from the small slip Mark made in the cloth of the package.

'Pity they're not the gem quality stones,' Kira said.

Harry was met by the MONA manager, who introduced himself, then Jason Petrie and another staff member who carried a tray of coffees.

'Thanks! You'd be the most popular man in MONA right now,' Harry said to the coffee bringer. He swiped a cup and swigged a mouthful.

'That's OK,' the manager said. 'I'm leaving you with Jason. He's informed me of what happened ... and now I've got to speak to the ousted patrons.' He looked at his watch. 'It's almost lunch time and we'll close for the day to assist you. We'll give the public a refund of their money and send them off. You'll have full access to MONA to complete your investigations, and I'm hoping you'll be done as soon as you can. I'll need a full report for my owner and hopefully be able to have customers back soon. By tomorrow?'

He shook hands with Harry and the three men entered the lift and it descended to an even lower floor. The manager hurried back to the people waiting in the rain in the evacuation area.

'It's no good yelling at me!' Sarah said. Her stance was defensive, hands clenched and her body turned to offer her brother a smaller target. 'It's not my fault.'

'Couldn't you have got the diamond packages when everyone fled the area? Couldn't you have fucking well done something?' Dieter hissed. He eyed the distance between himself and his sister across the kitchen. She was out of his reach. He slapped a hand hard onto the table and she jumped, shrank back.

Her fear was still better than nothing.

'I'd only just got there, I told you that. Just in time to see the bloody great dog and woman crash into the plinth and everything got crazy. People screaming. Yelling bombs… How in the hell could I do anything? I just had to get out with everyone else.'

Dieter turned away. 'We've lost the industrial diamonds. They were my fucking backup insurance. It's a bloody good thing I've got the gem grade lot ready for the next stage.'

'You've not told us what your plans are. Nothing. I got the diamonds in the first place. They're mine. Not just yours.' She was careful to remain out of his reach or to try to attach blame on him for the dramatic loss at MONA.

'Don't try to say they're yours. You'd never have got away with the grab in Sydney without me.' The hiss was back.

'Petra and I would have pulled it off. I don't know what went wrong?' her voice became a choke. 'We could have. You and Sean were just our insurance to get away. Now bloody Sean hasn't helped by losing the money you promised to back everything…'

'Shut your face woman. You and that slut are nothing without me. Nothing!' The hiss became a shout. 'Just you be careful with that mouth of yours …'

Chapter 65

'Did the CCTV cameras pick up Sarah Wilkes as she left MONA?' Harry asked Mark as he came into the office next morning. Slinging his suit coat onto the back of his chair he loosened his blue tie then stopped as he saw Kira already also at her desk. 'Hey! The heroine of the moment. And your dog ...what a performance! I saw shown the CCTV tape.'

Kira laughed. 'Duke had the best time. For an old mutt, he still has it and he seemed to enjoy the excitement. Couldn't have done it without him.'

'Well, you retrieved the industrial diamonds. Well done! The Argyle people will be over the moon. Good publicity for us and enough to keep the hierarchy happy with our results.' Harry grinned. He turned towards Mark. 'Well, did you get anything on Wilkes? What she was driving? Wearing? Are we sure that's who it was?'

Mark turned his computer towards the others. 'Lex's just coming up on Skype. Howdy,' he said in an imitation of Lex's South African accent. 'How are you this morning? Show yourself. Are you still in your jammies?'

Lex's eyebrows raised in a look of horror on his dark face. 'Who me?' He laughed as he realised that Mark was joking. 'Couldn't find my good superman ones and you wouldn't want to see me in the hospital gowns again. Ana copped an eyeful... Ooops!' he said and clapped a hand over his mouth as he saw

Mark's eyes open wide with questions. 'Back to you with the jokes.'

'OK, you two. Knock it off. You'll embarrass Kira.' Harry stood behind Mark into the Skype picture. 'You're certain of the Sarah Wilkes' ID yesterday.'

'Yes. Certain that she was a person leaving the Sydney bombing. Certain that the scan is as close as can be given that we don't have a very clear picture from Argyle's records. I'm certain that she is the Hood brothers' sister. Sister or half-sister.'

'You'd go that far?' from Mark.

'Yes, I would. The FBI scanner is that good on facial recon and tie in with the Sydney investigation. Remember the Perth boys got that DNA link from the bathroom sink at her home, even though the house was burned down. Amazing bit of pathology.'

'Good, so we've got that and now the recovery of the industrial diamonds. Next all we need are the rest of the gem stones and getting the murdering thieves.' Kira said. 'Not sure how and when but we're on the way.' She looked towards Harry. 'Where to now, boss?'

Harry glanced across at Kira. She was so part of the team. He grinned before his face became serious again. 'Yes, and we're at an interesting point. You've now been seen by Sarah Wilkes and ...' He held up a hand in a 'wait' movement '... so you can't pull an undercover slot again. Both Mark and I have confronted the Hood brothers face to face before this, in Adelaide and Cooper Pedy, so anything we do will have to be out front and hopefully we'll be in an arresting situation.'

Kira leaned forward, so keen to put her view. 'Boss, I wasn't dressed as a cop. My hair was loose and I wore dark glasses. She was only there for a moment and hers and everyone's eyes were on Duke. He was the focal point. Not me - the blind woman who sprawled face down and thrashed about.' She laughed and rubbed her shoulder. 'I hit that plinth and bird hard. I meant to knock the damn thing flying and was pleased to have it get smashed up. Got the bruises to prove it in the line of duty... want to see?'

'OK then, you're still anonymous to them. I always like to have someone at the crunch of an investigation that I can send in...' Harry said. 'And I'll believe the bruises...'

'You sure about the bruises... the shoulder. Do you need it seen by the medicos? You're OK?' Mark was always careful of his team mates.

'I'm fine...' Kira stretched and flexed her arm and shoulder. 'So where to next? Do you want me to check the CCTV of the MONA area again?'

'I've already done a huge sweep trying to find Wilkes. She's canny. I haven't been able to see her or what car she was driving. There's a huge area not covered by the cameras. Near where they land the people, the walking wounded, people with wheelchairs etc and who can't climb the steps up to MONA, from the river boat. I think that's the only place she could have put her car away from the usual parking areas.' Lex spoke again from the Skype screen.

'You still there?' Harry said.

'I'm part of this investigation. Don't leave me and my Solitaire out,' Lex responded. 'MONA have given me access to the last weeks of CCTV, inside and out, and I can have another go at them. I think that either Dieter or Sean had to put the packages into that plinth. Not Sarah.'

'Why,' Harry asked.

'Well, for starters just the physical weight of the industrials. Not something that she could have put into her handbag like she did with the gems in Sydney. With due deference to you, Kira, on this occasion I think it was a strong man who did the job rather than a woman.' Lex, as usual, spoke in a courteous manner to his female colleagues.

Kira smiled at the computer screen as Harry said. 'OK, that's reasonable. But it's back to square one or two. We still don't know where they are in Hobart. They're clever at keeping their heads down and away from surveillance cameras.'

'I hate waiting for the opposition to make the next move, but I think that's what we have to do.' Mark said as he signed off from Lex and Skype. 'See you later.'

Chapter 66

Ana pushed her hair back from her face and sighed. She swirled a large silver spoon through vanilla custard before spreading the sweet dollop over stewed peaches for the elderly lady who stood waiting for her to serve the dessert course of lunch. 'There, that looks good. I wouldn't mind a serving myself,' she said. 'How was the roast lamb today? It smelled delicious.'

'It was and I loved the mint jelly. You should have some too.'

'I may just do that,' Ana said with a smile.

The lady shuffled off on her walker, with her dish of sweets on the tray, to a table by a window.

Emily used to sit there, Ana thought. That strange episode seemed a long time ago... but it wasn't. They had only been in Hobart a couple of weeks although it did seem a long time. So much had happened. And Pietie had grown up even; going to kindergarten and making a new friend in Lyn's boy. She missed him; his gentle boy-ness and she was still wary of him out of her sight for more than a moment after his kidnapping at Cooper Pedy last year. He was well over the clinging time as he recovered and matured from a baby to a little boy. Ana wasn't sure that she had recovered but she and Pietie were a family with Mark. The honeymoon period wasn't over and she felt that it could continue forever when she was with him.

But Mark and Harry were totally caught up with the diamond robbery investigation and pursuing the criminal Hood family.

Rhette had her Egyptian studies and so, on many days, Ana was at a loose end.

Ana had returned to assist at the nursing home with the lunches but she was missing her new friend Lyn, who was completing a week's leave after the arsenic scare instigated by the said Emily, but work was just not so interesting without her. They had been in phone contact and Lyn, completely recovered, had added that her neighbour had invited them both to the opening of her first wine vintage. That should be fun and perhaps Mark could accompany her, make an evening away from his investigations.

I'll ask him tonight, she thought. Perhaps they could have dinner somewhere before then go on to the wine launch. Rhette would babysit.

Dieter came out of his bedroom carrying the diamond pouch. His scowl toward Sean was as dark as the shadow of rain clouds that hung down from the shoulders of Mount Wellington almost down to the river. Indoors and out the cold permeated into the atmosphere with threat. 'If you do anything to lose these I'll kill you,' he said. 'You've got one job. One job only. Get these stowed where and how I told you this morning. Get that one thing right just once. Or else!'

'Veronica's doing the wine bottling and packing tomorrow… it's not going to be easy what you're wanting me to do…' Sean glanced towards Sarah.

She moved toward Dieter as though she was going to snatch back the bag. 'I think your idea's stupid…' she said. 'Risky and stupid! I could do better just getting on a plane with them.'

'I didn't ask for your fucking opinion.' Dieter turned his shoulder against her. 'It was different when you had to steal the load of industrial diamonds as well. Greedy bitch. Then coming to

Tasmania was such a good idea. Then I was the clever one. Then my ideas were fine,' he jabbed the air to punctuate the words. His jaw thrust forward, eyes hard as he glared at her. 'Then you couldn't even come up with anything to save them at MONA.'

'Me! O - You are a shit! You lost them at MONA. Not me. I don't know why that bloody great dog went mad and smashed over the plinth. Something attracted him,' Sarah said.

Her eyes flicked towards Sean. She remembered the line of coke on the table when she had been packing the diamonds for Dieter. Her mouth opened to respond before she saw the look of pleading that flashed across his face from across the room.

'Don't tell him,' Sean mouthed.

'Well, it wasn't anything I did,' Dieter said. He played the blame game like an old pro. Put the blame elsewhere.

Under hooded brows Sarah looked back at her half-brother. 'O - so it couldn't possibly have been your fault? You're always perfect.' The sarcasm leaked from her mouth like acid. Her face was smug. 'You would've been struggling to survive without me providing a haul this time. I learned about your last shit faced efforts. Some master then. You lost everything. On the run from the cops, both of you,' She glared at both brothers. There was no way she was going to let Sean off the hook as well.

Dieter came at her across the room.

She scooped up one of the shoes she had discarded when she came home last night, and threw it at him. It stopped him in his tracks.

There was a sharp gasp from Sean and he turned away. Bloody hell! He thought. Not shoes.

Not at Dieter.

Dieter flicked the shoe away to bang into the wall. 'Never do that, you whore! Never! I'll kill you if you try that again.'

'We've confirmed that the Hoods are still here in Hobart.' Harry said as the detectives met for the morning update on the investigation. 'That pleased the hierarchy in Sydney. We had to prove it and now we've done it...'

Kira dispensed coffees to the men and at Harry's nod he and Mark tossed ten dollar notes on the table. 'It's on me,' Kira protested.

'Not this time. You did a great job at MONA. Our shout to pay.' Harry said. An idea formed and he grinned in satisfaction.

Lex was on Skype as before. 'Where's my coffee?' he said.

'Next time. And we've stopped them sending the industrial diamonds overseas to Egypt. Quite a feat,' Kira grinned at Mark. What an achievement she thought. And I've been part of it, she was still relishing her first major achievement with the special forces.

'I've got onto Interpol as you requested.' Mark said. 'The mummy and the falcon will be packed and they'll go back as planned. MONA's kept the incident as quiet as possible as we asked them to, although the media's caught a bit from witnesses.'

'Mostly they've accepted the explanation that it was all about a guide dog having a hissy fit and knocking the falcon off the stand.' Kira laughed. 'But mostly there's been no blame on Duke in the internet. Face Book comments have been on his side. Guide dogs can do no wrong.'

'It was a good disguise,' Harry said, letting Kita have her moment. He brought the subject back. 'Interpol will meet the shipment to try to make an arrest that end. They were intrigued with the whole case and it's mainly because it's not drugs, but diamonds, that were being smuggled. Not that they expect drugs from here but Australia's been known as a staging post for narcotics in the past.'

'They'll be lucky. The Hoods'll get a message to the gangs over there to stay away from Interpol's sting. I'll bet they'll be mad as hell losing that deal,' Mark commented.

'OK. Got another job for you, Lex, one you can do from Adelaide. I'm sending the CCTV taped from MONA. This time maybe we'll get something on Sarah Wilkes's car as she drove off and, just maybe, we'll find where they're hiding out. Hobart's not a big place but they've managed to stay out of sight. I'm getting bloody frustrated with them,' Harry said.

He stood from his chair and paced the room, coffee cup in hand. His stare ignored another day of cold Hobart weather where the rain battered against the police headquarters window.

Chapter 67

Free of Dieter and in the arms of Veronica Lewis, Sean was as happy as he had ever remembered being. Outside the day was bleak with mist hanging over the river. Veronica's son Simon was at school and would be away for hours but, nestled in her warm bed, Sean never wanted to move again.

'Damn,' he muttered as his mobile buzzed. It was across the room in his trouser pocket. For a moment, he thought to ignore the call but he knew it was his brother and he dared not do that. He shook his head as though the movement would clear the post coital sleepiness away enough to respond to the demand Dieter would make. He padded naked across the room and picked up the mobile phone.

'Is it done?' Dieter demanded.

'Not yet. I'm just about to...'

'Well, get on with it.' There was a smirk in his brother's voice, 'unless you are consolidating your position there...'

'Yes, that's right...' Sean's answer was evasive for Veronica's ears. He wanted their relationship for himself and was too aware that he would betray Veronica in the days ahead. Somehow, he wanted to string their relationship out for himself without setting Dieter's anger ablaze. It didn't take much to get him going. Sean stretched tall showing off for Veronica as she pulled the doona up around her chin. He could parade in his younger sexiness but she was still shy, being an older woman.

'Dieter's asking how the wine bottling's going,' Sean said as he hung up the mobile and reached for his pants. 'I guess we should get on with it. I'd rather stay here.' He made a play as though about to shed his trousers again.

'No. How about you get on with finishing in the shed while I get some lunch ready,' she said. 'There's only a couple of dozen bottles to go and then we can label and pack them into the boxes. It's all done then.'

'Right.'

'It's exciting having a partner and the bulk of the wine already sold overseas. Just enough left for the launch and a medium local market.' Veronica's voice sang with anticipation.

'Right,' he said again. This was exactly what Sean wanted. Playing right into Dieter's plans and instructions.

Sean went to the winery barn and did what he was asked to do with plenty of time to make love to Veronica again before Simon returned home from school.

The boy was accompanied by his new friend Cleo.

'Do you think your mother will let me serve the wine or the nibbles at her opening tomorrow night?' Fifteen year old Cleo hung on Simon's arm and gazed up adoringly at him with her question.

'That would be fun,' Simon said. 'We'd have to behave though. This's important for mum, she's got her first overseas order of wine.'

'Well, do you think...'

'I'll ask. She's had new special labels made for this shipment. With the gold label, she won at the Hobart wine exhibition, and it has a different red bottlebrush on the design. It's cool. Her new bloke has been great and mega helpful. He's even had the van painted with 'Veronica's Vineyard' on it. Mum's so pleased.' The pride Simon felt echoed on his beaming face. He touched Cleo's hand; his first real girlfriend. 'I'll ask her.'

'Tell her I've got a black skirt and a white blouse to wear. That'd look OK with your black slacks and white shirt. We'd match as servers.'

'You've got it all worked out, haven't you? I think Mum'll go for it. She mentioned about paying professional wine servers but I said I could do it all. Now you can help. It'll be fun and we might earn a bit of pocket money.'

'It'll be great,' she said and entwined her fingers with his.

'We'll have to be careful though. Mum's serving the same wine from bottles she's not sending away. The labels are similar and we're not to mix them up. I'm helping Sean with the final packing of the boxes and setting up the display so I'll know everything.'

'So, you'll ask...?' She twisted a lock of her long blonde hair with her free hand then flicked it back over her shoulder. A gesture way beyond her years.

He melted. 'I'll ask...'

Chapter 68

Mark stared at the computer screen.

There had to be something that would tell them more. He rubbed the back of his neck in frustration and noted that he could probably do with a haircut. Harry hadn't teased him, yet, so his longer locks hadn't been noticed. His hand went to his chin. At least there his skin was smooth and neatly shaven, all the better with a new wife. He stopped daydreaming and brought his mind back to the case and away from the enticing Ana.

He had gone over all the notes and reports of the Sydney bombing again and again. Nothing jelled on why the Hoods had come to Hobart as part of getting out of Australia. The bastards certainly had that intent to get away, he though. You couldn't get rid of that quantity of diamonds in Australia.

He paused. Sam's report. He flicked through the screens. There, that may be the something that was nagging at his memory.

'Harry,' Mark said in the general direction of Harry's chair. 'You remember when Sarah Wilkes got rid of the merc and the driver, the two old men, outside Sydney, and then went to a post office in the shopping centre?' It was a statement as well as a question. 'Did anyone follow that up?'

'Samantha was going to,' Harry said.

'There's nothing new about it in her reports. I'll give her an email and see if she did.'

'She's been on other cases but I'd guess she did look into it if she said she was going to.'

'It was early days after the bombing. We didn't have the ID on Wilkes then so she probably couldn't have asked many questions.' Mark said. 'I still wonder what Wilkes did in the post office. Bought stamps or did she post something? If she did, what was it and to where?'

Harry pushed the papers he was signing away and reached for the cold cup of coffee that was congealing on his desk. He tasted it and grimaced.

Kira sauntered over and raised a questioning eyebrow to him. He looked up, grinned and nodded, rather pleased that he had made an effort and bought a coffee machine in his lunch break. They had set it up and now the smell of freshly ground beans brought deep inhalations as it hissed two coffees into new china mugs. She waited for the third as Harry found the DAF computer files and scanned the lines of Sam's reports.

'She went back, as I expected, but no one remembered Wilkes or the incident. OK, let's hypothesize she posted something. We'll take it a step further and suggest that she was sending something to Hobart. Did she send the diamonds or her gun?'

Mark nodded. 'We never found the gun that killed the guards.'

'No, we didn't. We assumed that she'd chucked it off the bridge or whatever. They did search the area where the merc was dumped. Nothing.' Harry changed tack. 'Was she worried about travelling by air after the bombing and robbery. Let's face it we were thinking terrorist then and the airports and luggage was getting edgy and scrutiny was tight.'

'The mail service is good. If the gun was sent and packed properly the drug dogs at the mail exchange probably wouldn't have picked it up. They wouldn't be looking for firearms. Cripes, fancy sending millions of dollars of diamonds through the mail...'

Kira said. She sipped her coffee and gave a huge sigh of appreciation. Yum, she thought. No more instant...

'The end delivery would have to be a post office box...' Harry looked towards Kira and grinned at her beaming coffee face. 'One for you to look into. We've got her licence photo now, maybe a scout around Hobart's post offices might find something.'

'On it... at least it's something to do. Can it wait until tomorrow?' Kira said.

Harry laughed as he looked at his watch. 'Sure. Time to go anyway to give our women their girls' night out.' He stretched, stood from his chair and switched off his computer. 'Ready?'

'Girl's night out,' Harry teased. He turned to Mark waving his fork, with a big bite of buttered potato on it, across the table. 'That's what they get up to when we have to work.' He bit into the potato and licked the butter off his smiling lips.

'You're right,' Mark agreed. He helped himself to green salad from the bowl. 'I'm even bringing work home so that I can look after Pietie. Kira's coming to help with the baby-sitting and we'll probably talk shop. Just so you girls can have a night out.'

Rhette laughed as Ana started to protest. 'Ignore them. They're just jealous. They probably want a medal for babysitting Pietie,' she said.

Harry was suddenly serious. 'You're heading out before dark when there could be roos on the road. You're going to have to be careful.'

'I'll drive. I'm a country girl, I know to look out for them. And we're only going across the Derwent, then onto the Richmond Road, about half way towards Cambridge. The winery's new, sheds and a tasting area and an office,' Ana said. 'Veronica's still living in Hobart, next to Lyn's place.' She nodded towards Mark. 'The invitation came from Lyn and she knows Veronica well. I've not met her new boyfriend yet. He's apparently a spunk, so Veronica says, and he's the one who's helped her get the overseas sales.'

'So, he's a spunk,' Mark teased. He flashed a toned forearm at his wife. 'Got to watch out for the spunks.'

Ana could feel a flush creep up her face, 'That's what Veronica says. I'll tell you after I see him...' She tried a tease back at Mark.

'Hey, we'd better get ready if we're going.' Rhette pushed her plate away. 'That was good steak even if I say so myself. And you guys cooked it to pink perfection on the BBQ,' she said.

'You're taking credit for the steak...we did the cooking,' Harry said. He gathered the plates and set out for the kitchen.

'I bought that fillet from my special butcher. I've been cultivating him since we got here and that's the result,' Rhette said called to him. 'Bring in the apricot pie will you, and there's cream in the fridge.'

'A girl's night out...with a spunk and there's no chance the cultivated butcher will be attending?' Harry said.

Rhette gave a snort of derision. 'No chance. Just new wine to test and seeing Veronica's vineyard. It should be fun.' She turned to Ana, 'Let's go!'

Chapter 69

Night had drained the Derwent River Valley of colour as night settled in with the snap of a chilling breeze.

'You're not going to the wine launch? Why ever not?' Sarah asked her brother, amazement in her voice.

Dieter lounged on the settee apparently settling in for a night of TV watching. Newspapers were spread on the floor by his bare feet and the TV guide section open to the programs. 'No. Sean's been fucking the Veronica woman and now it's his turn to finish the deal.'

Sarah could see his annoyance in the jaw tight and the clipped tones of his voice.

'She doesn't like you, does she? That'll be a first won't it? Someone not liking you? Getting old and losing your charms with women.' Sarah gloated. She flicked a tea towel she was using to dry the dinner cutlery and saucepans towards him.

'Shut your face, woman,' he said.

His voice was flat and mean.

'You got your part of the business wrong at MONA and we lost the industrial diamonds. They were worth millions, but we're not allowed to mention this to you. Not allowed to talk about it. You play the blame game against us but we have to take your crap...' Sarah stood hands on hips, chin thrust out.

'I said shup up!' Dieter's voice had risen a notch.

'You seem to forget that those are my diamonds that Sean's

dealing with tonight. My diamonds. But you aren't fussing. Are you too tense to go yourself.' She stopped short. 'Are you expecting trouble?'

'No, you stupid bitch! Just leave me alone.' He kicked at the newspapers and shoved the TV guide to the floor.

'You're always ready to push us around. A hundred million worth of diamonds being moved and you're just sitting there like a stale bottle of piss. What lost your nerve?' The towel flicked again. This time the air snapped close to Dieter's ear.

'Fuck it! Stop that!' he shouted making a grab for the moving towel. He twisted his body to face her. 'You'll be sorry when we get out of here. Out of this fucking place where women are allowed to be un-natural… disgusting…'

'Do you mean me and Petra? I know you had her killed, you bastard. I don't know how you did it but you killed her. I'll hate you forever for that,' Sarah's face crumpled. She pushed the tea towel into her face and turned her back on him. 'I loved her…' she would not let him see her cry.

Dieter sat back, arms folded and his face clenched forward. A smirk wrapped his mouth into a pout. 'No!' he said. 'You fucking killed her.'

'Admit it. She was that person arriving in the lift. Just as I detonated the bombs. She wasn't supposed to come up,' Sarah's voice was brittle. 'You sent her.'

He waggled a finger at her. 'No, it was your voice told her to come to the diamond showroom. Not my voice. Yours! I'd taped your voice … and she went like a little lamb when you called. A lamb to the slaughter…'

Sarah grabbed a cup from the dish rack and threw it across the room. It missed and thumped into the back of Dieter's settee. She grappled about for something else to throw as her voice and whole body convulsed into a moan of mourning. An animal sound;

deep and guttural.

Bending to the floor, her hand closed over a shoe.

Dieter's discarded black shoe. She threw it and it struck the side of his head.

'Bitch!' he shouted and heaved himself to his feet. In a second he had crossed the room. 'I said I'd kill you if you did that again, you stinking whore!'

His hands closed around her neck.

She tried to ignore the pressure on her wind pipe. Past defensive training she had done in the mines flashed into her mind. Do something!

Don't pull at the hands stifling her. She'd never loosen the grip. That was part of the training.

With one hand, she scratched and clawed at Dieter's face. Her instincts were still to go for his strangle hold on her. No. No, she thought her mind a tumbling jumble.

With the other fumbling hand she reached behind her body, back to the sink.

Her hand grabbed a large serrated knife. Her fingers found purchase on the handle. She pulled herself away from her brother's body and struck!

Struck him hard in the belly. A desperate upward stroke that parted his shirt like tissue paper.

His hands dropped away from her throat.

Air! She dragged air into her lungs.

'This's for Petra,' she gasped in a mouthed whisper.

Dieter staggered backwards; his blood making an ignoble flower on his shirt front.

He stared down at the wound. The knife was still imbedded. His hands clutched at himself.

Sarah went with him, her other hand gripping his shoulder.

'Fucking bitch,' he said, his voice almost conversational in his disbelief. His stunned gaze switched upwards. Her face was now close enough that her breath hissed into his face through her clenched teeth.

Sarah pulled the knife free of Dieter's hands and body. She struck him again.

Blood covered his hands and the sharp blade slashed easily through his defences. Bloody hands grabbed at her shoulders.

The long knife thumped into his belly. Theirs was a weird dance as she clutched him to her body to strike and he held on to keep to his feet.

She slid the knife into him again, deliberately aiming up through his diaphragm for his heart. 'That's for deserting me at the camp all those years ago.' The knife thumped again. 'And this's for taking over from us ... all the rat-shit broken promises you made. Most of all this's for Petra,' she repeated; her tears finally flowing now that he couldn't see her cry. 'This's from Petra.'

Sarah pushed him away as blood welled up and pulsed out of his mouth in a bubbling red foam.

'You know nothing...' her voice was gloating through the sob of her tears. 'You got it all so wrong...'

'Bitch!' He muttered his breath fading.

Dieter's eyes glazed; his knees gave way and he slid to the floor.

Chapter 70

'I think we're ready,' Veronica said. Everything looks just as I planned and imagined it.'

She rubbed her palms together then down the sides of her jeans. This was her first proper wine launch and she was excited. Nervous. A first time when her wine was going overseas to Arabian wine connoisseurs, to princely families who enjoyed wine despite the non-alcohol decrees of their countries. Sean and his brother Dieter had arranged it and the shipment would be collected and leave tomorrow.

'Well, you'd better get changed into something better than those old jeans,' Simon said, a laugh in his voice.

'Yes, I'll off... plenty of time to get fussed up.' Veronica was a jeans and t-shirt woman who would get dolled up only when she had to.

'You'll need all the time you can get,' Simon teased.

Simon was happy.

His mother had agreed that his Cloe could work as a server and it would make the work fun. All they had to do was serve the wine and pass around the platters of cheese and nibbles. Piece of cake!

The late afternoon was now balmy and the breeze had dropped and the avenue of bottlebrush were flowering in spikes of red splendour giving shelter to the area. The grass was cut to a lawn of soft lusciousness but a possible trap for very high heels that most of the women attending could regret if they ventured away from the paved areas in front of the packing shed.

Cleo's father pulled into the area in his four by four. 'You do as you're instructed. No wine for you either, and I'll be back at ten. OK?' He said through the door that his daughter exited in an excited scramble of long legs. '...and have a good time...'

'OK, Dad,' she said.

Simon waited until the car was out of sight before he pulled Cleo into his arms for a quick kiss. Her long legs were shown off delectably in slim black trousers above ballet type shoes and her white shirt was crisp cotton with a delicate pattern of flowers. Her ensemble was expensive and looked it. Her makeup was a trace of lipstick, she needed nothing more, and her hair was a jumble of golden curls.

'Wow,' Simon said as she pulled away. He laughed, 'OK, I won't mess you up. Come on I'd better tell you what we have to do. Mum will tell you again but me first. It's really quite important but it's a bore...' He led her into the packing shed. The majority of the export stacks of boxes were front and centre of the array of wines. 'Veronica's Vineyard' emblazed in elegant script with flowering bottle brush as her logo.

'It looks great,' Cleo enthused.

'We have to be careful of one thing,' he said dragging his eyes away from her face long enough to pick up two bottles of wine. 'This one, see it has three bottle-brush on the label, is export and is not to be served tonight. It's the same wine and vintage as this,' he adjusted another bottle so that Cleo could see a differing label better, 'and we'll serve this tonight.'

The second bottle had five flowers in the design.

'I see the difference. But what and why?' Cleo was an

inquisitive girl.

'It's Mum's business partners ideas. A slightly better printed label mainly. They think they know it all and Mum agreed.' Simon shrugged his teenage shoulders and ran a hand through his carefully manicured hair. 'It's just a business thing.'

Chapter 71

'Wow! Look at you!' Ana said. 'Your shoes! Jimmy Choo! They've got to be.' She said as she looked at Rhette's outfit. 'And your bag too. Watch it girl, the millions are showing,' she teased.

Rhette did a pirouette showing off the red Romy 85 shoes she wore with a navy jacket, jeans and a floral blouse. 'I love them. Got them in Sydney when I bought your wedding shoes. I always wanted Jimmy Choo but he was way out of my range until I inherited. Fabulous aren't they and so comfortable.' She rolled her eyes in ecstasy.

There was no envy in Ana's eyes.

Her friend Rhette looked amazing, her head of lush red hair curled to her shoulders and her green eyes sultry were above a sprinkle of freckles she made no effort to hide. In easy contrast Ana's mid blue pant suit was tailored and stylish with the blouse patterned with navy and white. Her own hairstyle was a sleek fall of black with the broad streak of natural white that framed her face.

'I think we'll pass,' Ana said. 'And Mark's gone all copper on us. He wanted to drive us out there and pick us up when the launch is over. He says we can sample the wine all we want then phone him, but I've insisted that he's to have a night off too. I'll toss you for designated driver.' She opened her coin purse and picked out a dollar. Tossed it. 'Heads,' she said. 'OK you win, I'll drive. But anyway, there's nowhere else to go to afterwards except than come home...'

'Sounds like a plan to me,' Rhette laughed. 'We are two mature women and we can attend this wine launch without problems on the way home.'

'You can get as giggly as you want,' Ana laughed. 'I'm happy to drive and I've got to get Pietie off to kindy in the morning so no hangovers for me...' As an afterthought she added, 'Lyn will be there. She's one hundred percent fit after the arsenic scare. And Kira's coming for the evening with the boys so they can talk shop out of office. I think Kira wants to see the house too, and meet Pietie. They mentioned a Skype call to Lex too.'

'Good. They don't need us. Let's go.'

Their car sped north and east along the Derwent River estuary towards Veronica's Vineyard.

Each time the road was close to the waters they could see dozens of black swans, ducks of many varieties and a myriad of waders exploring the shallows, the reeds, and banks. Pelicans fished for their supper in groups and black cormorants, breaking their flight formation, splashed down into the river to fish and rest for the night. Ana pointed in excitement when she saw smaller slender cormorants in feeding flocks with a tall white-faced heron. A great egret took to the skies, disturbed by the car, its long legs extended way beyond its body in flight.

Their road from Bellerive joined Richmond Road, from the lights of Hobart on the other side of the river. Later they could see the Mount Pleasant Radio Telescope off to the right of them as they travelled on towards Cambridge. The Veronica's Vineyard entrance was signposted and Ana pulled onto the track and into the well-lit parking spot.

Simon came forward to welcome them with Cleo by his side. 'Mum'll be out soon. She's in the shed doing something but Lyn's here somewhere,' he said. 'We'll be serving wine now and after the speeches.'

Ana grinned. 'Thanks.' Somewhere. Something, she thought. The speech of the young.

Lyn rushed out of the shed. 'You're here! It's great to see you.' She swirled Ana into a hug and planted a kiss on her cheek. 'My heroine!' she said before Rhette could be introduced. 'And you have to be Rhette. Ana saved my life you know...'

'Yes, I know,' Rhette repeated her words. 'Ana's quite the detective and I'm pleased you've made such a good recovery. She's kept me in the loop.'

'Damn right. Back to work and I've been waiting for Veronica's launch. Come this way and I'll introduce you to her.' They followed Lyn, her flat shoes made easy work of the grass. Her black slacks and red top echoed the colours of the bottle brush flowers.

'Mr Choo doesn't like this lawn,' Rhette said, in an aside to Ana, as she pulled the slim heel of her shoe loose from the grass and tip toed across onto the pavers towards the set-up tables.

'I'm not having so much trouble,' Ana whispered back. 'I think this is just your way of staying close to the wine and all the food on the tables. Look at it all, we probably shouldn't have eaten dinner before we came out here.'

A large crowd had gathered, sipping the wines and wandering in the area lighted with fairy lights. A soft honey sweet smell of the bottlebrush flowers mingled well with the more astringent plants and people took advantage of the scattered bench seats as they waited. Magpies and willy wag tails whistling and calling was in a pleasant contrast with the hush of expectant voices.

Simon and Cleo circled with trays of wine, going back into the shed area to replenish from the bottles they were told to open and serve. An example of the contracted wine boxes was on the table as decoration with a couple of the actual export wine to show the special new labels. These would be packed later.

'Show time,' said Veronica. Her nervousness showed in the flutter of her hands in her hair. 'Come on.'

Sean kissed Veronica. 'Go on,' he said. 'They're waiting. I'm staying here – it's your night and you look stunning.'

'No. Come on out. How can I thank you as my financial backer if you're not here?' Veronica protested.

'Go, woman. I'll try Dieter again. He's not replying to my phone calls. Maybe he's actually close and hasn't pulled over to answer.' Sean laughed. 'He's usually not so correct, but he mightn't want a fine.'

That sounded a good excuse, he thought. Dieter wouldn't give a shit about breaking the law but he wouldn't want any police to notice him. Not even down here outside Hobart. So far, they hadn't been discovered. It'd been close at MONA and even the car accident in Salamanca had brought no cops knocking on their door. The doors that had been changed as they moved from motel to apartment to motel on an irregular basis to avoid being seen as anything other than tourists in Tasmania.

But where the hell was Dieter! He said he was coming to make sure everything went as planned.

To check on me as usual, Sean grimaced.

Always checking. Never trusting.

Chapter 72

Her silken dress, as soft as moonlight, flowed around her as Veronica stepped forward to welcome her guests and the short line of dignitaries who were seated beside the microphone system Sean has arranged for her. With a gesture of persons uncomfortable with public speaking she tapped the mike.

'Can everyone hear me?' she said as she looked over the waiting crowd of about seventy persons. There was an amused chorus of response and she launched into her speech, explaining the wines, her sponsors and her excitement at having such a good harvest and the excellent wines that were produced. She looked around wanting to thank Sean in person before them all.

Sean stayed back in the work shed still trying to contact Dieter.

Nothing. The bastard was probably sulking, he thought. He'd insisted that Sean seduce Veronica but was less than agreeable to him enjoying the experience. He was all smooth and complimentary to Veronica in person, but totally the reverse in private, while she was in awe of him. Maybe she was even a little afraid, Sean concluded.

Outside photographs were being taken, the other dignitaries and the co-ordinator of the wine tourist area spoke glowingly of Veronica and her current vintage. The labels were explained and a large bunch of flowers that Sean and Simon had organised were presented to her. The wines were served and sipped, canopies and finger food eaten, and Simon and Cleo were kept very busy.

There was a hum of contentment and compliments.

'There's more people here than mum expected,' Simon said an hour later as he put yet another bottle of red wine on the table ready to open. 'We've gone through heaps of bottles and I've opened three boxes of the home vintage.'

'And I've been serving the white wine and I had to stack more bottles into the fridge,' Cleo trilled. 'Boy, some people can drink.'

Simon laughed. 'They sure can. Have you had something to eat? And there's soft drink in the fridges too.'

'Yes, all good. My feet are sore, but I'm staying away from one of the newspaper reporters. He's trying to do a bit more than flirt with me when I serve him,' she said. 'All stinking shitty hands...'

'Stay away from him. He's a known perv.' Simon bristled. 'I'll serve him. But be especially nice to Ana, she's the one with the white in her hair, she's been special to Mum's friend Lyn.'

'OK. I know the one. She likes the white wine and her friend drinks the red. I got it too about the perv. Don't worry I can handle him.' With a flash of a smile and a sweep of her golden hair she was gone.

Simon looked after her with a smitten look as he reached for the bottle of red from the table to open and to refill glasses. His second call was to Rhette who was standing next to Ana and being served her second glass of wine for the night by Cleo.

With their eyes on each other the servers poured wine.

'Careful,' Rhette said as a splash of red wine overflowed her glass.

'Sorry! I'll get another glass,' Simon insisted his eyes wide. His voice louder than his careful serving manner.

'No, don't worry. It's OK,' Rhette said. Her eyes laughed as she saw the young boy-man flush. 'See, I'll sip away the extra.' She took a large swallow and stopped. 'Careful though, there's something in the wine.' She spat a fragment into her hand and looked down. It's glass... did you break the bottle when you opened it?' She flapped her hand onto the nearby grass to get rid of the fragment.

'No. No. I didn't...' Simon started to say.

Ana took the bottle from Simon and followed Rhette to the edge of the pavers and poured the rest of the red wine into her hand over the grass. Two more larger fragments appeared. ''Those weren't glass... These are diamonds,' she whispered to Rhette. 'I'm going to ring Mark. Something's up. This may be in connection with their case...'

'You mean Sydney?' Rhette said, an eyebrow raised.

'Yes, Sydney.'

At the same moment, a taxi pulled up beside the shed, Sean appeared at the doorway. Maybe this was Dieter, finally.

Two people got out of the car explaining in loud voices that they were sorry they were late for the launch. The third paused by the driver looking into the car. Veronica moved towards them in welcome.

Rhette looked into the eyes of Sean in instant recognition. He'd briefly been her many lover years ago and he was the brother of Dieter who had tried to kill her in Alice Springs.

She would know him anywhere.

Fear and surprise stopped her in her tracks. She turned away so that her back was towards Sean. Her shaking hand rested on her friend's arm. 'Ana,' she said in an urgent voice just above a whisper. 'Phone Mark right now. That's Sean Hood over there. I'd know him anywhere. He's a killer.'

'What! Get out of the area and keep your heads down,' Mark snapped into the phone. 'We're on our way.'

'What's happening,' Harry's body on the sofa snapped from

relaxed to totally on alert.

'Sean Hood and diamonds. At the launch? Shit those women are bloody magnets for trouble!'

The detectives grabbed for their service Glocks, vests, radios and car keys.

Harry shouted over his shoulder as they went to the door and out to the car. 'Sorry Kira, you're here; baby sitting and co-ordinating. Get the local boys from Cambridge to the winery. This could get nasty.'

Chapter 73

For an instant Sean Hood froze.

Rhette! What in the hell was she doing here? She was near the top of Dieter's hate hit list. And where the hell was bloody Dieter?

Sean moved back into the darkness of the wine shed then his panic increased as he realised that the front doors were the only way out. Veronica had insisted that the small back door was locked against anyone trying to steal anything. Her precious wine. Shit!

He might have to shoot his way out of this and he reached down and released the gun he carried strapped to his calf muscle. He hated guns, that was Dieter's department when he couldn't get someone else to kill for him, but Sean had killed. Rhette here! His mind flashed to her sister Kate. Other informants that Kate had died for...

Where the fuck was Dieter?

He moved towards the door and the wine launch. Get away, his thoughts screamed at him. He looked out. The taxi was still there as the driver was fiddling about on his computer. Grab the taxi.

'Mark says get down and stay out of sight. They're on their way.' Ana said as Rhette started towards the wine shed door. 'Wait...'

Sean appeared in the doorway again, one arm hidden.

He started towards the taxi.

'You! Grab him...he's wanted by the police. A murderer!' Rhette shouted to the crowd. Red hair was flying she charged towards Sean.

'No! Rhette come back,' Ana said. 'That's not what we were told to do...' She followed her friend's heels.

Veronica and Lyn stared at Sean as his gun came up, aimed in their general direction. Then the gun swung in an arc to cover everyone. An opening appeared in front of him as the group instinctively backed away from a man waving a gun.

All except Rhette and Ana. Rhette snatched a bottle from the table in her rush towards him and threw it at Sean.

It missed him and smashed on the pavers.

Sean fired wildly and the bullet passed above Rhette's head and away into the night. But now she was on him in her rush for vengeance. He seized her by the shoulder and swung her around, grabbing a handful of her hair. Rhette yelped as the pull of her hair brought her to a full stop. He jerked her by the hair down to her knees.

'Don't anyone move! Don't be a fucking hero now! I'll kill anyone who moves!' Sean shouted. With Rhette as his shield, his gun was up and it circled back and forth against the stunned crowd.

Ana gasped as her own run towards Sean, in Rhette's wake, was stopped. She stood helpless as Sean yanked Rhette to her feet and pulled her, still by the hair, towards the idling taxi. In an instant, he had opened the car door, pulled the driver out and thrown him to the ground. He pushed Rhette into the car and shoved her over to the passenger seat. Before she could react and do more than grab for the door handle Sean was in the driver's seat and had pushed the button locking all the doors.

Sean had a hostage.

A hostage who was screaming, like an out of tune violin, and cursing him.

He took one hand off the wheel to thrust the car into gear, then back handed Rhette. 'Shut the fuck up!' he shouted at her.

The car skidded through the gates and turned left, back to Hobart.

Automatically Rhette did up her seat belt.

Chapter 74

'He's got Rhette!' Ana gasped into the phone to Mark as everywhere around her people stood stunned. It had all happened so fast. There was a silence. Even the birds had hushed. A babble of voices started up as Ana clutched the mobile to her ear. 'He's gone towards Hobart and I'm in our car and following…'

'No! Stay clear, darling! Please stay safe.' Mark's voice was urgent.

Harry had obviously taken the phone from Mark. 'OK, Ana, follow but stay well back. Keep them in sight and have your phone open and talk to us… What's he driving?'

The question was important but came after the warnings. 'He's got a taxi. A black Mercedes with Hobart plates. I didn't see the numbers. Sorry.' Ana looked back. The winery was a bright glow in the distance as she followed the track back to a main road. 'I'm almost on Richmond Road now.' She placed the phone into the mobile cradle on the dash board. 'Can you still hear me?'

'Yes. Good girl. We'll get the local boys from Bellerive to follow us, Kira, you copy?' Harry said.

Kira said from within the link she had set up. 'Boss, I've alerted the Glenorchy station, they're closer than Sorrel boys. They're too far. Best the locals and you.'

'Stay back Ana - at least half a kilometre. Please do that,' Mark's voice was louder in his need to emphasise his concerns. He looked across at Harry, his lower lip drawn by his upper teeth, and shrugged his worry.

'Bitch! Shut up!' Sean shouted. He reached across and punched the shouting protesting woman. The savage blow caught Rhett's ear, the side of her face, and pushed her long diamond ear-ring into her neck. 'Shut the fuck up.'

Rhette flung herself against the locked door, away from Sean. His voice had sounded just like his brother's voice. Hard and brittle cold. Just like Dieter. A chill went through her, stamping down her fire into a freezing pit of fear. She reached a hand to her face and neck. There was blood.

His hand was back on the steering wheel and his attention was now on the dark road ahead. The car raced into the night and speedo on one hundred and fifty kilometres an hour on the winding road.

'You'll kill us,' she shouted as the car swung onto the wrong side of the road. Sean had yanked the wheel hard and over corrected on a bend.

'I told you to shut up,' he said. His fist raised. She pulled against the window, back out of his immediate range.

'You fired at me back there and missed. I thought you're a better shot than that.' Why the hell was she goading him, she thought.

'I've still got the gun and I won't miss next time. So, shut up and be quiet.' Sean's eyes flickered from the road to his side by his door. The gun was there. He couldn't think why he had missed. Maybe he was getting soft in his old age. Maybe Veronica... 'Shut up bitch!' he spat at Rhette.

He slackened his speed as a car approached him from ahead. It passed and his foot pushed the accelerator harder again. Another two cars came towards them and passed without incident.

Sean took a deep breath and fumbled for his mobile, pushed

redial. Nothing. The dial tone went on and on until it automatically cut out and a voice asked him if he wanted to leave a text message. Shit, he thought in panic. Where the hell was Dieter? In fury, he thumped the distracting taxi computer on the high edge of the driver's window. It stayed lit up, numbers rolling and a controller's voice droned on and on. 'Shut up,' he growled at it. He hit it again but the voice continued.

'I can't keep up with them. They're going too fast... A couple of cars have passed me from ahead and there's no feeling of trouble on the road.' Ana said. Her voice was faint but clear into the police car with Harry driving and Mark as passenger.

For now, Harry was using lights and sirens but would cut them when they got closer to the turnoff onto Richmond Road. Harry expected Sean to go to Hobart, across the causeway on the Derwent estuary but no matter how fast they went under lights he thought they couldn't get to the turnoff before the hostage car did. It could be up to the local patrols. He put his foot down, go for it, he thought. There were few other cars on the road they were travelling. Hang the rules. This was Rhette who was in terrible danger at the hands of a brutal man. The speedo crept up.

'Don't go above the speed limit. No heroics you hear,' Mark said to Ana. 'Just stay behind them and if they stop then go past. Don't think that you can do anything. Just be our eyes there. OK?' His voice was tense and she sensed his anguish. His love and fear for her.

Mark exchanged glances with Harry. Both men felt helpless. All they could do was get there. Wherever there was.

The taxi headlights picked up the warning lights of the causeway across the Derwent River.

The road arched away in a long curve, the red lights strung

along the road like a necklace of rubies. Rhette glanced at Sean. He was concentrating on the road, keeping the car on the road as the sweep began.

She reached down as though to get her foot back into her shoe. Instead she grasped the red stiletto by the toe and swung it hard at Sean.

Again, and again she smashed the sharp steel Choo heel into his face, his neck, anywhere going for his eyes. By the third blow his arm came up to protect himself against her silent fury. One handed he tried to grab the shoe from her hand. She pulled it away and struck out yet again, hitting his face. On her next strike, he battled to get the shoe out of her grip.

Now both his hands were off the steering wheel, one protecting his head and the other hand reached into the side pocket searching for his gun.

'I'll kill you...' Sean was cursing as the car missed the curve of the causeway.

It hit a red light post a glancing crash of metal on the passenger side.

It bucked and skewed again as it struck the kerbing, and flew into the air towards the dark waters.

Chapter 75

With no aerodynamics, the Mercedes pitched into the water with an almighty splash sending a bow wave racing across the wetlands.

The heavy engine roared power. The air bags exploded and the bonnet dipped, driver side down, towards the mud of the Derwent estuary before the flying waters had even settled.

Rhette, restrained by her seat belt and the airbag, sat stunned trying to draw air into her body and squashed lungs as the car settled. She braced herself as the world swung her side of the car higher and she hung in the seat belt. It's going to roll all the way over a rational part of her mind screamed.

Get out! Get out! Her instinctive self-preservation part of her brain screamed and instructed. Get out of this car.

Her hand, clutching the Harry Choo shoe was still trapped against her breast by the deflating air bag. She wiggled it free as what had happened before the crash came back into her mind. The car door, get it open. Get out. By the light of the taxi computer she saw the waters outside. 'Get the door open...' she found herself saying aloud.

It was locked. He'd locked it to keep her in she remembered. The window. She smashed the heel against the window, it held. Again, and again she pounded at the door. The window. The strong glass held.

Only then Rhette looked across at Sean Hood.

His head was a bloody mess. Half his once handsome face was smashed in and she had no idea if it was from hitting him with her shoe or the crash. The airbag had flattened somewhat and his body slumped against the door. Rhette shook him. No response. She shook him harder and his head lolled and bumped with a dull sloppy sound against the glass window.

In one cold moment, she had the vision of her sister Kate as she's last seen her laying on a mortuary slab and Rhette had the impulse to smash that face again with her shoe to make sure he was dead. She shuddered it away. If the man next to her had been Dieter she wasn't sure if she could have resisted.

Rhette was brought back to the moment as the car settled further onto the driver's side. Water less than two metres deep, acted as a buffer and kept the car at that angle. Like cola in a tipped glass the water was half way up the front windscreen but so far, the sealed Mercedes held the blackness out.

Rhette drew back to her side of the car. She had turned off the engine as her fingers reached the ignition key, but she needed the button to unlock and open the door. Sean's body trapped it and she couldn't reach it. Fear threatened to overwhelm her. Would the car tip more or over if she grappled past Sean to find the button? She knew many expletives and she voiced them in a torrent as tears, of frustration and fear, slid down her cheeks.

Water gained access through buckled panels to the car's systems. The lights, first the powerful headlights, then as the computer system failed, the interior lights slowly faded away.

Swans disturbed by the crash settled and their resultant musical trumpeting calls murmured to silence.

Darkness washed over Rhette like the hushed waters outside as she huddled, strung in the safety belt and the passenger seat, afraid to move.

'I'm just over coming to the causeway. I'm afraid they're gone.... I couldn't keep up. Hang on.'

Ahead Ana saw one of the posts, now with white flashes showing the direction was missing. She slammed on the brakes but she had passed the spot by the time she pulled up. She could see a huge boulder in the water... 'I'll reverse and have a look.' Reversing wasn't an option on the two-lane road so she did a neat three-point turn hoping that no other car would arrive to smash into her. She stopped with her headlights pointing towards the suspect rock.

Immediately, even without getting out of the car she could see the post pushed over and the damaged road edge. Letting her eyes line track out onto the water there was the Mercedes.

'I've found the car,' she said. 'It's in the water, part submerged. Doesn't look deep and I can't see any movement. I'll wade out...'

Harry shouted into the mobile. 'No! Wait for us. We're almost with you. Wait, Ana.'

'I'm trying the phone,' she said. 'Maybe Rhette's can answer...'

'No! Damn the woman! Can't she take instructions?' Harry said, his mouth a grim hard line. His foot slammed down on the accelerator. 'Kira – Get ambulances and accident recovery people out there, quickly.'

'Already ordered, Boss. I'm also getting an officer out to the vineyard to put a hold on the wine as diamonds were mentioned.'

'Copy that. Good,' Harry acknowledged.

Ana ran into the water and stared to wade towards the Mercedes along the tunnel of her own car lights.

Her shoes squelched into mud and rubbish. The water was cold and quickly rose higher up her pant suited legs. She felt nothing of the goose-bumps snapping out on her arms in response, only her eyes seemed to be connected to her brain looking for movement in the car. Her ears registered pinging and crackling noises of an engine cooling in the water and the slap of small waves against her legs and the car.

So far nothing.

No movement.

The wine she had drunk rose as fear choked her stomach and her gorge rose to bring acid to her throat.

Then something.

It was on the passenger side and she prayed it was Rhette alive and moving.

A hand! A blur of a face. Rhette.

'Rhette's alive! She's alive. I can see her...' Ana yelled into her mobile.

Another step and she could touch the car. Raw metal greeted her and sliced through a finger as she reached up for the door handle. Ana yanked. Nothing. The door stayed shut. Her purchase was all wrong as the car was higher in the water on the passenger side. Ana had to stand on tiptoe to try to see into the car, she braced herself again and immediately saw that her friend hung in her seat belt. She banged on the metal to get Rhette's attention.

Rhette's face registered seeing her.

Rhette shook her head. No. Stay back.

Ana waded to the front of the car where she could immediately see that it was on a perilous angle. The driver's side well down and the outside water level cut across the windscreen. The driver's side was under water, although as far as Ana could see the interior of the Mercedes was dry, there seemed to be no corresponding level of water lapping the inside. Better car better seals, she thought. That was something.

She mimed to Rhette. Open the door.

Rhette responded with a vigorous shake of her head.

No! Can't!

Ana shivered as the cold water, now higher than her chest at the front of the skewed and half submerged car, registered itself. She tried to give Rhette a thumbs up and felt for her mobile. It was in her pocket and wet. Damn. She clicked to speak. Nothing. Damn again and damn again, she thought. What to do now?

All she could do was wait.

Looking back to her car she saw another car just pulling up on the road. Maybe they could help but all she wanted was the lights of the police car and Mark and Harry. She tried to signal to Rhette that she was going to her car. The pale face nodded in response and flopped chin to chest.

An elderly man waded towards Ana. 'Cripes! Are you alright?' he said as they met in the waist deep waters. 'Them?'

'My friend's alive and trapped. I don't know about the driver…,' and I don't care about him either, she thought. 'The police are on their way. I've contacted them,' she shivered and realised that she was saying things back to front.

'We'd better get out of this cold water and wait,' the man said as a cold wind puffed at the remnants of his grey hair. 'There's a blanket in my car. You can have that to warm yourself.' He offered his hand to help Ana from the water. As she took it she looked more closely at this helper. He had to be in his seventies, thin of build and he was shivering as much as she was.

'Thank you,' she said. 'You have your blanket. I've got one in my car too.' As they slushed out onto the road she saw flashing lights in the distance. They seemed to come from all directions.

'Here comes the cavalry,' he said with a smile of obvious relief.

Chapter 76

'He's dead!' Mark said. 'From his injuries or drowning. Only the post mortem will tell us that. Not that it matters... dead is dead.'

Rhette's rescue had taken an hour and brute force from the police, the state rescue crew and the ambulance personnel to right the Mercedes and break into it.

'If this was an ordinary car we could've used a tin opener to get in but these buggers are tough,' one of the men said as they heaved and heaved at one stage. With the doors locked they were forced to break the windscreen to get to Rhette. Then water cascaded inside the car Sean's bloody face was under for a few minutes.

Harry hauled Rhette out and she collapsed into his arms before being bundled into the ambulance crews and Ana's care. Her cuts and bruises were superficial and, like all present, her main problem was the cold. Hypothermia was treated with thermal silver blankets and the warmth of the ambulance.

As the car was righted and the driver's locked door was jemmied opened from the outside to get the crumpled body of Sean Hood out. His gun was found still wedged by the driver's door.

When Ana's elderly helper had looked incredulous at the attitude to the trapped driver one until of the officers said, 'The bastard held that woman hostage and he's a killer. Better off dead for all of us, the courts and prisons. He'd be in for life.' Ana's hero went to the ambulance and quietly held both women's hands for a moment and left the scene.

A very young policewoman, who arrived in a third car and was still dry, said. 'We'll need him as a witness at the inquest.' She shivered and watched wide eyed at the activity around her. 'My first fatality,' she admitted, then almost remembering her academy instructions she said. 'I got his name and number.'

'And I can thank him too,' Ana said, her voice strained, tired and shocked. 'He was a comfort to us both before everyone arrived.

By two am the police had photographed enough, the pathology van had taken Sean's body away, the road cleared of emergency vehicles, and the foursome were home.

Rhette absolutely refused to be taken to hospital as she was checked by the ambulance crew as non-critical. She relented and they did go home by way of the hospital where she had the cut to her neck from the blow to her diamond earing attended to and another deeper one on her arm sutured. Ana wore a band-aide on her finger and many others of the attending officers would sport the same from handling the torn metal of the car. Ana and Rhette were given tetanus booster shots but most of the others' immunisations were up to date given the job type.

Kira met them at the door. 'Pietie hasn't moved. Sleeping beautifully.' She had the kettle ready, tea in a teapot and sandwiches made. 'Thought you might be peckish after all that,' she said as she hugged the two women. She offered a handshake to the detectives and got a hug from them too. The men headed for the food and tea while the women, showered for warmth, and changed into dry night clothes. 'I've organised a full crime scene situation for the winery and it's tight as a drum. Ready for a full investigation in the morning, Kira said stifling a yawn. 'You're sure the vic was Sean Hood?'

'Yes. Totally. Rhette ID'd him and we'll check his prints and licence photo at the post mortem tomorrow. Not that there's much left of his face but we've got DNA. Got the bastard,' Harry openly yawned back. He looked sideways at Rhette. 'Lady,' he said, 'I'll never get into an argument with you wearing shoes like you wore tonight...'

'My Jimmy Choo shoes had lethal steel stiletto heels, I had the perfect weapons,' she said, 'and I smashed him in the face with them. I was so angry... and so afraid...' Rhette nestled into Harry's arms on the sofa.

'Lex has been on Skype with me throughout this. He's ripped at what happened. With the diamonds lost to them he reckons that Dieter and Sarah will try for the airport in the next days. He's patched a loop with security at Hobart airport to see if he can spot them from Adelaide. He'd prefer to be here for this but the SAPOL powers say not yet.'

'That would be right. They'd be worried about Lex's return to work and any medical aspects. But Kira, you've done an excellent management setup for the scenes.' Harry said, his mouth full of a ham sandwich. 'Glad you made ham and not cheese, it's always cheese sandwiches...' His voice trailed off. 'God, I'm tired.' He jerked awake. 'Rhette remembered about the diamonds and the bottles...should be interesting and we'll follow up in the morning. Now all we've got to get are Dieter Hood and his sister.'

Chapter 77

Sarah left the flat after cleaning all traces of herself she could find. She knew that a police forensic team would find evidence of her eventually but she had the previous experience of doing a thorough clean-up.

Dieter - she left as he lay. His blood saturated the carpet. His shoes his pillow. Fitting she thought, whatever his thing was about shoes, he'd have to go to hell where he belonged with them. She felt nothing for the man, her half-brother and was only mildly interested that Sean would find him when he got back from sending the diamonds away.

A smile flickered about her lips as she contemplated the diamonds...

An hour later she had visited a chemist before booking into another motel, close to the airport, shitty that she could not get plane tickets to fly out until tomorrow. She would have to wait until late tomorrow with connecting tickets to Lebanon via Melbourne. It was better to stay away from Sydney, and she would have only a little luggage.

A small suitcase that should pass through Customs without trouble.

Her only concern would be to get safely through the domestic terminal to the overseas one without being spotted by the police. But she was a seasoned traveller due to her past work and this wasn't going to be a problem, not the way she presented now.

Working for Argyle Diamonds seemed like a long-ago dream.

Local police detectives and a patrol car had arrived soon after Sean and Rhette had fled the festive wine launch. They found the crowd in a terrified turmoil. A version of calmness ensued with their presence and the wine stack was cordoned off and the officers had taken names and addresses of most of the people there. Others, like Veronica, Simon and Cleo, and the dignitaries were questioned more closely before they were allowed to leave, detoured to sit in the seats waiting for they didn't know what.

The reporter was sent on his way with the first group of guests protesting that he had evidence photos. He should stay and get the story. Before he left Simon and Cleo advised a police woman of his conduct and he was stopped and given an official warning for touching an underage girl. There would be a follow up, she advised. His camera was confiscated and he, red faced and furious, threatened legal action against the police and everyone there. 'I don't think so,' the police woman said as she watched him roar off into the night on his motorbike.

To Cleo she said kindly, 'I'll want to see you too. Please give me a written statement and I'll talk to his newspaper editor…' She stopped as the girl pulled herself away and frowned in embarrassed horror. 'This isn't the first time that man has been reported and it will be his last with your help. No, No, you won't have to give evidence in any court. There's other witnesses of him, his actions, and his days are numbered, certainly as a reporter in the public domain.' She tapped the camera she held. 'I suspect that there will be interesting photographs here that he'd rather we didn't see. It all helps to make our case.'

'I'll come with you,' Simon said, his arm around Cleo.

The police woman shook his hand. This was her special area of training. 'Good,' she said, thankful that finally the public and especially schools were teaching the young people that they didn't have to be molested by anyone.

With the early morning news, there was no sign of that reporter but other TV vans and the like had ferreted out a story. They were kept at a distance by a police patrol car stationed at the gate. In additional police procedure cloth tents were erected over the working scene to keep hovering drones from getting their shots for the evening newscasts.

Back at the car crash scene the investigation was concluded and tractor pulled the Mercedes out of the estuary waters. It was loaded on a flat bed and taken away for further forensics appraisal.

All that remained of Sean Hood's death was a skerrick of crime scene tape caught on one road marker. Painted evidence marks on the ploughed up and scuffed road pointed to the broken white post with the red reflector, sparkling on the ground as the sun caught the shattered glass.

Birds, waders, ducks and swans picked through the debris of weed and minute swamp life that had been churned up now that the car and the feet of the rescue teams were gone, revelling in the bounty of torn up reed banks and dirty waters. A flock of Cape Barron geese lifted from the waters and winged away to the north in vee formation.

Chapter 78

Harry and Mark left the house on time for work in the morning and went immediately to Veronica's Vineyard.

Veronica was still distraught.

She had arrived back at dawn to the chaos of her dreams.

'No! No!' she cried as bottle after bottle of her packed wine was pulled from the boxes. Every inch of the packing was searched and searched again and the wine, her beautiful wine, was opened and poured through fine sieves into buckets. Every drop was collected as evidence. The red wine bottles produced coloured stones and the white's clear diamonds. Carat after carat of cut beautiful stones were held in the mesh.

'Clever. Bloody clever,' Harry conceded as he watched yet another red poured away leaving a yellow stone, large and glowing as it was displaced from the wine. Another plopped into sieve. 'These wouldn't have been spotted in the wines by even by the cleverest of checking eyes,' he said.

The gloved forensic officer nodded. 'We've retrieved about fifty stones so far and there's more than half the reds to finish and most of the whites.' He nodded towards the official cameras set up. 'It's all being filmed, sir, we'll have a complete chain of evidence, including fingerprints on the bottles, by the time we're finished. This's every woman's dream. A treasure trove.'

'The Argyle people will be advised from Sydney, and they'll be stoked,' Mark came to stand next to the tables. 'The Hoods almost got away with it...'

Sarah hacked at her hair with a pair of nail scissors.

Over-night she had bleached it blonde taking her natural shine and gleam from her dark shoulder length tresses with the harsh processes. Looking into the small bathroom she saw that it certainly was now less than stylish. She cut away another hunk making it into a ragged pixy urchin type cap of hair that hugged her skull. This was essential as one of her fake passports had her photographed with blonde hair. It had been a soft golden wig then and she no longer had that wig, and now her hair reflected the persona on the passport, an actress going overseas for a part in a film. The change'd be explainable to nosy customs officers, she thought.

With the same sharp scissors, she shredded her original passport, plus two others, and other documents into tiny pieces. She flushed the bits down the toilet and drain, flushing again and again to make sure it all went away. Anything to do to make the time go until she could go to the airport and leave this cursed place, this cursed country. The orderliness of her past life, as the scientist, the management consultant kicked in. Arriving at an airport too early attracted attention as did arriving at the last minute, she knew. She would time the taxi run for the required two o'clock flight departure.

She flicked on the TV and watched the local news of brief reports of a car accident, before it switched to a report of a new exhibition coming to MONA. So, the renovations there were done there, she thought. What a shemozzle bloody Dieter had made of that plan. The industrial diamonds lost. Gone.

Part of the haul, gone.

Serves him right that he was dead...

Ana tapped at Rhette and Harry's bedroom door; tea and toast in hand.

It was nine thirty on a cloudy cool morning.

The men were well gone to work and she had taken Pietie to kindergarten as usual, and called the nursing home to apologise for not being available for the lunch time service. She knew that Lyn had an afternoon shift and wondered how she was getting on after the excitement of the previous night.

'Come in,' Rhette called, her voice sleepy.

The doctors at the Royal Hobart Hospital had patched her up and insisted on a sleeping tablet before they would allow her to leave last night. They would have preferred that she stay in for observation, but Rhette being Rhette had refused and only reluctantly took their tablet.

Ana smiled as she opened the door. She recalled Rhette last night as she went over and over the experience and her voice had got slower and more slurred as whatever they had given her took effect. Harry had carried her into the house and bed, and it was now eight hours later.

'You are awake,' Ana said. 'I thought you might be still out to it.'

'I've been dozing since Harry got up. Cripes he's a noisy bugger, especially when he's trying to be quiet.' She attempted a stretch and gave a small moan. 'I ache all over.' She fingered the plaster covering the sutures on her arm, 'This hurts too,' she said.

'I've got your jewellery,' Ana said. She put the tea and toast on the bedside table and fished into her pocket. 'There, your earrings and necklace and I cleaned the earrings. Your blood was on the diamonds. Left them a bit ikky,' she said with a smile.

'Thanks. He's dead, isn't he? Sean?' At Ana's nod, Rhette continued. 'He was a bastard. Brother Dieter Hood's side-kick. He'd do what he was told and he enjoyed it. Only things Sean loved in the world were sex, money and aeroplanes. He piloted Dieter's planes while stuff, drugs and people were chucked out over the sea by Dieter if things went bad with a deal. Him or some other henchmen.'

Ana sucked in her breath. 'I'd never have believed it possible that people could be that evil. It's unimaginable those last moments of the victims, no matter what or who they were. Other gangsters... It happened when they fled from Cooper Pedy. Mark told me and I was horrified. The images in my mind...'

'One of them was Johnnie Fox, as bad as all Dieter's gang, but he'd saved my life once.' Rhette lay back on the pillow. 'I don't know if he fancied me, or maybe he was a police informant too, I wasn't ever told. Someone gave my sister Kate the final fatal dose of pure heroine. Don't think it was Johnnie. I'll bet it was Sean on Dieter's orders after they cottoned on to me working with the cops. The bastards...'

'Well, they've confirmed him dead. ID'd by fingerprints. Harry rang a few minutes ago asking how you were and he told me then,' Ana said. She had never heard Rhette say so much about her past. She knew most of it as it had come out in the Coroner's Court on the enquiry into Rhette's father's death and others of Dieter's gang after Cooper Pedy, but it was a closed book as far as they were concerned.

Rhette swung her legs to the side of the bed clutching a sheet to her naked body. 'I'd better get up.' She attempted a laugh almost joyous that Sean was dead and indicated her breakfast. 'This is nice but it isn't going to get my assignment finished. I'll eat this, shower and then take a walk to get all the kinks out of me. Then back to Egypt and the Queens.'

'Good. I'm free today. OK if I come walking with you?' Ana laughed relieved that Rhette seemed OK. The post trauma reaction could still come but Rhette was a resilient person with a past, and now she had Harry, she thought.

'Sure, be great… I can hold off my assignment and we could walk to the coffee shop. Buy some sushi for lunch, maybe eat it on the river.' Rhette nodded to the door. 'Get going now. I want to go to the shower,' she said.

Ana laughed. Since when was she coy about nudity? She stopped short. Rhette had to be covered in bruises from last night and she wasn't about to let see them. Or me know about it. Typical Rhette.

Chapter 79

The investigation was going very well for Harry and Mark.

They knew they were winding the case up.

Still the big fish to get, but they had the diamond haul.

Nothing was easy but their determination was fired up.

The sieving process had captured a small heap of diamonds that were now graded by colour into clear evidence bags. 'There's millions of dollars' worth here,' the Senior Sergeant from Hobart said as he collected them together. 'I'll see them back to Head Office and all checked out, sir.' He packed the bags into a secure case and Harry signed a receipt for them before he loaded them into the boot of a patrol car. 'We'll only need one empty bottle of each of the wines, and perhaps they can refill another bottle of each and reseal them for the Coroner's Office. No-one'll believe how this was done without proof. It was clever rort if I may say so.'

'Can do with the bottle evidence. But what'll we do we do with all the rest?' Harry said. 'They ran out of sterile buckets ages ago and the wine's just running away wasted down the drains.'

'I've got all the evidence I'll need, sir. I suggest that what you do with all the wine left is up to you and the vineyard owner...'

'Thanks a heap for that suggestion. Veronica's still in shock and outraged about what's happened. Not just the wine but that bastard Sean Hood swept her off her feet and her friends say she was the happiest she's been in years with him.' Mark said as he joined the officers. 'She should get some sort of compensation surely for the wine?'

'What compensation can she get for the trauma of betrayal by Sean Hood?' Harry said.

'Well, he won't do that again.' Mark ran a finger into a puddle of red wine. 'Pity this's ruined. But that's what happens.' He tasted the wine. 'Hmmm tastes good. Pity...'

'Compensations' not up to me, sir, thankfully... and look at the mess we've made. My officers got a bit drunk on it all, tasting a drop or two and even the wine fumes got to some of them. They mightn't touch wine for a while. Some of them prefer beer anyway,' he laughed as he got into the patrol car and drove away.

'Organise a forensic clean-up crew out here to help Veronica, would you please. We can do that at least.' Harry stopped. 'Anything else happening in Hobart that we should know about?'

'There's been a stabbing in a motel room. A cleaner raised a screaming ruckus when she found the body. Usually it would be of no interest to us, but the male vic's described as a stocky white, Caucasian, well dressed with a scar on one leg. Like from a bullet wound... Sounds a bit familiar to me.' Mark raised an eyebrow to Harry and they decided to follow the sergeant's car back to Hobart and the scene.

Just maybe the crime gods were helping them wrap up their case.

An hour later Harry and Mark had their ID.

Both detectives had previously interviewed the dead man at their feet. Harry in Sydney concerning drug trafficking and Mark, in Adelaide, when he'd warned Hood about expanding his crime businesses into South Australia.

They had no doubts. The victim was Dieter Hood.

His body had been stabbed multiple times in what looked like a frenzied attack. He lay in a pool of congealed blood and the estimated TOD, time of death, was in the period of twenty to thirty hours previous. Cause of death was obvious but motive and perpetrator or perpetrators were debatable.

'My first thought was maybe the drug cartels have caught up with him,' Mark said as they stood near Dieter's body still in situ in the motel room. The forensic team had been and the mortuary van waited for them to inspect the area. Purely a courtesy until they had made the ID. 'No,' he continued. 'They would have gone for the neat bullet in the forehead after they'd smashed his knees with baseball bats to give him pain and the knowledge that his time was up.'

'Yes, I'd rule them out. This looks personal. Do you reckon that Sean could've turned on him before he went to the vineyard? Getting Dieter out of the picture would equal a better share for him,' Harry said. He did not seem at all perturbed about the death as he stood, chin in hand looking at the body. 'It's either him or Sarah. Maybe they were in it together.'

'I don't think they've played happy families, not them. Dieter was a controlling bastard by all accounts. The sister, the half-sister,' Mark corrected, 'was pretty well a genius given the complexity of the Sydney Argyle robbery and Sean was the pretty boy manipulator. Killer too. Cross and double cross has been Dieter's pattern with the drug gangs. Maybe he was trying it on his family.'

'Rhette is going to be pleased that this one's dead,' Harry said in an aside to Mark, quietly just in case they were overheard by the mortuary men who still waited outside the room. His bulldog face was almost happy. 'Now she's free and I'll add it was lucky she was with Ana at the wine launch during the time frame of this.'

'You don't think you'd ever consider that she could've done

this?' Mark eyes widened in amazement. 'Surely not?'

'I'd have hated to get her in a dark room with him, armed and dangerous after what that bastard did to her sister Kate. And think about how your Ana reacted in Cooper Pedy when Quinn grabbed Pietie. Rhette was in that too. A woman can be dangerous when they're threatened – especially if their family is at risk.' Harry was almost serious.

'Well, we'd better watch our backs,' Mark quipped. 'OK then, my guess is on Sarah Wilkes. Her motive would be malice against the Hood men, remember her partner Petra was a probable bomb victim. Revenge probably and then just pure greed.'

Chapter 80

'Kira's on the phone. She's in contact with Lex who's still trolling the CCTV camera links here in Hobart. He won't be left out, and neither will she. Reminding me to tell you that you promised she'd be in on the kill when we get that far.' Mark said as he poked his head into Harry's office and peered over the great pile of papers and documents on the desk that Harry was trying to sort into some sort of order.

'What's Lex got?' Harry said. He pushed back in his chair. He was drawn, still tired from the previous night's dramas when Rhette had been abducted but he looked pleased to be interrupted.

'A late link from yesterday at a shopping centre and right now he's got a possible face recognition, at the airport,' Mark said.

Kira appeared at Mark's shoulder. 'You did promise,' she said, her face alight.

'Well, what are we waiting for? Get the car organised and we'll do what's necessary on the way to the airport. Not sure why you're still here instead of in the car already.' A jauntiness had returned in Harry's attitude and step as he grabbed his coat and followed the sprinting Kira along the passage to the elevators.

The trip to Hobart Airport, seventeen kilometres northeast of Hobart, was fast. They collected a patrol car and for the first ten kilometres they travelled under lights and sirens.

'There's a blonde...' Lex said by mobile.

'Sarah's not blonde...' Harry cut in. 'She's dark.'

'Ever heard of a dye bottle, sir,' Lex cut back on the Skype link. Getting a sir out of the tall black South African was unusual. He was as excited as they were.

'Sorry, Lex. Go on,' Harry would be contrite and apologetic later if all came out right.

'She's just checking in and the face recognition app likes her. Not sure where she's going as there's a couple of flights leaving Hobart in the next hour,' Lex's voice, on speaker informed them.

Kira leaned over and snapped off the lights and sirens and the following car did the same. 'Don't want to freak her,' she commented. 'In my experience freaking people's not a good way to get anywhere...'

Mark from the back seat had his iPad linked in with the Hobart terminal's Federal Police. 'They've spotted a woman answering her description and are keeping a watching brief. Cripes,' he muttered,' don't say they're learning after my Adelaide experience.'

'Stop gabbing on about your experiences, you two. Get the feds to remove her luggage from wherever it's booked to and be ready for us.'

'Yes, I'll do that,' Mark said.

Kira pulled into the back of the terminal and all three jumped out of the car and sprinted to the automatic doors. A patrolman from the following car moved to the driver's seat to properly park the car, shrugging enviously about lax detectives getting all the action.

'Easy,' Harry was breathing heavily. 'Kira, she could remember you from MONA, let's take it easy.'

A Federal police officer met them and they made a huddle with her inside the terminal doors but shielded from immediate view by a money changing booth.

'The woman we've been advised about, is in the line for security. Just along there.' The slim tall officer pointed.

The 'there' was close by in the single-story building. The line for the security examination was crowded with at least two plane loads of passengers ready to go through to the kiosks and vending machines inside the boarding areas. With the mounted tensions at airports and new rules applied, since the terrorist threats were averted earlier in the year, people had arrived early and were resigned to wait around.

'Got her,' Mark said. 'The short haired blonde. She's at the security checkpoint. I'm going through too. I look less of a copper than you do, Harry.'

'Hang it, Kira, go! We've got to have a female arresting officer and you're it.' Kira was gone before Harry could say, you've earned the job.

The two officers sauntered to the line waiting before the scanners like passengers about to board their plane. Kira grabbed a newspaper as something to carry and Mark had his iPad. Looking totally empty handed could warn their suspect.

Ahead of them the blonde woman went through the scanners and her handbag passed inspection also guided by a Federal Police woman who nudged the civilian operator. 'No weapons,' was signalled as the suspect looked away.

While they tried not to appear as though they were peering ahead too much Mark linked in with Lex. 'That's her!' was typed on the screen. Mark laughed as though the picture he was looking at waiting in line was something comedic. He pointed the image out to Kira and she shared the apparent joke. He surrendered the iPad briefly for security inspection.

Once in the lounge they watched the suspect walk to the coffee area sit on a tall seat. She leaned on a table and placed her handbag beside her legs. A waitress came, just as Mark was through the screening and about to make the arrest. He paused, waiting while the woman gave her order and also until Kira was at his side. She had to take off her shoes because the metal buckles had set off an alarm. The offending shoes were inspected by an innocent surveillance operator not in the know, and she was allowed through. She arrived looking daggers back at the man.

'Right, let's just quietly go there and make as little fuss as we can and just make the arrest,' Mark suggested.

Harry had come through the screening and was standing seemingly looking at newspapers in a kiosk. He wore an almost indiscernible earpiece.

The two arresting officers moved forward.

'Wait,' said Kira, as another dark haired woman after enquiring if she may, sat down next to their suspect. They appeared to be talking small talk when the waitress returned with two coffees and placed them down in front of the women.

Kira raised an eyebrow. She wasn't aware that the other woman had placed an order for coffee. Why, she thought.

Had the suspect ordered two initially?

Moments passed. The women finished their coffees and a when a boarding call for the Qantas flight for Sydney was announced, the second woman picked up a handbag. She seemed to say a friendly goodbye and rose to join the queue for that destination.

'Now,' said Mark.

'No wait,' Kira said 'There's something odd here.'

'Explain quickly...' Mark said.

On the iPad Lex typed. 'The blonde's Sarah Wilkes. I'd stake my badge on it. And arrest her. Arrest them both. They held hands, just for a second. They're not strangers.'

The second suspect moved to the Sydney boarding queue.

Harry left the paper kiosk, stepped up to the dark-haired woman and presented his warrant card. 'Excuse me, madam. I'm police Chief Inspector Harry Shaw. Would you please come with me?'

'Whatever for?' the woman said in a loud voice. She looked back towards Sarah, who remained sitting as before, then seemed to appeal to the others nearby. 'I've done nothing wrong.' She was attracting interest and people were peering in her direction. 'No! No! I've got a plane to catch. Leave me be.'

Mark and Kira faced the blonde woman with the words, 'Police. Sarah Wilkes, you are under arrest for murder. Please come quietly.'

'What? You're mistaken. I'm not this...Sarah...person.'

Sarah hesitated, seeming ready to come quietly as instructed. She stood, then swung her handbag at Kira's head and lunged her body in the opposite direction. Mark caught her trailing hand and twisted it behind her back while Kira caught the swinging bag and wrenched it out of Sarah's hand.

'I said come quietly,' Mark admonished his own voice clear and calm.

Sarah sat back down hard, all the sting out of her. Mark sat beside her, his grip pinioned her hand hard beside her body. The Federal Officer slipped into the seat on Sarah's other side, effectively restraining the captive. Mark nodded his thanks to the officer.

Sarah's glanced over to where Harry was still dealing with the woman, in the boarding line, who continued to protest the detainment. Her words were loud and provocative, his quiet and calm in contrast.

What colour that had been in Sarah's face drained away. 'She's nothing. A new lover. Nothing to do with anything. Let her go...'

'Not going to happen,' Mark said. He wasn't ready to advise that they had seen the hands holding in case it had been an accident due to their nervousness. 'Not going to happen,' he repeated.

Kira sped over to the confrontation that was still going on in the Sydney Qantas barrier. Others in the line were muttering, even taking sides, as the woman protested in an ever increasing voluminous voice that had risen almost to a screech. 'Go away, damnit,' the woman said.

Kira tapped her on the shoulder and with her other hand thrust her own police card before her eyes and face. 'Listen! Enough!' She said, her voice volume as if she were addressing a parade ground of cadets. 'Enough. I'm not as nice as my superior, so be quiet and come right now. You are under arrest for making a disturbance in an airport. So that's it.' She pulled handcuffs from her pocket and expertly cuffed the struggling woman. 'Stop that or I'll add resisting arrest to the charges.'

They led her away and the other wide eyed passengers boarded their flight.

Chapter 81

Sarah Wilkes had been taken to an adjoining interview room where she too was cuffed, and read her legal rights.

She was silently watching as Mark checked into his iPad for a report he was seeking. An aside note that he and the team had overlooked and not considered as important previously. The Federal officer came into the room and agreed to stay with the prisoner until Mark returned. He took Sarah's handbag as evidence and as a precaution against it going lost.

As Mark passed a jubilant Kira in the hall between the interview rooms, he said. 'Remind me never to get into an argument with you. What a bellow! You'd start an avalanche of snow on Mount Wellington with it.'

She tapped his shoulder. 'Just you remember it, my friend... Harry's given me the OK to check the handbags. I've got a Fed to assist and witness it.' Mark handed over Sarah's bag and went back to the room where Sarah Wilkes was hunched into her chair and staring into a distance only she could see.

'You OK to stay here?' he asked the Federal Officer, Jane Forsyth, reading from her name tag.

'Sure, as long as you need me,' Jane said. She was revelling in the excitement of the arrests.

Mark went to find Harry. He was still with the other woman who had been detained in a room where Federal Police cameras and automatic taping were under way.

The woman was now quiet, staring into her own depths.

'I'd like you to meet Petra Joyce,' Mark said to Harry.

'Rot! I'm not her,' an indignant response.

'Well, if you're not Petra then you're her twin sister, Odele,' Mark said.

'Odele?' Harry enquired.

'The information was in the records. Petra has, or was, a twin. We just didn't put her twin into the equation.'

Harry's eyebrows raised. He stood still taking it all in. The murder pieces started to fit, ducks in a line. 'Yes...' he said.

'Did you sacrifice her like Sarah did that young school girl to confuse the inquiry?' Mark insisted to the prisoner. 'It must have been worth it. But to let her die like that - your twin sister.'

They watched Petra's face slowly begin to crumble. Tears edged out of her eyes, beautiful eyes sinking into the darkening shadows of her cheeks.

They waited a moment. Silence often acted as a catalyst for confession for many first time persons being interviewed.

Petra Joyce shifted in her seat her chin quivered.

She was ready to talk.

'That bastard Dieter was going to double cross us,' she blurted. 'Like an idiot Sarah asked for his help and, O yes, he'd help but he took over all our plans. Make the decisions. My twin sister, Odele was straight but she was influenced by the Hoods. She actually took a liking to both of them. The seducer Sean and the smarmy Dieter.' Her face screwed up now in disgust. 'They convinced her to double cross us. We were the bad lesbians. She'd never been against us. Then they brought Odele into the raid. Gave her the job of helping Sarah...'

'As the woman in the burka?' Mark said.

'Yes.'

'So, she became the body in the lift, ID'd as being you the

identical twin by DNA?' Harry said. He looked away sickened. This'll make the arrest murder for her as well and we'll make sure that the prisons would never let Sarah and Petra be together, he thought.

Mark interrupted Harry. 'You realised that the Hoods probably thought that they had killed both of you. That's right, isn't it? And Sarah let them, to keep your doublecross going.'

'The night before the robbery, Sarah thought that Dieter could kill me. He didn't like me or my relationship with her. His sister a lesbian? It shitted him off. He got religion on that one. He'd manage to get me into the bomb zone.' Petra looked at them. Her look was defiant. 'I swapped my mobile for Odele's and he called her to the salerooms instead of me. Sarah had to pretend she was upset. Grief stricken. She's quite an actress ... she told me about it.'

'Did she say how they explained the missing Odele?'

'I guess they thought she'd just shot through. Got scared. Sarah was sure that they would've killed her anyway when it was all over. Kill her like they'd kill us, the bastards.' Petra's mouth was a hard thin line as she spat out the words.

'So, she told you she'd managed to steal the real diamonds from Hood. I can't imagine he would've let the out of his sight or possession. Or did she take them after she killed him...? Harry said.

'We hadn't gone to all the trouble to get the diamond replicas to let bloody Dieter Hood keep the real diamonds.'

Above the woman's head Harry and Mark exchanged looks.

These women had to be psychotics in their disregard for the death of a twin sister. For all the people who died in the diamond sale room. Even the of killing Dieter Hood had nothing to do with a lesbian relationship, except on Hood's part. It was all about their greed and making a plot to satisfy themselves.

They were common criminals and murderers.

Kira came to the door and beckoned Harry. 'Come in and say it,' he said to her.

She nodded. 'Yes sir, the real diamonds are in Sarah's bag.'

He turned to Petra. 'The bag contains the real stolen diamonds. Of course, it does. How many copies of the diamonds did you have? One for the bombing, yes? And one for the Hoods? This has been planned in detail all along, hasn't it, Ms Joyce?'

As Harry left the room Petra slumped down further into her chair. Her face as well as her body slumped. She took a deep breath and straightened. 'I want a lawyer. Sarah said we had to be lawyered up if we were arrested. I haven't told you anything. I'll deny everything...'

'It's a bit late for that,' Mark said. 'We read you your rights and it's all on record.'

Harry Shaw stood from his chair. He had heard enough. Time to go to see if Sarah Wilkes had broken her silence.

She would prove to be the stoic one, unlike Petra.

Chapter 82

Harry ran a tired hand through his hair.

Tie and coatless, he stretched back onto his chair in police headquarters. His body demanded sleep although he felt exhilarated by the end of the case. A case that tied up years of investigation and endless workhours in the pursuit of the Hood Brothers.

'Sarah Wilkes wouldn't talk, not until you let her get a glimpse of Petra in the hall. A clever idea. She saw her lover beaten and now it's all coming out,' he said to Kira and Mark.

'So, we have the whole story. The massive robbery with overtones of terrorism to provide doubt and confusion. Clever in its own way,' Mark said drawing a deep breath to stifle a yawn. He straddled a chair leaning forward so he appeared the chair back held him up and awake. It was. They had spent the day interviewing the two women, trying to tie up loose ends.

'I still don't understand why Sarah contacted the Hoods to help them?' Kira caught the yawn and rubbed her face. 'Shit, stop that Mark,' she said as she yawned an echo yawn.

Mark chuckled.

'Sarah said that they weren't confident they could make a getaway after the Sydney robbery. Before that Dieter had found her and emailed her. Made contact. Petra hated the Hoods on sight and the feeling was mutual, but the women needed gangland drivers and guards who wouldn't be curious. Dieter provided those and he managed to scare them into believing they couldn't just hop on plane and go, not immediately. His Tasmania plan was contrived to get the diamonds to overseas buyers but they had to be sold on it. Had to trust him so that he had time to do a double cross.' Harry said.

Kira said, 'So once the Hoods were on board they needed another set of replica diamonds for them. They never trusted Dieter and Sean, that's why they were slow getting things going in Tassy. Waiting for them to arrive from the states. And a first set of fake diamonds were always to be substituted for the real ones before the bombing robbery. Complicated. The second set to do their own double cross against the Hoods. Charming lot.'

Detective Inspector Chad Lennox knocked briefly on the door. 'Anyone home?'

The three detectives scrambled to more erect positions as the tall man came into the office. 'Yes sir,' was muttered from both Harry and Mark.

'Congratulations all. Sorry to do this but a press conference is essential given the brilliant wrap up of this case,' Chad said. 'That's you Harry….'

'And Kira, sir. Detective Regan has been paramount in the investigation,' Harry insisted.

'I think all three,' Chad returned. 'Into your best gear then asap. I've booked it for four o'clock in time for the evening broadcasts. Best news out of Hobart in a while.' He left the office looking very pleased.

'Tassy one – the mainland love,' Mark squared off a tennis forehand volley as he called the shots.

Chapter 83

Ana turned to her husband as the foursome sat on the front deck overlooking the Derwent River enjoying a pre-dinner drink after the press conference. 'So, you're telling us that the Hood brothers, or family, virtually self-destructed due to mutual double crossing?'

'Yes. Criminally psychopathic, the lot of them!' Mark said. 'It's no wonder they left a trail of murders and bodies scattered everywhere all these years.'

'I saw Sean briefly at the wine launch when he took Rhette. For some reason I felt I'd seen him before … not recently...but...' Ana paused as Harry and Mark exchanged glances. She ran her hand through her hair, through the natural white hair that framed her face. The distinctive white strands, spread by her fingers, fanned out like lace on her black hair. It was a signature that had followed her life. 'There's more to this isn't there?' she said.

'Yes, there sure is,' Harry said. 'We think that the Hood family were in the same Middle Eastern camp that you were as a child. That they were expatriated to Australia about the same time you were too, adopted as you were, and...'

'Sean and Sarah? They could've got fruit like my sister Kari and I did every day. That's where I recognised him from before. It had to be from then. Dieter would have been too old. He might've been in the camp attack.' Ana's hand moved to cover her mouth in amazement. She looked wide eyed at Mark. 'I didn't see any of them after that time. I can't believe it. Those days have come back to haunt me again. First on the River Murray and now here.'

'The body identified as Dieter Hood had an old bullet wound in one leg…it could've come from then. We'll never know now he's dead although the Coroner may want a fuller explanation of his past,' Harry said. 'Something we may have to further investigate,' he said to Mark.

Rhette held the wine bottle up to the evening light, enjoying the colour of the pinot noir red, before she refilled their glasses. 'I'm so sorry for Veronica losing all her beautiful wine. It was delicious. I'm going to see if she has a case or two left somewhere still for me to buy.'

'Looking for the odd diamond we might've over looked as a souvenir? They are replicas remember,' Harry teased.

'No but she must have taken a terrible loss when your forensic team poured it all away down the drain.'

Ana cut in. 'Veronica has to be feeling bad. She said she thought that she and Sean really had something together. To be used as a dupe. Horrible. Then to lose most of her wine… I don't mean to sound all psychologist but I hope she is getting some help.'

'Kira is looking to that. She's ordered the police psychologist to see her. And the young lass who was groped by that reporter. Turn over one stone and you find more than one squashed bug,' Harry said.

Ana gave him a look that was in agreement with him. She understood his comment.

Rhette sipped her wine. Rolled it around her mouth. It would be her last glass of wine for a while. 'Yes… and I wouldn't mind offering Veronica a business partnership. Help her and use some of my money as an investment. It'd be worth it for her and me.'

'What a fabulous idea,' Ana said as she smiled across the table at her friend.

'A reason to come back to Hobart on holiday? Sounds good to me,' Harry commented. He stretched back into his chair, looking with concern at Rhette. Her bruises were ripening into patches of purple and yellow on her face and neck from the abduction and crash. 'It's almost over...'

'Surely this's the end of this case. There's winners and losers. The Argyle Diamond people will get their diamonds back and keep their position on the stock market. That'll please them. You blokes have been chasing the Hood brothers for ages. Never mind that there was a sister as well. OK, she's in custody and unlikely to ever be released, but as I see it as far as the Hoods go - they're dead and done,' Rhette said specifically to Harry. 'The losers. All the people who died in the bombing, especially the school girl and the delivery lad on the bicycle. Breaks my heart they do. Always the innocents. The others. The criminals they took the risks and they paid the price. So, it's over at last? We can get on with our lives...'

'It is, all except reams of reports and paperwork for the Coroner and to wrap up this case.' Harry leaned forward and took Rhette's hands. 'I'm going to see if we can do it here in Hobart.'

'Good, sounds like a great idea. You men've been working around the clock and must have some time off... we need time too,' Rhette said. 'We still have a month or more on this house lease so we could stay here on holiday. It's big enough for Lex and his family to visit, and we can get to know Kira better. Sydney and Adelaide can wait, for a while at least.'

They watched as Lyn's car pulled into the drive. 'That'll be Pietie home from his play-date with James. There goes the quiet,' Ana laughed. 'I'll get the door.'

Piet rushed to Mark as they returned. 'Jimmy and I made a rocket ship out of big boxes!' he said. 'It was fun and we had pancakes with jam.' He stopped. 'Have you said yet?' He asked his mother.

With a smile at Mark, Ana said. 'Trust Pietie to tell. We've got news.'

'You too?' Rhette said with a laugh towards Harry. Handshakes and hugs greeted her words. 'Congratulations! And I've got a wedding to plan. And soon. Harry's determined that we're not going to have our baby without a ring on my finger. Even if it's in a registry office. He's old fashioned that way...'

'A wedding? Can I give the bride away like I gave Mummy away to Mark?' Piet's eyes danced as his feet were doing. 'Can I?'

'I think that can be arranged. There's no one else...' Rhette smiled then paused. There was no one else left of her family. Everyone gone thanks to the Hoods. Now they were done and she had a future that would be everything. 'It would be a pleasure if you all gave me away to Harry,' she said.

End

ABOUT THE AUTHOR

Rendezvous at Lock 6 began the journey to *Rendezvous on the Opal Fields. These stories were set in South Australia and with this novel I went to a wider Australian field..*

All my mystery thrillers are 'stand-alone' books that are not essential to be read as a continuum. However some of the characters do continue from one book to the next ... and as I have suggested this is because the characters were not 'finished' with me or their stories. With this book I have completed the Rendezvous Trilogy and I hope the characters are content, or not, depending on what I did to them. So be it.

After many years of writing poetry, short stories and film scripts in many genres - including Sci-Fi - retirement finally gave me the time to follow my inclination and to write those first novels. Like many before me I had un-named and unfinished piles of writings that, in film parlance, ended up on my editing room floor. They would never see the light of any day given their limitations.

However sometimes a little success came my way with competition wins; *Walking with Granddad* was read on ABC National Radio and an added thrill of a short animated film, *The Long Beach,* which I wrote was made and shown in film festivals all over the world.

My previous working and general life experiences include a degree in Social Work; work in the prison system, the Criminal Court, housing, domestic violence and general counselling areas. On the medical side I've been a nurse, a St John Ambulance officer 'on the cars' and as an Air Attendant, instructed with the Royal Life Saving Society, and taught children to swim over many years.

Study in diverse areas included archaeology and history have coupled with travel and life as a wife and mother have all given me arenas to stretch my writing wings. I write about places I know - except in Sci-Fi where the Universe is hardly enough in space and time - and the Australian landscape, flora and fauna, is where I belong.

I am very appreciative of comments I have received from readers of my work, and welcome more - praise naturally, but constructive critiques are welcome.

My email address is: helenvr@southernphone.com.au

Helen van Rooijen
Port Lincoln 2017

www.ingramcontent.com/pod-product-compliance
Lightning Source LLC
Chambersburg PA
CBHW070053120726
47909CB00002B/376